A LADY OF RARE QUALITY

Anne Ashley

MILLS & BOON®

First published in Great Britain 2006
Harlequin Mills & Boon Limited,
Eton House, 18-24 Paradise Road, Richmond, Surrey TW9 1SR

© Anne Ashley 2006

ISBN-13: 978 0 263 19054 0
ISBN-10:   0 263 19054 4

Set in Times Roman 12 on 15 pt.
08-0906-77458

Printed and bound in Great Britain
by Antony Rowe Ltd, Chippenham, Wiltshire

HISTORICAL ROMANCE™

Novels coming in October 2006

AN IMPROPER COMPANION
Anne Herries

Daniel, Earl of Cavendish, finds the frivolity of the *ton* dull after serving in the Peninsula War. Boredom disappears when he is drawn into the mystery surrounding the abduction of gently bred girls. His investigation endangers his mother's companion, Miss Elizabeth Travers. Tainted by scandal, her cool response commands Daniel's respect – while her beauty demands so much more…

THE VISCOUNT
Lyn Stone

The young man who appears late at night at Viscount Duquesne's door is not all he seems. Dressed as a boy to escape the hellhole in which she has been imprisoned, Lady Lily Bradshaw must throw herself on the mercy of a ruthless rake. Viscount Duquesne soon finds himself captivated by this bold lady – and he can't resist her audacious request for a helping hand…in marriage!

THE VAGABOND DUCHESS
Claire Thornton

He had promised to return – but Jack Bow was dead. And Temperance Challinor's life was changed for ever. She must protect her unborn child – by pretending to be Jack's widow. A foolproof plan. Until she arrives at Jack's home…and the counterfeit widow of a vagabond becomes the real wife of a very much alive *duke*!

MILLS & BOON®

Live the emotion

HIST0906 HB

'Whatever are you thinking of? I'm sure I can walk.

'Oh, sir, put me down at once, do!' Annis demanded, in a voice now decidedly hoarse after all attempts to gain someone's attention during her confinement in her temporary freezing cold jail.

She didn't quite catch the muttered response, but felt sure it was neither polite nor a promise of compliance, as he merely continued striding purposefully towards the house. Although it had been some little time since she had been carried in a gentleman's arms, she remembered the occasion quite well. What she couldn't recall experiencing, however, when she had foolishly gone and twisted her ankle all those years ago, was the peculiar sensations she was feeling now. There had been no odd fluttering in the pit of her stomach or beneath her ribcage during that one previous occurrence, she felt sure. And why there should be that pulsating heat in the area directly below her cheekbones when the rest of her was still experiencing the lingering effects of the atmosphere in the icehouse, she simply couldn't imagine.

When at last she felt herself being lowered carefully onto her bed, and those strong arms were no longer providing their support, Annis didn't know whether to feel relieved or disappointed.

Anne Ashley was born and educated in Leicester. She lived for a time in Scotland, but now makes her home in the West Country, with two cats, her two sons, and a husband who has a wonderful and very necessary sense of humour. When not pounding away at the keys of her word processor, she likes to relax in her garden, which she has opened to the public on more than one occasion in aid of the village church funds.

Recent novels by the same author:

A NOBLE MAN*
LORD EXMOUTH'S INTENTIONS*
THE RELUCTANT MARCHIONESS
TAVERN WENCH
BELOVED VIRAGO
LORD HAWKRIDGE'S SECRET
BETRAYED AND BETROTHED

*part of the Regency mini-series
The Steepwood Scandal

A LADY OF
RARE QUALITY

Chapter One

It was a full minute before Miss Annis Milbank could recover sufficiently from the shock to exclaim, 'But, my dear ma'am! What in the world makes you suppose that I am the most appropriate person to aid you? For all that I endeavour to behave as my dear mama would have wished, I remain shockingly outspoken on occasions. In consequence, I'm ill equipped to take upon myself the role of mediator, most especially in such a delicate matter as this.'

Lady Pelham merely smiled that serene smile of hers, as she raised her eyes to study the delightful features framed in a riot of glossy chestnut curls.

Beautifully candid as ever, her goddaughter had spoken no less than the truth. Yet, even though her manners and behaviour were somewhat unorthodox on occasions, and there were those who considered her a little too self-reliant for someone of her tender years, Annis had been blessed with her mother's serenity, not to mention kindness and understanding, and her father's determination and sound common sense. These admirable traits, coupled with an abundance of roguish charm, made her the ideal person to adopt the role of envoy.

'You err, my dear,' she countered gently. 'Your not being afraid to speak your mind in this instance might well prove advantageous.'

Annis betrayed her misgivings by lifting one fine brow in a de-cidedly sceptical arch. 'Ma'am, if the present Lord Greythorpe re-sembles his predecessor in character, is it likely he'll listen to anything I might choose to say?'

'The truth of the matter is, child, I've no notion of what manner of man the current holder of the title might be,' Lady Pelham confessed as she rose wearily to her feet and went across to the window. 'Opinions vary. I've heard it said that he's very like his late father in so much as he has a tendency to be cold and unapproachable on occasions; others, so I understand, hold a very different view of him. I myself am endeavouring to keep an open mind.'

Her expression suddenly grave, Lady Pelham swung round to stare at her goddaughter. 'Please do not imagine I ask this of you lightly,' she revealed at length. 'In fact, if I could have turned to any other, a member of my own immediate family, or some close friend here in Bath, I should never have written in such a melodramatic fashion, begging you to visit here without delay. You must have been a little concerned when I offered no explanation in my letter.'

Her lively sense of humour coming to the fore, Annis couldn't help smiling at this gross understatement. The instant she had received the communication, she hadn't hesitated to make all haste to Bath. The journey from her Leicestershire home had been achieved swiftly enough, but even so she had been granted ample time to imagine the worst.

On her arrival a short time earlier, she had half-expected to be met with the intelligence that Lady Pelham was gravely ill, or at the very least that some shocking misfortune had befallen Helen, her godmother's niece. Never in her wildest imaginings had she supposed she had been summoned for the sole purpose of acting as go-between and spokesperson, a role for which she had had no previous experience. Therefore she could only assume the situation must be more dire than she had first supposed.

'Ma'am, perhaps I have not perfectly understood,' she felt obliged to admit. 'You say you received a communication, quite out of the blue, from Helen's half-brother, inviting you both to spend a few weeks at the family's country residence in Hampshire, and that Helen herself was not altogether enthusiastic about accepting.' Annis found it impossible to suppress a wry smile. 'Well, ma'am, I for one can fully appreciate her feelings on the matter. She appears to me to have gone on well enough without being acknowledged by any member of her late father's family throughout her life.'

'Helen feels neither bitter nor resentful towards any member of the Greythorpe family,' Lady Pelham assured Annis, before subjecting her to a thoughtful stare, as she resumed the seat opposite. 'Which is something I have strongly suspected that you yourself have experienced increasingly over the years towards your mother's relatives, my dear.'

Annis's refusal to be drawn on the irksome topic of her late mother's close relations ignited a glint of respect in Lady Pelham's eyes. 'Do not misunderstand me,' she went on. 'I for one felt nothing but admiration for your mama. Unlike my sister and myself, she at least possessed the strength of character to go against her family's wishes and marry a man of her own choosing. How different Charlotte's and my life might have been had we possessed the courage to follow a similar path!'

Although she knew a great deal about Lady Pelham and her late sister's marriages, neither of which had been even a moderately successful alliance, though both blessedly of short duration, Annis felt obliged to have one salient point confirmed at this juncture, and so did not hesitate to ask that all important question.

'There has never been any doubt in my mind that the Sixth

Viscount Greythorpe was indeed Helen's sire,' Lady Pelham answered, the conviction in her voice unshakeable. 'My sister's behaviour might not have been altogether wise, though understandable in the circumstances. Married to a highly cynical and unapproachable being, many years her senior, was it any wonder she responded to the gentle attentions of the young man commissioned so early in the marriage to paint her portrait? Charlotte freely admitted that she sought the artist's company frequently during those few weeks he stayed at Greythorpe Manor. But she swore their association never went beyond mild flirtation. It was perhaps unfortunate that Helen was conceived at that time,' Lady Pelham felt obliged to concede. 'More unfortunate, still, was that she should have been cursed with the red hair that has not infrequently crowned the heads of certain members of our family down the generations, myself included.'

'It does seem strange that the late Lord Greythorpe didn't appreciate this fact himself,' Annis remarked.

'He might well have done so,' Lady Pelham acknowledged, after a moment's intense thought. 'A gentleman prone to moods of deep depression he might have been, but I never heard it said he lacked intelligence. He might have taken into account too that it is not uncommon for two people with very dark locks to produced auburn-haired offspring. It was just unfortunate that the artist himself had Titian hair.'

'Unfortunate, indeed,' Annis agreed. 'But if, as you say, Helen feels no bitterness towards her late father's family, why is she so unwilling to accept the invitation to visit the ancestral pile?'

'Oh, she isn't wholly against the notion,' Lady Pelham corrected gently. 'It is simply that we had previously accepted an invitation to spend a few days with a friend of Helen's in Devonshire at the end of February, which was the time Lord Greythorpe proposed for the commencement of the visit to Hampshire. So I wrote back explaining this, and suggested a shorter visit might be more appropriate for Helen's first stay at Greythorpe Manor.'

'Is Helen against a protracted sojourn in the country?' Annis queried when her godmother relapsed into silence.

'Oh, no. I think, had circumstances been a little different, she might well have been quite happy to oblige her half-brother,' Lady Pelham revealed, her expression suddenly grim. 'As things stand, however, it doesn't suit Helen at all to remain away from Bath for a lengthy period at present.'

Annis's attention was well and truly captured, for she felt that at last they had arrived at the crux of the matter. Consequently she did not hesitate, yet again, to have her curiosity satisfied.

'Because shortly before we received Lord Greythorpe's invitation, Helen's path was, regrettably, crossed by a handsome, silver-tongued young rogue, who has been paying her marked attention ever since,' her godmother revealed without a moment's hesitation.

Annis wasn't slow to comprehend. 'A fortune-hunter, ma'am?'

'Undoubtedly!' Lady Pelham concurred. 'Surprisingly, Helen has yet to see him for precisely what he is. However, as you know yourself, she is not prone to folly, and is mature for her years. It is my belief that, given time, she will overcome this foolish infatuation of hers and common sense will prevail, providing she is granted that all important time.'

Once again, Lady Pelham rose from her chair, only this time to pace about the room, clearly revealing her troubled state of mind. 'My one great fear is that, if forcibly removed from Bath, while she remains utterly besotted, she just might be persuaded into an elopement. Then, I'm afraid, there would be nothing either her trustees or I could do to prevent that young ne'er-do-well, Mr Daniel Draycot, from getting his hands on at least part of her inheritance.'

Such was her perturbed state, she appeared to find it necessary to adjust one of the ornaments on the mantelshelf a fraction of an inch, only to return it a moment later to its former position. 'You see, my sister Charlotte was determined that Helen, like your own mother, should marry for love. Helen will come into her inheritance unconditionally upon marriage, at least the money left to her by her mother, which is not insubstantial.'

Although Annis perfectly understood her godmother's concerns, she still considered the problem could be easily resolved. 'Why not simply do what Helen herself wishes, ma'am, and write to Lord Greythorpe suggesting a shorter visit later in the year? Surely that will satisfy all concerned?'

'That is precisely what I did do, my dear, and my reply most definitely did not satisfy his lordship. He sent me this in response.'

Lady Pelham went over to the escritoire, and, quickly locating a certain letter, promptly presented it for Annis to read. A moment later she watched her goddaughter's finely arched dark brows snap together, and the green flecks in the strikingly lovely grey eyes intensify, as they avidly scanned the missive written in a bold and unmistakably masculine hand.

'The arrogance of the man!' Annis tossed the letter aside in disgust. 'Who on earth does he imagine he is, insisting his half-sister pays a visit when it suits his purposes? His maternal grandmother...?' She paused to consult the missive once more. 'This Dowager Lady Kilbane is no relation to Helen, after all, so there is no necessity for Helen to be present at the proposed birthday celebration to be held at Greythorpe Manor early in the spring. If I were you, ma'am, when the carriage he clearly intends sending to collect you arrives next week, I'd send it back immediately, with a letter stating in no uncertain terms that you will decide when your niece shall visit Greythorpe Manor.'

'Believe me, my dear, nothing would afford me greater satisfaction,' Lady Pelham divulged. 'I very much fear Lord Deverel Greythorpe is not unlike his father, imperious and uncompromising, having scant regard for the feelings of others. Sadly, though, he is well within his rights to insist upon Helen visiting whenever he chooses.' She smiled as Annis's expression turned to one of consternation. 'The late Lord Greythorpe, for reasons best known to himself, never took steps to divorce my sister after their separation. When he died, guardianship of the daughter he never acknowledged as his own, along with everything else he possessed, passed to his only son and heir, the present holder of the title.'

Misguidedly, Annis had always assumed that, after Charlotte's demise, Lady Pelham had become Helen's guardian, and didn't attempt to hide her astonishment. 'I never knew that, ma'am,' she admitted. 'It makes one wonder what can have been in the late Lord Greythorpe's mind. Why did he not transfer guardianship to you after his wife's death, as he clearly wanted nothing to do with Helen?'

Lady Pelham's smile was twisted. 'Whatever the motive, I cannot imagine it was because he had his youngest child's best interests at heart. No, it is much more likely that he succeeded in putting her very existence from his mind.'

As this seemed highly probable, Annis nodded, before something else occurred to her as rather odd. 'Why, do you suppose, has the present holder of the title suddenly taken such an interest in his half-sister?'

Clearly at a loss to understand this herself, Lady Pelham shook her head. 'I do know that he has travelled extensively and was abroad when news of his father's demise reached him, which is perhaps why he waited almost a year before making contact at all. The ancestral home covers very many acres of Hampshire countryside. There is also a smaller estate in Derbyshire and a fashionable London residence, both of which he has visited in recent months. He must have been kept very busy since his return.'

As this, too, seemed a reasonable enough assumption to make, Annis didn't dwell on it. Instead she asked, 'Do you suppose that he, at least, now that his father is dead, is prepared to acknowledge Helen openly as his sibling?'

'If that is his intention, it could do the child nothing but good. I wouldn't attempt to suggest that Helen has suffered greatly as a result of her late father's unnatural behaviour, but there have been occasions when some heartless wretch has questioned her birth within her hearing.'

'We must hope, ma'am, that her half-brother's actions will check any future speculation, and that his wife too is disposed to look kindly upon your niece.'

'Oh, he isn't married, my dear,' Lady Pelham disclosed, with a quizzical smile. 'I cannot quite make up my mind whether that surprises me or not. I met him only once, when he paid an unexpected visit here, offering his condolences, shortly after Charlotte's death. Whether he did so with his father's full knowledge and approval, I'm not altogether sure, though I will say this, his expressions of regret at his stepmother's demise did seem genuine. Understandably, after almost ten years, my memory of him is a little hazy, but I seem to recall thinking him a very serious young man, though not unappealing in a darkly brooding sort of way. And I seem to remember too someone, quite recently, mentioning that he resides with his sister who, if I remember correctly, is close to him in age and, like himself, has never married.'

Lady Pelham once again lowered herself gracefully into the chair, and for several moments stared meditatively at an imaginary spot on the carpet. 'Helen knows nothing of Lord Greythorpe's most recent letter. She knows nothing either of the extent of his authority over her.'

Annis was surprised to discover this and didn't attempt to conceal the fact. 'Great heavens, ma'am! Why on earth did you keep his guardianship secret?'

Lady Pelham shook her head, as though at a loss to know why herself. 'The truth of the matter is that, even though I was informed, shortly after her father's demise, that Deverel Greythorpe had become Helen's legal guardian, I never gave the matter a second thought. Her father never once attempted to interfere in her up-bringing, never attempted to make contact at all, come to that. It never occurred to me to suppose that her half-brother might behave differently.' A further sigh escaped her. 'Believe me when I say that I didn't deliberately keep the guardianship secret from Helen. All the same, I cannot help feeling that it would be a mistake to reveal it at the present time, while she is still viewing a certain unscrupulous young rogue through a rosy haze.'

Annis, having no difficulty understanding this viewpoint, at last began to appreciate the extent of her godmother's grave concerns. 'You fear that Helen just might be persuaded into believing a pro-longed visit to Greythorpe Manor is a ploy on your and her guard-ian's part to separate her from her beau?'

Given her troubles were many at present, Lady Pelham managed a secretive little smile. 'Not only that, my dear, I sincerely believe it would be a grave mistake to cancel our visit to Devonshire, for I've recently discovered that Mr Draycot is, for reasons best known to himself, not at all keen for Helen and I to go there. And I feel sure his objection does not stem from a desire not to be parted from Helen.'

'How interesting!' Annis was intrigued. 'You suspect he fears that you might uncover something unsavoury about him there?'

'That is precisely what I do think, yes,' Lady Pelham admitted. 'And, to be perfectly truthful, what I am hoping. He did on one occasion let fall that he stayed for a short space in that part of the world, though whether in Okehampton itself, where Helen's friend resides with her parents, I'm not altogether sure. Although I believe Mr Draycot has attempted on more than one occasion to persuade Helen to cancel the visit, declaring he cannot bear to be parted from her even for a few days, she has withstood his pleas thus far, and remains determined to go.'

Lady Pelham returned to her chair as the sound of voices filtered through from the hall. 'Unless I am much mistaken, Helen has once again come upon Mr Draycot…er…quite by chance, you understand, during her walk in the park, and has, unless my hearing is defective, invited him back for refreshments. You may judge for yourself what manner of man he is. But have a care, Annis, my dear,' she warned in an undertone. 'Helen does not expect to discover you here. So you must say your visit is purely impromptu; that you are on your way to stay with friends, and that you simply couldn't pass so close without visiting us for a day or two. On no account must she discover that I have sent for you.'

As a direct result of that one and only encounter with Mr Daniel Draycot, Annis did not linger in Bath. Within the space of two days, she was travelling across the country again in a hired post-chaise, only through Hampshire this time, a county she had never visited before.

Ordinarily Annis would have found sufficient to capture her attention, even this early in the year, when the countryside was most definitely not looking its best, had it not been for the fact that she was more interested in reaching her destination without delay.

Unfortunately, since her departure from that once-fashionable watering place, the weather had taken a definite turn for the worse. Within the space of twenty-four hours the temperature had plummeted, the country was now being buffeted by a biting-cold east wind, and the leaden sky, which had looked grimly threatening all the morning, was finally adding to the sufferings of hapless travellers by liberally scattering frozen droplets across the landscape.

'I ought to have bespoken rooms back at that posting-house, instead of foolishly attempting to reach Greythorpe Manor today,' Annis confided to her sole travelling companion. 'Both you and the post-boys predicted snow before too long.'

'You're not one to ignore sound advice,' Eliza Disher, ever loyal, countered, 'leastways, not unless you have good reason. I know well enough that you're not at all comfortable with this task Lady Pelham has set you. So the sooner it's over and done with the better you'll feel, my lamb.'

'That's assuming his lordship is willing to receive me,' Annis responded, smiling despite the fact that she was under no illusion about this herself.

Of course, there was a very real possibility that she might be denied admittance, and the discomforts she had suffered during the past days, travelling about the country at a most unseasonable time of year, would have been for nought.

'It is true I carry a letter of introduction from my godmother. Whether or not it will suffice, and I shall be granted the interview I seek with the Viscount, is a different matter entirely. Furthermore, as what I wish to discuss is of a very personal nature, I might well be shown the door long before I'm able to state my godmother's case fully.'

'I see it this way, Miss Annis, you can do no more than your best,' the lifelong maid encouraged, thereby winning herself a loving smile from the young woman whom she had helped bring into the world almost twenty-four years before. 'I know you better than most anyone else does, and know that unless you believed you were doing right to speak up for Lady Pelham, you wouldn't be here now.'

Silently, she acknowledged the truth of this. Lady Pelham was one of the few members of her own mother's social class whom Annis openly admired. A widow of many years, Henrietta Pelham was intelligent and good-natured, a lady who had taken her responsibilities as a godmother seriously indeed. It was mainly thanks to her that Annis had been able to sample those entertainments enjoyed only by the most privileged class during the many visits she had made to Bath, both before and since her beloved mother's demise.

Undertaking this mission now was a way of thanking Lady Pelham for the many kindnesses she had shown towards her over the years, but even so Annis had not made her decision without giving the matter a deal of thought first.

'Well, Dish, every instinct tells me that Lady Pelham has good reason to be suspicious about Mr Daniel Draycot. A rogue and no mistake! I don't doubt my godmother's ability to manage things, providing of course she is granted the opportunity. It's up to me to do my utmost to ensure that she is given sufficient time to reveal Draycot's true—'

Annis broke off as the carriage came to an unexpected and abrupt halt in the middle of the road. The snow was nowhere near heavy enough to contemplate abandoning the journey quite yet. So she could only assume that the post-boys, not quite certain of the precise location of Greythorpe Manor, were debating between themselves which fork in the road to take.

Drawing her cloak more tightly about her against the inevitable blast of cold air, Annis let down the window, and demanded an immediate explanation for the delay. An apologetic post-boy was before her almost at once, appearing decidedly ill at ease as he revealed the surprising intelligence that there was what appeared to be a body lying in the road, just up ahead.

Naturally surprised, but not unduly alarmed, Annis alighted

from the carriage the instant the steps had been let down, with the fiercely protective Disher close on her heels.

She had grown accustomed throughout her life to being compared with her father. Not only did she resemble him in looks, but, to a certain extent, in character too. Undeniably she had inherited the late Dr Milbank's acute powers of observation, which she put to good use as she approached the clearly masculine form lying prostrate in the road, and the handsome chestnut gelding standing a mere few yards away from his evidently injured master.

After casting a cursory glance over her left shoulder at the trees that edged the road, Annis dropped to her knees in order to examine the stranger more closely. The blood oozing from a scorched portion of his jacket sleeve, between shoulder and elbow, told its own tale, as did the slight swelling and gash on his forehead. With her maid's assistance she managed to turn the stranger over on his back. Unfortunately a brief examination of his various pockets did not reveal his identity, merely the fact that the motive for the attack was unlikely to have been robbery.

'Begging your pardon, miss,' the agitated post-boy said as Annis, after a closer inspection of the area surrounding the injured man, rose at last to her feet, 'but we'd best not linger. No saying as who might still be about, lying in wait,' he added, before he turned, eager, it seemed, to rejoin his colleague and remount his horse.

'You are not proposing, I trust, to continue the journey and leave this poor fellow here?' Annis asked, raising her fine, expressive brows in faint hauteur, a gesture that never failed to put Disher in mind of her young mistress's aristocratic grandmother, in her time a fearsome matriarch whom one had defied at one's peril.

The look had the desired effect. The injured man was subsequently deposited in the carriage by the two stocky post-boys, though not without a deal of grumbling, and muttering of colourful oaths. Not disposed to linger herself, Annis did not hesitate to order the resumption of the journey once the stranger's fine gelding had been secured to the back of the conveyance.

'Are you hoping someone at Greythorpe Manor might know who he is?' Disher asked, after watching her mistress's attempt to make the stranger more comfortable by placing a fur muff beneath his injured head, and covering him with a rug.

'If he's from around these parts, and I have every reason to suppose he might well be, then, yes, there's every chance he'll be known by someone at the Manor.' Annis took a moment to study the evident aristocratic lines of a face that, although not handsome, was ruggedly attractive and full of character. 'His clothes alone suggest a man of some means. His mount too is a fine piece of horseflesh. Moreover, gentlemen with funds aplenty at their disposal usually travel great distances by carriage, not on horseback. That is why I'm inclined to believe he's local.'

Disher smiled. 'How you put me in mind of your sainted father at times like these, Miss Annis.'

If she had suspected this praise to be received with any degree of pleasure she was doomed to disappointment. When she attained no response whatsoever, she turned her head, and was surprised to discover deep lines of concern furrowing her young mistress's intelligent brow. 'What's troubling you, miss? Do you suspect the gentleman is badly hurt?'

'A more thorough examination is needed to be sure, but I wouldn't have said so, no,' Annis answered promptly. 'Clearly he's been shot, but that I suspect is nought but a scratch. The gash to his head is the more serious injury and, unless I'm very much mistaken, was sustained when he fell from his mount.' She frowned again, perplexed. 'What I find hard to understand is the motive for the attack. It certainly wasn't robbery. You saw yourself the size of the purse I drew from his pocket.'

'Perhaps we happened along before the robber had time to search for the gentleman's valuables,' the maid suggested, 'and he made a quick getaway before he was seen by the post-boys.'

'Unlikely, Dish,' Annis countered. 'As we didn't hear the sound of a shot—and neither, I suspect, did the post-boys, otherwise they wouldn't have been quite so surprised to discover our friend here in the road—it's reasonable to suppose the incident occurred some little time before we arrived on the scene. This is corroborated by the lack of footprints in the snow. Apart from our own, and the chestnut gelding's, there were no prints. It began to snow some fifteen minutes ago, no more. So the attack, I imagine, took place shortly before then. Ample time for a would-be robber to rifle through the gentleman's pockets, I should say.'

As the carriage slowed yet again before passing between the stone pillars of an imposing gateway, Annis's thoughts turned to more mundane matters. Since their return to the carriage the weather had deteriorated further. It was almost impossible to distinguish between the sweep of the drive and the grass verges, and she couldn't help feeling a deal of unease about the return journey to town. Time was of the essence. In consequence she didn't waste a precious second in studying the architectural splendour of the Restoration mansion, when the carriage came to a halt outside the imposing front entrance a few minutes later, but marched resolutely up to the solid oak door.

The footman in smart green livery who came in response to her imperious application of the door-knocker was not slow to divulge his master's absence from home, or the fact that Viscount Greythorpe rarely saw strangers without an appointment.

Annis, undaunted, merely announced her intention of leaving a

letter of introduction, and returning on the morrow, weather permitting, before revealing the more pressing concern of the stranger
in her hired conveyance.

Although naturally taken aback, the footman braved the
elements and accompanied her back down the steps to the waiting
carriage. 'You evidently recognise the gentleman,' Annis said when
the footman's jaw dropped perceptively the instant after he had
peered into the carriage.

'Know him, ma'am? I should say so... It's his lordship!'

Chapter Two

After silently acknowledging how incredibly stupid she had been not to have considered the very real possibility that the injured gentleman might just turn out to be none other than the very person she had travelled so far to see, Annis took command of the situation by ordering the stupefied young footman to assist one of the post-boys in lifting his lordship from the carriage.

Even though by no stretch of the imagination had things gone according to plan that day, Annis was determined to maintain the dignified calm that she never failed to exhibit in times of stress, and for which she was much admired. Without experiencing the least reluctance to do so, she followed into the spacious hall, where she caught immediate sight of someone crossing the chequered floor, heading purposefully in her direction, whose mien strongly suggested that he might well turn out to be none other than the iron ruler of the household staff.

Surprisingly he exhibited no shock whatsoever at the means by which his master had entered the Manor. Only when he fixed his steely gaze on her did his expression alter to any significant degree, and he betrayed what looked suspiciously like a flicker of distaste, as though he had detected a slightly unpleasant odour.

"Never, ever, betray diffidence when dealing with servants, Annis," her mother had once counselled her, "most especially high-ranking ones. Good servants are extremely discerning. They rarely fail to recognise persons of quality, and will respond accordingly."

Consequently, Annis returned the major-domo's rather supercilious regard without so much as a blink, even going so far as to raise her pointed little chin slightly, as her mother's excellent advice filtered through her mind.

'I came upon this gentleman, whom I am reliably informed is none other than your master, along the road. I do not believe him to be seriously injured. None the less, he will need to be warmed and made comfortable without delay, and quite naturally a doctor must be summoned,' she advised, and was rewarded a moment later when the butler, seemingly having no difficulty in detecting the dignified authority in her voice, carried out the instructions by summoning several underlings into the hall.

Once she had watched the unconscious master of the house being safely conveyed to the upper floor by way of a handsomely carved wooden staircase, she turned her attention again to the major-domo. 'Is his lordship's sister at home?' she enquired, thereby proving that, although a perfect stranger, she wasn't completely ignorant about the Viscount's family.

'Miss Greythorpe is at present paying a visit to a retired servant residing on the estate, ma'am.'

Annis had no difficulty herself in detecting the slight note of reserve as the butler volunteered at least this snippet of information. In the normal course of events she didn't doubt for a moment that he would never have dreamed of revealing his mistress's whereabouts to a complete unknown. The fact of the matter was, though, that circumstances were anything but normal, and protocol must be set aside at least for the present.

The steadfastness of her gaze succeeded in retaining the punctilious servant's full attention. 'If your mistress left the house any length of time ago and, more especially, on foot, I would strongly recommend that you take it upon yourself to send out the carriage without delay in order to collect her. The roads are still passable at present, but this, I fear, will soon not be the case. The wind is strengthening as we speak, and drifts will not be long in forming. Which reminds me,' she added, turning to the post-boy who, having been relieved of the strenuous task of carrying his lordship, had remained in the hall. 'You must return to town while you're still able. Secure rooms at the posting-house, and there await my further instructions.'

Finally, Annis focused her attention on her personal maid, who had witnessed proceedings with an appreciative gleam in her kindly eyes for the no-nonsense and dignified manner in which her young mistress had conducted herself in what might have turned out to be a most embarrassing situation.

'Ensure our overnight bags and my small travelling case are removed from the post-chaise, Dish. Naturally, we cannot think of leaving before Miss Greythorpe returns. No doubt she would appreciate an explanation of how it came about that a complete stranger took it upon herself to convey his lordship back to his home in a post-chaise and four.'

The light of battle replaced the appreciative gleam in Disher's eyes when the butler looked as if he was about to proffer an alternative suggestion. 'She'll appreciate your presence here a deal more if the doctor is unable to visit, Miss Annis. Leastwise, we can see to it that his lordship is as comfortable as may be until the doctor arrives. I'll take a look at him first if you're agreeable?'

'By all means do so, Dish, once you've supervised the removal of those bags necessary for our comfort from the carriage,' Annis urged her. 'I, in the meantime, intend to await Miss Greythorpe's return.' She turned her attention to the butler once more, her own eyes now flashing a challenge. 'But not in this hall.'

Annis didn't doubt that even though the iron ruler of the household staff must be troubled by recent events, not to mention puzzled by her unexpected arrival on the scene, he had by this time made up his mind that his lordship's somewhat unconventional rescuer was, if nothing else, clearly the daughter of a gentleman, for he didn't hesitate to show her into a small, homely parlour, where Annis wasn't slow to take advantage of the chair placed by the comfort of a roaring fire, before divulging her full name, and then enquiring his own.

'Yes, Dunster, I should very much appreciate a dish of tea while I await Miss Greythorpe's return,' she promptly replied, after the butler, thawing marginally, had responded to her question and then had made the offer of refreshment. 'But nothing to eat, I thank you. With luck your mistress will not be long delayed. Then I shall make my way back to town as soon as may be, and eat my dinner there.'

Although her voiced desire to be gone from the Manor without undue delay, thereby not attempting to take advantage of his lordship's hospitality, had won her a further flicker of approval from the punctilious retainer, Annis wasn't unduly surprised to be forced to revise her plans a short time later when, having been furnished with the promised refreshment, she was informed that her presence was required immediately in the master bedchamber.

Dunster took it upon himself to act as escort. Whether this singular honour had been bestowed upon her out of deference, or a simple desire to keep a watchful eye on the many valuable items of silver and porcelain to be found gracing various positions en route, Annis wasn't at all sure. Nor, for that matter, did she care too much, for she took little interest in the richness of her surroundings, wanting only to answer the summons that she was well aware would not have been issued unless necessary.

One glance at his lordship's arm justified the trust she placed in her maid's judgement. 'Yes, Dish,' she said, settling herself on the edge of the richly draped four-poster bed, the better to examine the injury. 'There are some threads embedded in the wound. My tweezers, if you please.'

'I didn't dare risk probing myself, Miss Annis, not with my eyes,' Disher admitted. 'And the wound looks as though it could turn uncommon nasty if mauled about unnecessarily.'

'It's certainly inflamed, Dish. But it's still little more than a scratch, thank goodness! And at least I've been spared the necessity of having to probe for a piece of lead shot.'

Out of the corner of her eye Annis saw the butler and another male servant, whom she supposed must be his lordship's valet, exchange startled glances, as though amazed that 'a mere slip of a girl' would ever contemplate attempting such a thing, and smiled to herself before returning her full attention to the injured arm.

'That's as much as can be done for the present,' she announced, a few moments later, after successfully extracting the threads, thoroughly cleansing the inflamed area, and binding the wound up deftly. 'Has he regained consciousness at all, even for a moment?'

'Not since he was carried into this chamber, ma'am,' the valet volunteered. 'His lordship did not so much as stir when we removed his clothes and placed him in his nightshirt.'

Although not altogether happy to learn this, Annis betrayed none of her concerns as she turned to her maid. 'I'll remain with him for the present, Dish. You rest for a while and partake of refreshments. I'm sure Dunster, here, will kindly see to it that you are made comfortable.'

His slight bow in acknowledgement was sufficient to assure Annis that he was prepared, at least for the time being, to leave someone who had shown such presence of mind, and a certain degree of knowledge, in charge of the sickroom. All the same, she had no desire to give the impression that she had any desire to rule the roost, and so requested him to send word the instant his lordship's sister returned.

The valet, eager, seemingly, to undertake his normal duties, was not slow to follow the others from the room, shaking his head as he did so, while bemoaning the damage to his master's superbly tailored coat and expensive linen, leaving Annis free to study his lordship in private for the first time.

His straight-limbed and well-muscled physique clearly revealed a life of comfort, but certainly not one of overindulgence. A second and much closer perusal of his physiognomy did not persuade her to change her former opinion. His features, though undeniably regular, were too sharply defined for him to be considered handsome, though a generous breadth of forehead suggested strongly that he wasn't lacking intelligence. Although her godmother, Lady Pelham, had mentioned that he had attained the age of thirty in recent weeks, there wasn't a surfeit of lines about the eyes and mouth, which might well indicate, Annis thought, that he was a gentleman not given to smiling much. It did not automatically follow, though, that he went out of his way to be disagreeable or was totally lacking in humour, and it would be a mistake to assume that this might be so.

Leaning forward, she placed her fingers gently over that deep furrow between coal-black brows, further evidence, she quickly decided, of a serious bent rather than a frivolous one. But of nothing more, she reiterated silently, striving to keep an open mind.

Conscious all the while of the dry, yet not excessive, heat rising steadily through her fingers, she turned her head to gaze absently through the window at the slowly increasing pile of snowflakes gathering on the sill and the now totally white landscape beyond, before returning her attention to her patient, and discovering herself the recipient of a steady, albeit slightly puzzled, gaze.

'Welcome back, sir,' she said gently, while removing her hand and rising from the bed. 'Do you recognise your surroundings?'

'I do… But I cannot say the same for you, ma'am.'

'Nor should you,' Annis responded, instantly liking the husky timbre of the cultured, masculine voice. 'Suffice it to say that you sustained a fall from your horse and it was I who took it upon myself to return you to your home.'

There was a slight grimace as he raised one of his black brows a fraction. 'An angel of mercy, I perceive!'

Annis couldn't forbear a smile at the thread of scepticism she clearly discerned. 'I have been called many things in my time, sir, but an angel has never numbered amongst them until now.' She became serious again. 'How do you feel? As though you have been kicked by a mule, I dare swear.'

'I feel as if someone is pounding my head with a mallet, certainly.'

'How many fingers am I holding up?' Annis asked, after raising one hand.

A faint look of boredom flickered over his features. 'Three.'

'And you can see me quite clearly?'

There was a slight pause while blue eyes, of a particular dark and striking shade, travelled over the mass of glossy chestnut curls that framed her face. 'Perfectly.'

'In that case I shan't plague you further for the present.' Reaching for a certain bottle in her case, Annis carefully measured several drops into a clean glass and added water before slipping her arm beneath his lordship's broad shoulders. 'Drink this,' she coaxed, after successfully raising him slightly. 'It will help you to sleep. Hopefully your head will feel better when you wake again.'

His lordship required no further prompting. He swallowed the liquid meekly, as though unequal to the task of putting up any form of resistance. He certainly seemed disinclined to attempt further conversation, and during those few minutes his eyes remained open he spoke not a word, though Annis had the feeling that he remained very conscious of her presence, before his heavy lids finally lowered.

A moment later the tranquillity pervading the master bedchamber was broken by the reappearance of none other than the butler, who delivered the welcome news that his mistress had returned safely, and was awaiting Miss Milbank in the parlour. Once again he took it upon himself to act as escort, even going so far as to introduce Annis very graciously, before leaving the two ladies alone together.

As she came forward to take the proffered hand, Annis was immediately struck by the strong resemblance between the Greythorpe siblings. Then her perceptive gaze registered the worry and puzzlement in the blue eyes that the brief and tentative smile of welcome could not quite disguise.

'I do not know how much you have learned since your return, Miss Greythorpe,' she said, coming straight to the point in her no-nonsense manner in an attempt to allay what she suspected must surely be the sister's most pressing concern. 'But let me assure you that, in my opinion, your brother is not seriously injured. In point of fact, he regained consciousness a few minutes ago, and was quite lucid. He betrayed no signs of impaired vision, though he did complain of a headache, which is perfectly understandable in the circumstances. Furthermore, there are no signs of a significant rise in his temperature.'

Annis took a moment to stare once again through a window at the increasing depth of snow covering the landscape. 'In view of the fact that it is highly unlikely that the doctor will arrive in the near future, if indeed at all this day, I took it upon myself to tend to your brother's injuries personally and administer a few drops of laudanum to ensure that he sleeps at least for the next few hours.'

The troubled look that followed this pronouncement was not lost on her either. 'Do not be alarmed, Miss Greythorpe. My father was a practitioner. And an exceptional one, if I may say so. He saw fit to pass on some of his knowledge and skill to me, at least sufficient for me to do more good than harm.'

The concerned expression faded marginally. 'Please forgive me, Miss Milbank. You must think me quite rag-mannered. Do sit down. As you can appreciate, I am sure, I am somewhat puzzled by what I've discovered since my return. I understand that you came upon my brother lying in the road, and that he had been shot?'

Annis didn't doubt for a second that the tall, angular woman standing before her was finding it difficult to comprehend just why such a fate should have befallen the head of the household. No matter what others thought about Lord Greythorpe, his sister clearly considered him above reproach.

'That is correct, ma'am. Perhaps, though, I should begin by explaining why it was that I, a complete stranger, should happen along at a most opportune time,' Annis said, after once again making herself comfortable in the chair by the hearth. 'It was with the sole purpose of seeking an interview with Viscount Greythorpe that prompted my visit to this part of the country.'

She could see at once that she had captured her listener's full attention. 'Although I am not acquainted with his lordship personally, I have been acquainted with another member of your family for very many years—your sister, Helen. In point of fact, her aunt is my godmother. And it was at Lady Pelham's behest that I have made this journey into Hampshire.'

Although Sarah Greythorpe was clearly intrigued to learn this, her most pressing concern was to discover more about what had happened to her brother, as she proved when she said, 'And so it was while you were travelling here to the Manor that you came upon his lordship lying in the road?'

Annis nodded. 'Quite correct, ma'am. Naturally, never having seen him before, I had no notion of who he might be. It wasn't until I arrived here that I discovered his identity.'

'Yes, yes. I can fully appreciate that,' she said, placing a slightly shaking hand to a forehead that was deeply etched, betraying a lingering anxiety. 'I just cannot understand who might have wished Deverel harm.'

Although she could fully understand these concerns, Annis, being an immensely practical sort of person, considered the immediate future of far more importance.

'No doubt we shall discover more when your brother is up and about again. Which I do not envisage will be long delayed. All the same, I did take it upon myself to send for a doctor. What manner of man is your local practitioner?'

The response came without a moment's delay. 'Thankfully, an extremely conscientious one.'

'In that case, he will not hesitate to answer the summons, if he is able.'

All at once Sarah Greythorpe looked troubled again. 'I have already called upon his services once this day,' she disclosed. 'He was with me for a time, attending to an injury sustained by a retired elderly retainer. While on the estate, he received word that his presence was urgently required several miles away. He left just as the first flakes of snow began to fall.'

'In that case, we would be foolish to suppose that he will manage to call here. Furthermore, he would be very foolish to make the attempt, as the snow is falling harder than ever now. Which brings me to the matter concerning me most at present, Miss Greythorpe. I took it upon myself to remain here until your return, and sent my hired carriage back to town. I very much fear I must take advantage of your kind hospitality by seeking refuge under your roof until the weather improves and my maid and I can be conveyed to the posting-house,' Annis explained, a moment before the door unexpectedly opened.

She then watched a girl, not long out of the schoolroom, she judged, slip shyly into the room, thereby denying Miss Greythorpe the opportunity to respond, and obliging her reluctant hostess to make known the identity of the new arrival.

Although initially Sarah Greythorpe might not have been altogether happy about being compelled to house two complete strangers for an indefinite period, by the time the evening was well advanced, the slight misgivings she had once harboured had all but disappeared, and she was surprisingly experiencing, given the traumatic events of the day, a feeling of rare contentment as she paid her second visit to her brother's apartments in the west wing.

The surprising feeling of well-being that had increased with the passing of the hours was given a further boost the instant she entered the master bedchamber to discover the head of the family awake this time, and propped against a mound of pillows, sombrely contemplating the bowl of weak broth set before him on a tray.

As Annis had correctly judged, Viscount Greythorpe could never be accused of being light-minded. None the less, Sarah did not allow that inscrutable expression he invariably maintained to deter her from approaching the bed, for she above anyone knew that her brother was a master at concealing his emotions, and that it was nigh impossible to judge his moods.

'How are you feeling now, after your long sleep? Better, I trust?' she asked, showing a deal more animation than she had been wont to display in many a long year.

His lordship regarded her in silence, while he depleted further the contents of the bowl. 'I'd feel a good deal better if I hadn't been experiencing the increasing conviction that, during the past hours, my household had been taken over by a perfect stranger, and one who, moreover, I strongly suspect, is a very managing female withal.'

'Oh, no, no, not managing!' His sister was all delightful confusion, an attitude he had witnessed all too frequently over the years. 'I'm certain she has only your best interests at heart.'

He smiled grimly. 'I am pleased that you retain sense enough not to attempt to deny it, my dear. I should never have believed you had you tried. I know you too well. You would never have had the temerity to insist I drink only water, nor present me with only a bowl of weak broth, after I had fasted for most of the day.'

'Oh, well...Annis...Miss Milbank assured me it would be necessary to keep your diet light at least for today, as there was just the slight risk you might become feverish,' Sarah explained in what his lordship considered an unnecessarily coaxing voice, as though she were trying to reason with some unruly child.

'Doctor Prentiss has not called,' she continued, when he made no comment. 'Which is in no way surprising, my dear, in view of the fact that it has snowed for most of the afternoon and evening. And I'm reliably informed by Dunster that there are drifts hereabouts now of six feet and more. If it hadn't been for Annis's presence of mind, Louise and I might well have found ourselves stranded at Nanny Berry's cottage. I really ought not to have considered walking over to see her after luncheon.' She paused momentarily to make a little helpless gesture with her hand. 'But you know how difficult I find it, keeping our cousin Louise amused. I thought it would pass the time. And I cannot be sorry that I did so now, for Nanny Berry sustained a fall this morning and twisted her ankle rather badly. It was Dunster who informed me that it was Annis who suggested he send the carriage to collect us.

'She is such a capable person,' she went on hurriedly, when he maintained a stony silence throughout this recital of random snippets of information. 'I cannot tell you what a relief I have found it having her here. We have passed such a very jolly evening, too. Why, I've never seen little Louise so animated! Except for those initial few minutes, when they were first introduced, she has not shown the least shyness in Annis's company.'

His lordship took pity at last. 'That being the case, I do not imagine that it was your enterprising Miss Milbank who had the temerity to present me with this meagre repast in person a short time ago?'

'No, I expect that was Dish...I mean Disher, Miss Milbank's companion and personal maid,' Sarah explained. 'It was she who sat with you for most of the evening. But it was Annis herself who took care of you earlier in the day. It was, in fact, she who discovered you in the road, and took it upon herself to return you safely home.'

'Yes, so Flitwick informed me not so long ago,' his lordship responded, after his mind's eye had successfully summoned up a clear image of chestnut curls framing a highly pleasing, if not conventionally beautiful, countenance. 'I did not recognise her. She is not, I think, from around these parts?'

'No, Deverel, she is not,' Sarah confirmed, appearing slightly troubled again. 'She has lived all her life in the Shires. In point of fact, it was with the very intention of seeking you out that brought her here.'

He betrayed a marked degree of interest now. 'Indeed?'

Unfortunately the slight edge of disapproval in his tone was not

lost on her, and was more than sufficient to assure Sarah that he was
not altogether pleased to learn this; and although she fully appreciated his policy of not admitting perfect strangers to the house,
she found herself instantly coming to their unexpected guest's
defence.

'I would be the first to admit that Miss Milbank is not what
one might consider a...er...conventional young woman,
Deverel. In point of fact, I think it would be fair to say that she
is quite out of the common way. But let me assure you there is
absolutely nothing in her manner to suggest that she is anything
other than a very proper person. Why, even Dunster took it upon
himself to order her baggage placed in the green bedchamber,
would you believe? And as I have heard you remark on several
occasions, you can rely on our butler to know what's what.'

'The green bedchamber, eh? Approval, indeed!' his lordship
was obliged to concede, raising a brow.

Sarah quickly nodded in agreement. 'I cannot tell you the precise
reason why she wishes to see you, Deverel, and I feel fairly certain
that she wouldn't have satisfied my curiosity if I'd had the temerity
to ask. But what I can tell you is that Lady Henrietta Pelham is none
other than her godmother. So I can only assume her business with
you must have something to do with Helen.'

If she had expected this information to reassure him, she soon
realised her mistake when the line between his jet brows grew very
much more pronounced, a clear indication that his initial curiosity had been overshadowed by a strong feeling of annoyance. Those
who knew the Viscount well could testify to his being a fair and,
for the most part, tolerant man. The one thing he would not countenance, however, was interference in his personal concerns.

'In that case, Sarah, you had best go and assure our unexpected
guest that she shall be granted the interview she desires directly

after breakfast tomorrow.' The smile that curled one corner of his mouth was neither pleasant nor of long duration. 'Whether she enjoys the experience or not is a different matter entirely.'

Chapter Three

Whether or not it was having enjoyed a good night's rest in possibly the most comfortable bed she had ever slept in in her life that had resulted in a feeling of utter contentment, Annis wasn't perfectly sure. She only knew she felt not a whit disturbed at the prospect of being obliged to remain at the Manor at least for a further day, and possibly a good deal longer. In fact, she was very much looking forward to spending more time with those two charming females whose delightful company she would never have been privileged to enjoy in the normal course of events.

All the same, Annis was nothing if not a realist. She was well aware that perhaps not everyone residing at Greythorpe Manor might be pleased to be housing an uninvited guest. Nor was she prepared to forget what had necessitated her visit to the county in the first place. Consequently, after savouring the rare treat of a leisurely breakfast in bed, she didn't delay in answering the summons to join the master of the house in the library.

Seemingly content to maintain the role of personal escort, Dunster was on hand to show her the way to the handsome book-lined room on the ground floor, where the master of the house stood sentinel-like by the window, surveying his acreage of snow-covered park land.

For several moments, after his butler had announced his visitor and had withdrawn, his lordship didn't move so much as a muscle. Then, very slowly, he turned, and subjected Annis to a prolonged stare, which was no less disturbingly direct than her own could be on occasions.

Just what flaws in her person his thorough appraisal had managed to locate, Annis had no way of knowing, for his expression remained quite inscrutable as he came slowly round the desk towards her, gesturing towards a chair by the hearth as he did so and inviting her to sit down.

'Firstly, Miss Milbank, I must thank you for the singular service you rendered me yesterday. But for your timely assistance, my case might have become dire indeed.'

'You do not appear to be suffering unduly after your unfortunate experience,' Annis responded, having some difficulty deciding whether he was genuinely grateful, or merely adhering to the social niceties by offering his thanks.

'But for your intervention, Miss Milbank, I might well be suffering a deal more than a few bruises and a sore arm.'

'You make too much of it, sir,' she responded, raising a hand and moving it swiftly through the air, as though attempting to rid herself of a troublesome insect.

'Not according to what my sister and servants tell me,' he countered, his voice, like his gaze, revealing nothing of what was really passing through his mind.

'Then let us both thank Providence, sir,' Annis suggested, all at once sensing that Viscount Greythorpe was a gentleman who favoured plain speaking. 'The unexpected encounter has been as much to my benefit as yours. Had I not come upon you lying in the road, I might well have been denied, outright, the interview I'm being granted now.'

For an instant something that might well have been akin to approval flickered in the depths of deep blue eyes. It was gone too quickly for Annis to be certain. None the less, she considered it a modest victory. At least she had succeeded in piercing that inscrutable mask, if only briefly. Just what could lurk, hidden from the world at large, behind that impassive façade she might never be granted the opportunity to discover. There was one thing of which she was absolutely certain now, though—the master of Greythorpe Manor was not so coolly detached as he might wish to appear.

'It wasn't until last night,' she began, 'while I was lying in bed, that I began to appreciate, perhaps for the very first time, that any gentleman who places a high value on his reputation must of necessity remain on his guard. Females, of course, need to be extra-vigilant. But there are pitfalls for the unwary of both sexes,' she continued, gazing thoughtfully into the fire, and thereby missing the quite different flicker this time that glinted in his lordship's eyes. 'Here am I, a complete stranger... How can you possibly be sure I am who I say I am, seeking you out for a legitimate reason, and not some designing harpy out to entrap you for personal gain?'

If his lordship was taken aback by the indelicate choice of language, he certainly betrayed no sign of it. 'Be easy on that score,' he said, his intense gaze not wavering for a second. 'I have no doubt that you are Miss Annis Milbank of the Shires. And not, I am persuaded, come here for reasons of your own.' If possible, his gaze grew marginally more searching. 'Nor, I am persuaded, did you agree to come here altogether willingly, but at Lady Pelham's personal request.'

She could not help but admire his perspicacity. Seemingly his sister had passed on what little information Annis had been willing to divulge the previous evening, and he had deduced correctly that she was here at someone else's behest, though whether he was altogether pleased about it was a different matter entirely. She strongly suspected that he was not, and was doing his utmost to conceal the fact.

The suspicion did not, however, deter her from assuring him that he was perfectly correct. 'Indeed, yes, sir, a circumstance I should now be in a position to prove, if I hadn't foolishly overlooked the fact yesterday that I had, for safekeeping, placed my godmother's letter of introduction in one of those bags now awaiting my arrival at the posting-house in your local town. Furthermore,' she added when he made no response, 'you are perfectly correct in your assumption. I did indeed undertake this mission most reluctantly.'

Curiosity evidently had managed to get the better of him, because he put in rather sharply, 'Why so?'

'Because I consider I'm not the most suitable person to adopt the role of emissary. I am on occasions too plain-spoken for some people's tastes.' She shrugged. 'Lady Pelham, however, thought differently, possibly because her long and close friendship with my late mother resulted in my own extensive knowledge of her private concerns.'

'Miss Milbank,' he said after a further prolonged silence, during which she was yet again subjected to close scrutiny, 'I do not boggle at plain-speaking. You may fulfil your designated role with impunity.'

Thus assured, Annis didn't hesitate to reveal the dilemma besetting Lady Henrietta Pelham. She deliberately refrained from embellishing the reasons why her godmother considered it detrimental to visit Greythorpe Manor at the present time with explanations of her own. Yet, surprisingly enough, it was precisely her own views on the matter that he sought the instant she had revealed all.

'Come, Miss Milbank,' he urged, when she continued to regard him with just a hint of suspicion in what he considered a refreshingly direct gaze for one of her sex. 'I do appreciate you were in

Draycot's company for a brief period only, and on that single occasion. Nevertheless, I cannot believe he departed from your godmother's home without leaving an impression upon you.'

He detected just a hint of a smile playing about the sweet curve of her lips, before she turned her head to watch the flames dancing in the hearth. For several moments the only sounds he detected in the room was his own even breathing matching the steady ticking of the mantel-clock; and the strong suspicion that Annis Milbank was for the most part a very restful young woman passed through his mind a moment before she admitted,

'My every instinct tells me my godmother isn't very far out in her assessment of that particular person's character, sir. I cannot imagine Mr Draycot would ever concern himself overmuch about the feelings of others.'

She turned her head to look at him, her gaze so prolonged that his lordship had little difficulty in detecting the flecks of green contained in the depths of her lovely grey eyes. 'It is also my opinion that Lady Pelham has assessed the situation perfectly. It might indeed prove to be a grave error if Helen is forcibly removed from Draycot's sphere at the present time.'

'So, you too believe my sister might be persuaded to elope?'

'I sincerely believe it's a distinct possibility, yes,' she answered, scrupulously truthful. Her sigh was clearly audible. 'Yesterday evening, I found myself on numerous occasions comparing Helen with your cousin Louise. There is less than two years between them, and yet the difference is quite marked. Unlike Louise, your sister doesn't lack self-confidence and is mature beyond her years.'

'And yet, from what you tell me, she's singularly failed to appreciate she has become the target of some gazetted fortune-hunter,' he countered, rapier-sharp.

'True. But I didn't attempt to suggest she lacks any of those less favourable feminine attributes,' Annis parried, with equal swiftness. 'What female on the verge of womanhood would not feel highly gratified to become the sole object of a handsome man's attentions? Draycot's a veritable *Adonis*, sir! Why, even I found myself blinking several times when he walked into Godmama's parlour! And you may be sure that a handsome face hasn't caused so much as a fluttering in my breast for years!'

It could well have been a trick of the light, but Annis felt sure she detected what looked suspiciously like a twitch at one side of his lordship's mouth, before he raised a shapely hand to massage his chin, as though giving due consideration to what he had just learned.

'Sir, I wouldn't dream of attempting to suggest your sister is so well adjusted that she doesn't require guidance,' she went on, when he continued to gaze meditatively at some imaginary spot on the hearth rug. 'But what I do believe is that eventually sense will prevail and she will see Draycot for precisely what he is. Lady Pelham is wishful for Helen to attend the party here at the beginning of April, and become acquainted with her Greythorpe relations. What she's endeavouring to do is not reveal her opinion of Draycot, and give the impression that she has any intention of removing Helen from his sphere by insisting they accept your invitation to spend several weeks here.'

'Yet she is determined that Helen should spend those few days in Devon next week,' he parried, but Annis wasn't in the least discomposed by the sharpness of the response.

'And very well it was managed too,' she praised, determined to reveal her admiration for the method her godmother had so cleverly adopted. 'You must remember, sir, that that particular invitation was issued and accepted long before Draycot's arrival in Bath. And, incidentally, before your first communication was received by Lady Pelham,' she reminded him.

'Initially Helen had been overjoyed to think she would be present at her best friend's birthday celebration. Quite naturally, after Draycot had crossed her path, and tried his utmost to persuade her not to leave Bath, she did begin to have second thoughts about attending the party. Cleverly, Lady Pelham didn't attempt to remonstrate. She merely said she had no intention of changing her own plans, and that Helen was at liberty to remain behind, if she so wished, providing she stayed in the home of one of Lady Pelham's close friends. Which resulted in Helen finally deciding herself to accompany her aunt into Devon, despite Mr Draycot's opposition.

'Furthermore, during my short stay in Bath, Helen herself revealed that during the time she was still debating on whether to attend her friend's party, your invitation to stay here at Greythorpe arrived.' Annis couldn't suppress a half-smile. 'Even Helen herself considered it most odd that a gentleman who, in one breath, had been professing himself heartbroken at the mere thought of being parted from her for so much as a long weekend should, in the next, be actively encouraging her to enjoy a protracted stay with relations in Hampshire. I'm as one with my godmother. There is something decidedly smoky about Draycot. And he definitely has a very good reason for not wishing Helen and Godmama to visit Devon.'

The long silence that followed was broken when the Viscount unexpectedly asked, 'Okehampton is where this forthcoming party is taking place, I believe you said?'

Annis nodded as she watched him rise to his feet, his brow once more furrowed by deep lines of thought as he turned to take up his former stance before one of the windows. When he attempted to say nothing further, she took it to mean that he considered the interview at an end, and was not unduly sorry herself. She had completed the task for which she had been entrusted, and to press the matter further, she strongly suspected, would avail her nothing.

'Be assured, Miss Milbank, I shall consider carefully what you have told me, and let you know my decision in due course,' he announced, when the silence was once again broken by the rustling of Annis's skirts this time, as she rose to her feet. 'After all, there is no immediate hurry. You won't be going anywhere for a day or two, I suspect.'

Still unable to decide whether or not he resented this, Annis went across to the door, as content as he appeared to be himself to bring the interview to an end. Then she bethought herself of another matter, and delved into her pocket, capturing his full attention once again when she tossed the heavy purse down upon his desk.

'Yours, I believe, sir. I removed it from your pocket when you lay unconscious in the road, and omitted to put it back.' Annis found herself unable to resist a further smile as she watched his blue eyes focus on the filled leather pouch. 'Whatever the reason behind the attack upon you, it certainly wasn't robbery. A further mystery that requires solving, I'm thinking.'

His lordship watched her quietly leave the room before retrieving his property from the desk. 'Yes, Miss Annis Milbank,' he murmured, tossing the purse in one hand as though attempting to assess its contents. 'And no less intriguing than the young woman who retained my property for safekeeping.'

Annis was not destined to cross the Viscount's path again until that evening, when she joined the family in the small parlour just prior to dinner. Miss Greythorpe had once again proved to be a gracious hostess, keeping her entertained for the majority of the afternoon by taking her on a leisurely tour of the Manor. Louise in particular had proved to be lively company, chuckling constantly at Annis's less-than-flattering observations about the portraits of the Greythorpe ancestors lining the walls of the picture gallery.

So it came as something of a surprise to Annis to detect a degree of constraint in the atmosphere the instant she entered the comfortable little room where she had spent part of the day plying a needle, while conversing about nothing in particular, or listening to Louise's highly commendable efforts on the instrument in the corner of the room.

If anything, the atmosphere became a fraction more strained when they took their places in the small, informal dining room, and it wasn't too difficult for Annis to appreciate why this should be. Although Sarah Greythorpe had been gracious in welcoming a stranger under her roof, there was a definite reserve in her character. Like his lordship, Sarah was not garrulous by nature, and Annis suspected that brother and sister had been content to pass their evenings together in companionable silence. Perhaps both had put themselves out to make slight adjustments in their lifestyle with the advent of Louise's arrival, but even so it wasn't to be expected that two such reserved characters would have much in common with a girl of Louise's age, most especially his lordship, who was clearly finding his young cousin's natural shyness in his presence somewhat difficult to overcome.

Seized by a benevolent whim, Annis decided to come to his rescue by addressing a remark directly at Louise, thereby forcing the girl to make conversation. 'I believe you mentioned your parents are at present enjoying an extensive tour of Italy, Louise. When are you expecting them to return?'

'Late spring,' was the only response forthcoming.

'And I seem to recall you mentioned earlier today that you have a brother up at Oxford?' Annis persisted, determined to see at least a return of a semblance of the girl whose company she had enjoyed earlier in the day.

'Yes, Tom. In his last letter he said he would try to get down to see me quite soon.' If anything, she looked more forlorn than before. 'But I do not think it will be this weekend.'

'Unlikely,' his lordship agreed. 'Only a fool would attempt travelling any distance before a significant thaw.'

'And with luck that will not be too long in coming,' Annis put in quickly before his lordship, unintentionally or otherwise, could dampen poor Louise's spirits further. 'Then at least you will not be confined to the house, and will no doubt enjoy a good gallop across the park.'

She could see at once by Louise's crestfallen expression that she had blundered, even before the girl admitted, 'I don't ride. I—I don't like horses.'

'I'm afraid our cousin suffered a bad fall a year or so ago, and broke her collar bone,' Sarah explained. 'As a result she is somewhat nervous round horses now.'

'Very understandable,' Annis hurriedly sympathised, thereby successfully recapturing Louise's attention before the girl could observe the look of impatience that momentarily flickered over his lordship's features.

Annis strongly suspected he was one of those people who had little sympathy for anyone who made no attempt to overcome his or her fears, and to a certain extent she agreed with this viewpoint. Yet at the same time she could appreciate Louise's wariness, and decided to voice her further support.

'Horses, of course, even the most well behaved among them, can be notoriously unpredictable creatures—forever twitching and snorting when one least expects it. And if that isn't bad enough, you then get the biters and those that do their level best to tread on the toes of the unwary. Worst of all are the kickers!'

Annis wasn't at all surprised to have retained Louise's full attention. Evidently the girl wasn't accustomed to having someone speaking out on her behalf, and she continued to stare across the table in a mixture of gratitude and reverence. Sarah, perhaps finding it a pleasant change not having to seek out topics to keep the dinnertime conversation going, was lending more than a polite ear. His lordship's gaze too was firmly fixed in Annis's direction, though there was unmistakably more than just a hint of a suspicious gleam flickering in that razor-sharp stare of his—a suggestion, possibly, of staunch disapproval.

Undeterred by what she strongly suspected might be one listener's disapprobation, Annis warmed to the subject. 'My late grandfather once owned a notorious kicker, a beautiful grey hunter, fearless, but downright ruthless to any hapless soul who happened to approach him from the rear. Of course Grandpapa, being Grandpapa, didn't waste an opportunity to make use of the creature's failing. I recall quite clearly that morning, and I couldn't have been more than ten years old at the time, when a close neighbour by the name of McGregor came to call. Being aware of his neighbour's avaricious tendencies, Grandpapa easily tempted him by tossing a shiny golden guinea down in the line of fire, as it were. To this day I still don't know how the poor man avoided ending head first in the water trough.'

'Your grandsire would appear to have been something of a jester, Miss Milbank,' his lordship remarked drily, after his sister's ladylike attempts to stifle her chuckles and his cousin's more open merriment had faded.

'He could be an out-and-out rascal when it suited his purposes, sir,' Annis revealed, with total honesty. 'At the age of fourteen he took it upon himself to run away from school and spent months going about the country from fair to fair with a band of travelling entertainers, would you believe?'

'Good heavens!' Sarah exclaimed, appearing genuinely shocked.

'What on earth possessed him to do such a thing? Anything might have befallen him.'

Annis shrugged. 'I suspect much did. He always swore he learned more in those few months than at any other time in his life. And, of course, to a certain extent running away served his purpose.

'His father was intent on him pursuing a career in the church,' she went on to explain, when his lordship raised one black brow, a clear indication that he was curious to discover more himself now. 'It was a nonsensical notion, for a more inappropriate person to take holy orders would have been difficult to find. When eventually he was tracked down, his father and mother were so overjoyed to have him safely back in the bosom of the family that they allowed him his way and agreed to his joining the navy, providing he finished his education first. Sadly for Grandpapa, his dream of a career at sea was destined never to be realised. Fate intervened. His elder brother died in a smallpox outbreak, and Grandfather was then groomed to step into his father's shoes, and inherit the property. He became a considerable landowner who, to do him justice, took his responsibilities very seriously. All the same, he never forgot what he learned during those few months he spent with horse-traders, gypsies and entertainers.

'In fact, after dinner,' she added, addressing herself once again directly to Louise, 'I shall endeavour to entertain you by revealing a little something he learned during that period of unholy adventure.'

Whether it was simply because Louise found dining in his lordship's presence something of an ordeal, or she was genuinely eager to discover precisely what it was the late Josiah Milbank in his reprehensible youth had been taught by fairground folk that induced her not to delay in finishing her meal was difficult to judge. Nevertheless, it seemed to Annis that in no time at all she was returning to the small parlour with the ladies of the house. Surprisingly enough, the master himself was not far behind them, though whether this attentiveness on his part was prompted by a determination to prove himself the perfect host even to an uninvited guest, or a desire to keep a watchful eye on proceedings, was equally impossible to judge.

Once the tea things had been removed, Dunster, always on hand to cater for every need, was not slow to provide Annis with the items she requested; and although she might have wished that the three dainty porcelain vessels he placed down on the table in order for her to perform her trick might not have appeared quite so expensive or delicate, it wasn't long before she was concentrating hard and inducing the ladies of the house to part with their money.

'A perfect example of the quickness of the hand deceiving the eye,' his lordship drawled, after watching the pile of coins at Annis's elbow growing steadily taller. 'Or is it simply a case of fools and their money, etcetera?' he added, if not looking precisely amused by proceedings, at least not appearing wholly disapproving.

Annis raised the porcelain cup in her right hand to reveal the tiny pebble, which resulted in both Sarah and Louise having once again to dip into their purses for pennies to add to the pile on the corner of the table. 'Don't be too disheartened, ladies,' she said cheerily. 'It's all in a good cause, remember? I am relying on you to place my winnings in the poor box. There may be no sign of a thaw yet, but I very much doubt I shall still be here to perform the deed myself after church on Sunday.'

Receiving no response, Annis raised her eyes in time to see Sarah's smile fade and to discover Louise looking downright crestfallen. It was rather flattering to think that neither lady was eager for her departure. His lordship's thoughts on the matter of her leaving, on the other hand, were impossible to gauge. His expression remained as impassive as ever, as he continued to regard her steadily from beneath half-closed lids.

'Do you not care to try your luck, sir?' she invited, but he was not to be tempted.

'I do not object to games of chance, Miss Milbank,' he freely admitted. 'But I am not so gullible as to partake in those where there is not the remotest possibility of winning. A game or two of picquet is a different matter entirely, however.'

His lordship watched a dimple appear in response to this challenge, before a perfectly sculptured feminine mouth curled into the most natural, roguish smile he had ever seen in his life.

'You amaze me, sir! Dare you risk challenging a person who from the cradle has been tutored by a master of deception, and who is possibly conversant with at least a dozen ways to cheat at cards?'

His lordship's response to this deliberate provocation was merely to rise to his feet and saunter across to the gaming-table, from which he drew out a fresh pack of cards, before gesturing with one shapely hand, inviting her to join him.

After a moment's indecision Annis obliged, though she had little doubt he had definite reasons for singling her out for particular attention. That he was intent on putting her through some kind of test seemed the most obvious conclusion to draw. This was borne out when he quickly suggested a change of game, one involving a deal more skill.

It swiftly became obvious, too, that he was no mean player himself, skilled and, more importantly, remarkably controlled. Moderate sums of money certainly changed hands at frequent intervals, and by the time the evening was fast drawing to a close honours were more or less evenly divided.

'My compliments, Miss Milbank. You have proved a worthy opponent,' he announced, forestalling her as she made to rise in order to return to the ladies before finally retiring for the night.

He regarded her in silence for a moment, with just a suspicion of a twitching smile. 'Given what you've revealed about your grandfather this evening, and your evident close bond with the aforementioned worthy gentleman, I should have been astonished if you hadn't received a deal of instruction in how to fleece your fellow man,' he surprised her by saying, thereby finally responding to the provocative remark she had voiced earlier. 'And I should be equally astonished if you were ever to indulge in the reprehensible practice yourself for personal gain.'

'How well you know me already, sir!' Annis responded, raising her eyes to discover his lordship quite openly smiling now.

The sight was so unexpected that it caught her completely off guard, and although she would never have indulged in flights of fancy by admitting to a quickening of breath, or a suddenly increased pulse rate, she certainly felt something within her stir, a sensation that was totally novel and therefore impossible to define.

His lordship might never number among the most handsome men she had ever met, but his smile went some way in placing him among those that were quite out of the common way, she swiftly decided. And, she suspected too, not easily forgotten.

Chapter Four

It was after spending a third night luxuriating in the comfort of a four-poster bed that Annis woke to discover clear evidence that the thaw had at some point during the night well and truly set in.

She was in no way surprised to detect the gentle tinkle-tinkle of water running along the guttering, or to see droplets of melted snow following each other in rapid succession down the panes of glass on her bedchamber windows, for Dr Prentiss, having braved the elements and safely negotiated the numerous snowdrifts, had managed to pay a belated call the previous afternoon. After a brief and favourable examination of his lordship, he had joined the ladies in the parlour, and had assured one and all that he had detected a definite rise in temperature during his journey to the Manor, and had declared he'd be surprised if there wasn't a thaw before too long.

Although disinclined to make snap judgements about people, Annis had made up her mind long before he had left the house that she rather liked the good doctor. Conscientious, and possessed of a gentle reassuring manner that could not help but put the most nervous patient swiftly at ease, Dr Prentiss had put her forcibly in mind of her own father. Consequently his accurate prediction on the weather came as no surprise. What did rather astonish her, though, was the disappointment she was now experiencing at having no valid reason for remaining at the Manor.

'Ah, Dish!' she announced, turning her head as the door opened to discover her loyal maid-cum-companion entering the room. 'Time to pack our belongings, I think.'

'Can't see any reason not to set out for the town this morning, miss,' Disher responded, after depositing the pitcher of hot water on the washstand. 'According to one of the stable-lads, the roads are all clear, or clear enough for travel, at any rate.'

'That is good news,' Annis replied, lying quite convincingly. She had no intention of revealing how disappointed she felt at the prospect of leaving the Manor, especially as the reason for the un- expected swell of malcontent continued to allude her.

'Do you want me to ring for your breakfast tray, miss?'

'I'd much prefer to break my fast in the parlour,' Annis admitted. 'However, given the fact that I've been assured his lordship prefers his own company for the first meal of the day, it might be as well to pander to his whims, especially as I find myself obliged to take advantage of his generosity still further by begging the use of a carriage to convey us to town.'

'Do you imagine there's a chance he might refuse?'

'Had you asked me that very question directly after I'd perused the blunt letter he'd written to Lady Pelham, Dish, I would have been inclined to suggest there was a very strong possibility he might do precisely that. Now, however, I can safely say, "Cer- tainly not", with total conviction.'

Absently plucking at the bed covers, Annis began to consider his lordship's character still further. 'I should imagine only those select few who number among his closest friends are privileged to know his lordship really well. Notwithstanding, if I've discovered

anything during our enforced stay here, it's that Viscount Greythorpe is far from the austere, humourless being one might imagine
him to be at first sight. He's certainly an intelligent man who, I
suspect, rarely acts without due consideration. I think, too, that
anyone would be extremely foolish to underestimate him; it would
come as no great surprise to me, either, to discover that he could
be quite ruthless if crossed. First and foremost though, Dish, his
lordship is a gentleman, born and bred. He would never see a lady
stranded, or turn away without offering his support. Ergo, I harbour
no fears that we shall find ourselves obliged to walk to the posting-house in town later this morning.'

Although firmly convinced that her reading of his lordship's
character was accurate, as far as was reasonably possible to
judge on so short an acquaintance, Annis wasn't unduly surprised to be the recipient of that severe frown of his, when she
had the temerity to sweep into his private sanctum, unannounced,
a little over an hour later. After all, he was essentially a very
private man who, if his daily routine was any indication, preferred to spend much of his time alone. Personally she saw
nothing amiss with this preference for his own company and, as
a guest in his house, would never have dreamt of interrupting at
a time when he was clearly working had the need to do so not
been absolutely necessary.

'Forgive the intrusion, my lord,' she said, boldly slipping into the
chair on the opposite side of his desk, after he had belatedly risen
to his feet, acknowledging her arrival with the briefest of nods. 'But,
as I'm sure you'll appreciate, given the favourable change in the
weather, I didn't wish to delay in speaking with you this morning.'

For answer his lordship merely reseated himself, before placing
the letter he had been perusing to one side, and paying her the

common courtesy of at least favouring her with his full attention, even
if his expression remained serious, and not wholly welcoming.

'Loath though I am to do so, sir, I must beg another favour by
requesting the use of a carriage to convey me and my maid to the
local town, as there is no reason now for us to remain, and I refuse
to take advantage of your kind hospitality further by outstaying the
gracious welcome you and your sister have extended thus far to a
complete stranger.'

'There is absolutely no likelihood of your outstaying your welcome,' his lordship surprised her by responding, before confounding her further by adding, 'But is not your request of a carriage a
little—how shall I put it—precipitate? You had a purpose in coming
here, Miss Milbank,' he reminded her, when she made no attempt
whatsoever to conceal her puzzlement. 'You'll forgive my saying
so, but your attitude this morning is inclined to give the impression that you imagine you've been wholly successful in your endeavours, and that I shall be happy to acquiesce to Lady Pelham's
wishes on the matter of my half-sister?'

Annis couldn't help but admire his directness, and his quite remarkable perspicacity. If the truth were known, she supposed she
had been a little presumptuous. Having quickly come to the conclusion that he was in no way an unreasonable person, she
supposed she had, indeed, taken it for granted that he would oblige
Lady Pelham in this instance by not exerting his authority.

'Seemingly, sir, I have assumed too much in believing just that,'
she admitted, acknowledging the truth of the accusation without
preamble. 'However, if this is not the case, I cannot imagine there
is anything further I can do to make you change your mind, so my
remaining cannot possibly serve any useful purpose to either of us.'

'You err, child,' he returned swiftly. 'Your remaining would
serve a very useful purpose indeed.'

Startled though she was by the admission, Annis didn't fail to observe the same odd smile briefly pulling at one corner of his mouth as she had glimpsed on several occasions during the past two evenings, when they had been playing cards together. Whether or not his evident amusement this time had been engendered by her inability to conceal her bewilderment, she had no way of knowing. Notwithstanding, she decided to leave him in no doubt on that score.

'I am totally at a loss to understand why you should think so, sir.'

His immediate response was to rise to his feet and take up the exact stance by the window that he had adopted during their former meeting in the room. He was undeniably an impressive figure in both height and breadth, and yet surprisingly enough Annis had never found him in any way intimidating. In fact, the opposite was true. The Viscount exuded a quiet dignity that she found oddly comforting and unerringly familiar, because it brought forcibly to mind that special aura she had never failed to detect whenever her late mother had entered a room.

'Firstly permit me to deal with the matter of my half-sister. I shall not pretend to be overjoyed about the current situation,' he began slowly, as though choosing each word with extreme care. 'Nor can I bring myself to wholeheartedly approve of the way Lady Pelham hopes to deal with the matter of my sister's foolish infatuation. None the less, I do fully appreciate that she believes she is acting in the girl's best interests. It is beyond question too that her knowledge of Helen's character is second to none. Consequently, I am prepared not to interfere at this juncture.'

Annis felt a wave of relief wash over her. 'You will not regret your decision, sir.'

'I sincerely trust you prove to be right,' he returned almost brusquely, as he resumed his seat at the desk, his eyes never wavering from hers for an instant. 'But so that we do not misunderstand each other, I shall speak plainly. Unlike yourself, I am not well acquainted with Lady Pelham. I have never heard anything to the lady's discredit. In fact, the opposite is true. Common report would have me believe that, having been a widow for many years, she is positively shrouded in respectability. Even so, she would be a rare being indeed if she was without flaw. Therefore I cannot help wondering if this disinclination on her part to pay an extended visit here at this time stems solely from the honest belief that she is acting in her niece's best interests. It could also be an attempt on her part to continue caring for Helen without outside interference.'

Annis could quite appreciate these reservations, and did not hesitate to offer what reassurance she could, while maintaining the absolute truth. 'If you are asking me whether or not Lady Pelham resents the fact that you are Helen's legal guardian, then all I can tell you is that she never admitted as much to me at any time during my recent stay with her. The overall impression I gained was that she welcomes this interest you are taking in your sister.'

His lordship's regard had never been more keen. 'Does Helen herself know the extent of my authority over her?'

Annis could see no benefit in attempting to conceal the truth, and so shook her head. 'To be honest, sir, it came as a mighty shock to me, so I can only imagine how Helen herself will feel when she learns. But let me assure you that Lady Pelham has not deliberately concealed the truth from her. It was simply that it never crossed her mind to suppose that you would behave any differently than your father, so the matter of your guardianship was never really an issue. Given the stance you have adopted, though, my lord, she fully intends to tell Helen. But she will choose her moment with care.'

Again his look was intense, as he said, 'Clearly you hold your godmother in high regard, Miss Milbank.'

'Indeed I do,' she didn't hesitate to affirm. 'She is without doubt the most level-headed female of my acquaintance. Furthermore, I know her to be a person of her word. She fully intends to bring Helen here at the end of March in order that you may become acquainted in advance of the party.'

When he merely regarded her in silence, Annis thought he must consider the interview at an end, and was about to rise to her feet when he forestalled her by saying, 'You, I believe, have been honest with me, Miss Milbank, so I shall be equally frank. I have several reasons for wishing to become acquainted with my half-sister, not least of which is the benefit, I believe, a closer relationship will eventually bring to Sarah. It cannot have escaped your notice,' he continued in response to her questioning look, 'that my elder sister is essentially a very private person, very much the introvert. I thought a period of several weeks in which to become better acquainted before the rest of the family descends upon us could only be beneficial to them both.'

A sigh escaped him as he lowered his eyes to study the heavy signet ring on his right hand. 'However, I cannot in all honesty say that having our young cousin to stay during these past weeks has turned out to be the overwhelming success I had hoped. I do not think you need me to tell you that my sister and cousin have little in common, and although Sarah is genuinely fond of Louise, she finds entertaining the girl something of a trial on occasions, so perhaps I was foolish to suppose that she might find much in common with Helen.'

'Given that they were kept apart through no fault of their own, it would be nice to think that eventually they will rub along together reasonably well,' Annis said, feeling that some response from her was required. 'It will take time, I should imagine, for any deep sisterly bond to develop, however.'

'Quite so, Miss Milbank! And time, sadly, is not on my side.' Once again she became the sole object of that most strikingly direct violet-eyed gaze. 'But Providence, it would seem, most definitely is. *She* chose to bring to my door someone who is…' here his lordship paused to shake his head, and for the first time ever in her presence to smile broadly in what seemed to be genuine, wry amusement '…blessed with an innate ability to communicate with people on their own level, and make them feel almost instantly less inhibited. No one could have failed to notice that your presence here, Miss Milbank, has been nothing other than highly beneficial. You have, in the most natural manner possible, bridged the divide between my sister and our cousin, which has resulted in a far more relaxed atmosphere prevailing.'

Annis could never recall being complimented in quite the same way before, and while she felt extremely flattered, she had the feeling she had yet to hear the reason for the unexpected praise.

The Viscount chose not to keep her in ignorance for very long. 'If at all possible, I should very much like to maintain that atmosphere,' he continued, 'most especially for Sarah's sake. She will have much to occupy her during the weeks ahead, with all the preparations for our grandmother's birthday celebration. So, as I'm sure you can appreciate, having someone on hand to help entertain Louise would lighten her load considerably.'

Once again his lordship smiled, more broadly than he had done before. 'Not perhaps the most gracious invitation you have ever received, Miss Milbank. But I wish to be as honest with you as you have been with me. My invitation is not merely a gesture of politeness on my part. I do have quite definite reasons for wishing you to remain. Furthermore, I do not want you to harbour the notion that I am seeking some sort of *quid pro quo*. Nothing could be further from my mind. Be assured that whatever your decision, my resolve not to insist on Helen's staying with us during these next few weeks will stand.'

Annis continued to hold his gaze across the desk, until he unexpectedly rose to his feet and returned to the window to stare out at what she suspected was for him a favourite view of the estate. She was not quite certain whether it was altogether sensible for her to remain, at least not for the prolonged stay he was proposing. Yet, at the same time, she couldn't immediately understand why she should suddenly be plagued by uncertainty, when only a short time before she had been desperately striving to quell the swell of disappointment at having no valid reason for remaining at the Manor. It was so unlike her to be so contrary, not knowing her own mind.

He began speaking again, and she paid him the common courtesy of concentrating on what he had to say. 'I do appreciate, Miss Milbank, that you might have commitments back in Leicestershire that make it impossible for you to extend your visit, so I shall not press you. Will you at least do me the honour of taking a day or two to think it over. In the meantime, I shall deal with the matter of the expenses you may have incurred at the inn, and ensure the rest of your belongings are collected and brought here without delay. It is the very least I can do in return for the service you rendered me on your arrival.'

Receiving no response, the Viscount turned in time to catch a surprisingly arresting look in what he had considered from the first to be wonderfully clear and strikingly lovely grey-green eyes.

'Receiving no outright refusal leads me to hope that I may at least look forward to your company for at least a further week, perhaps?'

'Until then, sir, certainly,' Annis finally agreed, drawing her eyes away from the imaginary spot on the wall directly above his left shoulder. 'It will at least grant me the opportunity to attempt to satisfy what some have stigmatised as my insatiable curiosity.'

His lordship didn't attempt to curb his. 'I think I must ask you to explain, Miss Milbank.'

'I shall make a point, sir, of returning to the place where I came upon you three days ago. It's just possible I might uncover something that would offer a clue as to the identity of your attacker.'

His lordship shrugged, betraying his distinct lack of concern. 'I should imagine we have seen the last of the fellow. None the less, if you are intent on investigating, I shall escort you. In fact, I insist upon it, Miss Milbank, in the unlikely event that the rogue is lingering in the locale. Could you be ready to accompany me out in—say—an hour? We could travel in my phaeton. Or would you find an open carriage too cold at this time of year?'

'On the contrary—ideal, sir!' she didn't hesitate to assure him, as she rose from the chair. 'It shall enable me to see more of the countryside.'

Annis didn't delay in returning to the bedchamber. Nor did she delay in revealing her revised plans to her faithful maid.

'Staying, miss…? Whatever for?' Disher demanded, exercising all the familiarity permitted to a lifelong, devoted servant. 'I mind you were set against the whole idea of coming here in the first place. I would have thought you'd have been glad to be gone.'

'Yes, and so should I. But the truth of the matter is, Dish, when I awoke this morning, and discovered I had no valid reason for not packing my bags and leaving, I felt hugely disappointed,' Annis admitted, prepared now to reveal at least some, if not all, of the contrasting feelings she had been experiencing that morning.

She took a moment to stare about the room that, she had been reliably informed, was one of the best guest bedchambers in the house. And she could well believe it! The quality of the chintz curtains and matching bed hangings was unmistakable; the various pieces of walnut furniture dotted about the room had been produced by the finest craftsmen; and the wall and floor coverings had been selected without the least consideration for expense.

'Look about you, Dish,' she urged. 'This bedchamber must be four times the size of the one I use back home, and yet I feel not a whit out of place here. Almost from the moment I set foot inside Greythorpe Manor, I have felt inordinately comfortable in my surroundings, even in those sumptuously furnished rooms that are used only on special occasions. I simply do not understand it!' She shook her head, genuinely puzzled. 'I know that I'm the daughter of a gentleman, and have been accustomed to command most every comfort throughout my life. And I am fully aware that there is a great deal of difference between comfort and out-and-out luxury, Dish, and yet I feel completely at ease here… It's almost as if it's…it's my own home.'

The maid shrugged. 'Well, that's in no way surprising, Miss Annis, if you take a moment to consider. You're your mother's daughter, after all. It's in your blood to appreciate the finer things in life. There's no denying this is a very elegant house. But it cannot compare with the mansion your sainted mother grew up in, at least not in size. Tavistoke Court must be almost three times the size of this place, miss.'

'I'll need to take your word for that, Dish, because it's unlikely I'll ever receive an invitation to visit that particular grandiose dwelling,' Annis returned, before she paused to consider for a moment. 'And, to be truthful, I suppose rank curiosity was responsible in part for my agreeing to come here on Godmama's behalf. I wanted to more than just glimpse the kind of house Mama grew up in. Of course I never imagined I would be granted the opportunity to sample such luxury for so many days.'

An element of concern was easily discernible in the maid's homely features. 'That's understandable, miss. But it wouldn't do for you to become too comfortable with this way of life.'

Annis didn't pretend to misunderstand. 'Don't worry, Dish, I'm too much of a realist even to attempt to delude myself. His lordship's reasons for wishing me to stay are honourable enough, if not wholly flattering, as he himself was the first to admit. He believes my presence will be beneficial to the ladies of the house. He has no interest in me, personally.'

Disher, however, was not altogether convinced that her engaging young mistress, who had proved to be an exceptionally good judge of character in recent years, not to mention uncannily accurate in her predictions, was correct in her judgement about everything.

The loyal maid was by no means the only servant inclined to ponder that day over his lordship's actions. An hour later the head groom, Wilks, began to do just that when he caught his first sight of the young woman who had taken care of the Viscount in his time of need. This action alone would have ensured that Wilks regarded Miss Milbank in a favourable light; and he was forced to own, as he watched her trip lightly across the stable-yard, that she was a pretty enough young woman whose voluminous fur-lined cloak, he suspected, hid a trim, shapely figure. All the same, she was hardly in his lordship's usual style!

Wilks, like Dunster, was a devoted servant. He had worked for the Greythorpe family most all his life, and had sat the present holder of the title on his very first pony. Compared to the other servants of long standing, Wilks possibly knew his lordship's ways better than most, and had undoubtedly forged the closest bond with the present master of Greythorpe Manor. He invariably travelled with him whenever the Viscount took it into his head to visit the capital, so he had seen often enough the type of female who found favour in his lordship's eyes.

Undoubtedly the Viscount's tastes ran to golden-haired lovelies.

His mistresses, and there had been several over the years, had all been acknowledged beauties. Even his flirts, those ladies who might or might not have shared his bed, but who had been his chosen companions at the theatre and at leading social events, had all been sophisticated ladies of rank and style, not innocent young females who might easily misunderstand the reasons why they had been singled out for particular attention.

And that, if what the most recent household gossip to reach the realm of the stables was to be believed, was the truth of the matter, Wilks reflected, nimbly jumping up on the perch at the back of the phaeton, a moment after his lordship had taken up the reins. Astonishingly enough, it was none other than the Viscount himself who had wished Miss Milbank to extend her stay with the family.

It seemed to Wilks, as he kept his eyes glued to the rim of the jauntily worn beaver hat directly in front of him, that Lord Greythorpe was behaving most oddly. Not only was it a rare event, even in London, for his master to take up a female beside him when driving his phaeton, it was even rarer for him to go out of his way to make conversation, as he was clearly doing now. More surprising still was that the young woman seated beside his master didn't hesitate to answer in the most direct way to any question his lordship posed. Most surprising of all was that her comments and opinions were, unless Wilks much mistook the matter, being received with a deal more interest than politeness.

Wilks was astonished, and by the time they had arrived at the intended destination, and he had taken up his position at the horses' heads, he was firmly of the opinion that Miss Annis Milbank was a rare specimen of womanhood indeed. She instantly rose further in his estimation when she took the trouble, after alighting from the phaeton, to enquire directly of him the condition of the chestnut hunter his lordship had been riding on that fateful day.

'He be none the worse for having been left standing in the cold wind,' he assured her, while thinking that he couldn't ever recall seeing a sweeter smile than Miss Milbank's. And so natural too!

'That's a relief to hear,' she said, sounding as though she genuinely meant it. 'I shouldn't have liked to think that he had suffered any ill effects. A fine animal, if I may say so. And coming from the Shires, I should know. I've seen many a prize hunter in my time.'

It was clear to Wilks, simply by the easy way she was displaying affection towards his lordship's bays, that she had a fondness for his particular favourite creatures. 'You'd be most welcome to come to the stables any time, miss, and look over the other cattle we 'ave there, if you've a mind. All prime stock, even though I do say so myself.'

Having unashamedly listened to every word of this brief exchange, his lordship turned in time to see a lopsided grin adding more creases to his trusty henchman's weather-beaten face. Seemingly it had happened again, and his lordship couldn't say he was in the least surprised. If a punctilious, old stiff-rump like Dunster could fall victim to that wholly natural, ultra-feminine charm, then there wasn't much chance of many members of the male sex withstanding the spell of that bewitchingly lovely ladylike manner, and winning smile.

The Viscount turned again to discover the subject of his thoughts now squatting down on her haunches, avidly studying a section of road close to the verge. Then she rose abruptly and swung round, causing the cowl on her fur-lined cloak to fall away and to reveal a mass of glossy chestnut ringlets, loosely dressed, merely confined at the back of the head by means of a red satin ribbon.

Although coinciding with it, his lordship was well aware that his sudden intake of breath had not been generated by the same unexpected sharp gust of wind that had disarranged the magnificent mane sending tendrils whipping across the softly rounded curve of a feminine cheek and jaw. He watched her raise a hand to brush the strands away impatiently, while all the time avidly studying the copse on the other side of the road. So intent was her scrutiny that she appeared totally oblivious to the fact that she had become the sole object of a fastidious gentleman's close scrutiny and, more importantly, had not been found wanting. Quite the opposite, in fact!

'I'm so sorry, Miss Milbank, I was in a world of my own,' he apologised when he finally realised that she had addressed him and was regarding him now rather quizzically. 'Er—what did you say?'

'I asked whether or not you experienced the feeling you were being followed at any time while you were in town that day, or after you had set off on the homeward journey?'

Although his lordship paid her the common courtesy of giving her enquiry due consideration, deep down he remained firmly of the opinion that his unfortunate experience was purely and simply down to mischance, merely the result of being in the wrong place at the wrong time, that he had been the victim of an opportunist thief who had been denied the profits of his nefarious deed by her own timely arrival.

'No, Miss Milbank. It was a Tuesday, like any other Tuesday, except it was devilish cold. So it was a case of hat down, cloak collar up, and a dash for home before it began to snow. The only thing I can recall being aware of was how well my new hunter was performing.'

'Well, my lord, even taking into account the conditions of the day, and your attempts to keep out the cold and get home speedily, you'd need to be blind not to have noticed someone lurking in the copse, yonder, given the fact that there's not a sprout of foliage anywhere, and no tree trunk wide enough to conceal a child, let alone a man. So I think we can safely assume that he wasn't hiding there.'

After casting a wistful glance downwards at his highly polished boots, the Viscount felt obliged to follow his engaging companion to the far side of the copse. Despite the fact that within seconds his worst fears had been realised and the pride of his fastidious valet were covered with mud, he found himself smiling. Miss Milbank put him forcibly in mind of a favourite little terrier he'd had as a boy, a tenacious little thing who'd never give up once it had picked up the scent of vermin.

'Aha!' she exclaimed, looking very well pleased, as she peered along the ditch that was impossible to see from the road. 'A much more likely hiding place for our villain of the piece to have awaited the arrival of his quarry, wouldn't you say, my lord?'

The Viscount couldn't deny the truth of it, and began to think he had been foolish to take such a light-minded view of the whole business. 'I've lived here all my life and never realised until now that this field is partially edged by a deep drainage ditch.'

'Not your land then, sir?'

'No. It belongs to a man named Hastie, a neighbour of mine as well as a close family friend.'

This information drew her head round sharply. 'Not Colonel Hilary Hastie, by any chance?'

'Why, yes! Are you acquainted with him?'

'If it's the gentleman I think it is, then, yes. I've met him on two or three occasions. He was a close friend of my grandfather's,' she revealed. 'Hunting mad, as I recall. Never missed a season in the Shires, until years of overindulgence in port and brandy finally caught up with him.'

'Sounds like the old Colonel,' his lordship was forced to concede. 'He still breeds horses, but doesn't ride as much as he used to himself. In point of fact, the horse I was riding that day came from his stables.'

'I very much doubt your assailant's did…if he was mounted at all. A man could easily have concealed himself here, but not his horse. He could, of course, have left his mount over there, well out of view…' she gestured towards the wood edging the far side of the Colonel's field '…while he hid himself here, lying in wait for you.'

His lordship regarded her in silence, no longer prepared to dismiss this possibility out of hand, as he might well have done a short time before. 'You seem convinced that I was the intended victim.'

'I think it highly likely, yes,' she admitted, regarding him earnestly, and he found himself, after a further moment's intense thought, easily conceding it might be true.

'Yes, you could be right. As you've possibly judged for yourself by now, if only by the absence of any vehicles travelling along it, this is not a well-used road. Only those wishing to visit me are likely to use it. Those choosing to visit Greythorpe Magna, a sizeable village that borders my land on the eastern side, would stay on the main road. It's far quicker, and a much shorter distance from the town.'

'And the right-hand fork, back there?' she asked, as they began to retrace their steps.

'Leads only to the property of Lord Fanhope, and the cottages of those people working for him.' The Viscount considered for a moment before shaking his head. 'The countryside is far less open half a mile or so further along that lane. Anyone wishing to harm any member of the Fanhope family would lie in wait there, not in the ditch back here… And the motive for the attack was, you believe, a very personal one, someone wishing to inflict physical harm?'

'I wouldn't go so far as to say that, my lord,' she answered, appearing for the first time genuinely perplexed. 'But what I would suggest is that, before we begin to speculate on the likely motive, we examine the facts we do have.'

His lordship delayed only for the time it took them to make themselves comfortable once more in the phaeton, before begging her to proceed, for his interest now was well and truly captured.

'From what I have observed about you thus far, my lord, I would suggest that you are definitely one of those gentlemen who rarely deviate from a set routine. To put it bluntly—a man of habit.'

Despite the fact that he resented being described thus, honesty obliged him to acknowledge the truth of the statement. 'I suppose I have become increasingly so over the years, certainly.'

'And you invariably pay visits to the local town on Tuesdays?'

His lordship caught the faint twitch at one corner of that shapely, yet not overgenerous feminine mouth, before he once again took charge of his team and headed homewards. Unless he much mistook the matter, his delightful companion was very well aware that he was feeling slightly irritated by this line of questioning and was deriving no little amusement from the fact.

'Certainly every last Tuesday in the month, when I remain to partake of luncheon in the inn with my man of business.' He felt the need to clear his throat. 'I suppose you would say it has become a—er—ritual.'

'And anyone reasonably well acquainted with you would know this,' Annis pointed out, before enquiring whether he departed for home at the usual time on the Tuesday in question.

'No, a little earlier than usual, as it happens,' he derived some satisfaction in disclosing. 'It would have been earlier still, if Colonel Hastie hadn't walked into the inn, just as I was on the point of departure, and we fell into talking, mainly about the hunter he'd recently sold me.'

'On horseback you would have made good time, so it's highly likely that you did, in fact, pass my carriage somewhere along the road,' she suggested after a moment's silence. 'Not that you would have realised that, of course. But can you recall whether it had begun to snow before you were shot?'

'No, it had not,' his lordship answered at once, certain of this fact. 'I never saw a soul either, not after I'd turned off the main road. I remember the sudden burning pain in my arm, and then the next thing I recall is waking up in my own bed, staring up at a...a perfect stranger,' he finished, recalling too that he had thought her something rather more than a mere mortal. With the window behind her, her head had been framed in a bright halo of light.

'In that case I shall do my best to fill in the gap for you, my lord,' she returned practically, and unwittingly destroying the pleasurable memory by forcing him back to the present. 'I should imagine I could have been no more than ten minutes behind you, fifteen at most. I base this on the fact that you were still quite warm. Also there was a reasonable covering of snow, enough certainly to reveal prints. There were none about you, except the marks made by your horse. I noted these facts particularly. So whoever shot you had sufficient time before I appeared on the scene to have filched your belongings and to have made a swift departure. So we can be sure robbery wasn't the motive for the attack. Furthermore, if it had been someone bent on revenge, wanting to take your life, why on earth didn't he complete the task?'

Annis shook her head, genuinely perplexed. 'Whoever shot you, sir, was either inept in the use of firearms, or a very fine shot indeed...and I suspect the latter. Which leads me to suppose the intention was to incapacitate you temporarily, not cause lasting harm. What eludes me completely at the present time...is why.'

'It puzzles me even more, Miss Milbank, I assure you,' his lordship confessed, after quietly turning over what she had said. 'I'm on reasonably good terms with all my neighbours and tenants, some, of course, better than others. I certainly haven't engaged in any

disputes with anyone since coming in to the title. But I shall certainly give what you suggest further consideration,' he added, before
something occurred to him, and he found a smile coming effortlessly
to his lips. 'I must say, ma'am, your powers of observation are quite
formidable. Not many, I suspect, would have noted quite so much
when stumbling upon a complete stranger in the road.'

Annis's own smile of memory was no less spontaneous, and a
deal more tender. 'It was something I learned from my father, sir,'
she revealed. 'I believe I have already mentioned he was a physi-
cian. It was a game we used to play—a wager, if you like. I had to
diagnose someone's ailment by studying physical appearance.'

Intrigued, he asked, 'And could you?'

'In some cases, yes,' she revealed. 'Sadly it is all too easy to spot
at a glance if someone has survived smallpox, for instance, or
suffered from rickets as a child, or is prone to gout. The more one
practises, the more proficient one becomes at searching for the not-
so-obvious signs and symptoms, those little clues that begin to
reveal someone's state of health, the life he or she has led, and in
some cases character type too.'

Silently, his lordship was forced to own he had been doing precisely that himself in recent days, and had drawn certain conclu-
sions that he now wished to have verified.

'Clearly you were very fond of your father, Miss Milbank,' he
remarked, carefully beginning his inquisition. 'And your grandfather too,' he added, when she nodded before raising the cowl that
had fallen from her head a short time earlier. 'You have mentioned
them on several occasions within my hearing. But I have yet to hear
you mention your mother.'

The hand she was using to adjust the head covering stilled for a
moment. 'I loved my mother dearly, sir, and have missed her greatly
since her death, perhaps more so than both my father and grand-

father, simply because I spent much more time with her when I was growing up. She influenced my behaviour to a significant degree.'

'Yes, I can well imagine she did, Miss Milbank,' he returned, not doubting her for a moment. 'You are clearly the daughter of a gentleman who stemmed from good yeoman stock. But that unmistakable air of breeding you exude, unless I much mistake the matter, comes from the distaff side.'

Taking his eyes briefly from the road ahead, the Viscount caught the ghost of a smile, before she acknowledged the accuracy of his assumption by saying, 'How very perceptive of you, sir.'

'And may I be permitted to know your mother's maiden name?'

'My late mother was none other than Lady Frances Stowe, youngest sister of the present Earl of Tavistoke.'

All at once much of what had puzzled his lordship about his companion had become crystal clear.

Chapter Five

As a direct result of his very welcome guest's astute, not to say surprisingly nettling, observations, his lordship chose to deviate from routine and partake of luncheon that day in the company of the ladies. All the same, directly afterwards he returned to his normal practice of taking refuge in the library, and it was while he stood at his desk, poring over several sheets detailing the various branches of the Greythorpe family tree, going back through the centuries almost to the time of the Conqueror, that his sister took it into her head to pay one of those rare visits to what she considered his private domain.

Not in the least displeased by the interruption, he beckoned her forward with an imperious wave of his hand. 'Come and look at this, Sally,' he urged, resorting to the name he had always used in childhood.

She recognised at once what he had been perusing with such interest. 'I haven't seen those things for years.'

'No, and neither had I. So I merely asked Dunster to locate their whereabouts. Which he did of course without too much trouble. They were in the attic in one of the chests.'

Without conscious thought his lordship began to swing his

quizzing glass back and forth by its black ribbon. 'Do you know, Sal, I rather fancy I take those servants of ours somewhat for granted. Dunster, for instance, is a prince among butlers. As you remarked yourself only recently, if not in so many words, he is able to recognise an encroaching mushroom at a glance. And, it goes without saying, those who are quite otherwise,' he added, somewhat enigmatically. 'I should have realised, I suppose, the instant you mentioned that Dunster had taken it upon himself to allocate the green bedchamber, that there would turn out to be more to her than one might imagine. Dunster must have suspected as much on first setting eyes upon her, or very soon afterwards.'

'About Miss Milbank, you mean?' Sarah queried, having found her brother's conversation somewhat hard to follow. 'Oddly enough, she was the reason why I decided to seek you out.' She regarded him in silence, not for the first time wishing that they had spent much more time together, once they had left their childhood behind, so that she understood him rather better, and knew what he was thinking. 'I just wondered why you asked her to remain as our guest for a few more days?'

He lifted one black brow in exaggerated surprise. 'You've no objection, surely? I thought you'd be pleased.'

'Oh, I am. I am!' she hurriedly assured him. 'It was just that, misguidedly, I suppose, I gained the distinct impression that she would wish to leave at the first opportunity.'

'You were not wrong in this assumption. That, most definitely, was her intention,' his lordship disclosed, once again turning his attention back to the large sheets on his desk, 'but I managed to persuade her to remain at least for a few more days. And I sincerely hope I can repeat my success and encourage her to stay a good deal longer. Ideally, until after the party next month.'

When she did not attempt to hide her surprise, his lordship felt some explanation was necessary. 'Not only could Miss Milbank be invaluable in assisting us in becoming acquainted with our half-sister, when Helen eventually does arrive here, but also in the interim she could be of immeasurable help to you in bearing Louise company, thereby leaving you with more free time to concentrate your efforts on finalising the arrangements for Grandmama's birthday celebration next month.'

His lordship cast his sister a brief assessing glance, hoping that she wouldn't interpret his actions as criticism of her, for nothing could have been further from the truth.

No one knew better than he the isolated existence Sarah had been forced to endure, pandering to the whims of a parent who had been totally selfish and unfeeling for much of his life. At least by attending Eton and Oxford, and then taking over the running of the family's estate in Derbyshire, not to mention travelling extensively in more recent years, he himself had benefited greatly from lengthy periods away from a house whose atmosphere had been corrupted by a resentful man's attitude to life. Poor Sarah had not been so fortunate. After two Seasons in London, where she had failed to elicit even one offer for her hand, she had, prematurely in his opinion, resigned herself to spinsterhood and the care in his declining years of a father who had shown her precious little affection in return throughout her life. Was it any wonder that she had become an out-and-out introvert, much preferring her own company for much of the time?

'I do not deny that I've found Miss Milbank's presence here strangely reassuring, very beneficial,' she admitted with a wan smile. 'Cousin Louise clearly likes and admires her. And there's no denying she's such a capable young woman. Nothing seems to daunt her.'

'I do not know her well enough to comment,' his lordship responded, raising his head to fix his gaze on an imaginary spot on the wall opposite. 'But what I do know is this house has suddenly taken on a different personality with her presence under its roof. She has only to walk into a room for the atmosphere of rigid formality we both knew only too well as children to be lifted completely. It's like a window being thrown wide on a glorious spring day. She's quite simply a breath of fresh air...something this house has desperately needed for a very long time.'

Suddenly realising he was being regarded with avid interest, his lordship turned his attention once again to the large sheets spread open on his desk. 'If there is one other thing I have discovered about Miss Annis Milbank, she is full of surprises. We are, in fact, related to her—distantly, it is true. None the less, the connection is definitely there. We share the same great-great-great-great-grandparents. She is none other than the present Earl of Tavistoke's niece.'

'Good heavens!' Sarah was clearly impressed. 'Why on earth did she not mention it?'

His lordship smiled grimly. 'If I were to be uncharitable, I might suggest that it is because her uncle refuses to recognise the connection. But I strongly suspect it is simply because our—er—Cousin Annis is far too well bred to resort to name dropping.'

'Was there some sort of disagreement or rift in the family, do you suppose?' she asked.

'Apparently so. I needed to consult Dunster. A fount of wisdom on such matters, as I'm sure you're aware. He clearly remembers the scandal surrounding Tavistoke's youngest sister, Lady Frances Stowe. The chit had the temerity to elope with an insignificant country practitioner, after an extended visit to the Shires. The family, seemingly, could never bring themselves to recognise the match, and never spoke to the sister again.'

'Oh, poor Annis!' Sarah exclaimed, at once revealing the sympathetic side to her nature.

His lordship, on the other hand, thought he knew better. 'Your sympathy is misplaced, Sal, for unless I much mistake the matter, Annis doesn't care a whit, and possibly never has done, at least not for herself. She's made no secret of the fact that she enjoyed a wonderfully happy life up until both her parents sadly died in a typhoid epidemic, and even afterwards she was gloriously content in the care of that paternal grandfather whom she clearly adored. No, Sally, she was privileged to enjoy something that we were never blessed to have. And, unless I'm overestimating her powers of discernment to a very significant degree, she already suspects as much.'

His lordship's judgement had not been flawed: Annis had indeed already come to the conclusion that the Greythorpe siblings' childhood had left much to be desired. All the same, as she sat in the parlour at that moment, assiduously plying her needle, it wasn't so much the distant past occupying her thoughts as more recent, puzzling events.

Normally, she found sewing an aid to concentration, and would have recourse to the contents of her sewing box whenever taxed by a particular problem. Unfortunately her needlecraft skills had proved singularly unhelpful on this particular occasion. Try as she might, she simply couldn't perceive why anyone in his right mind would lie in wait, or go to the expense of paying someone else to do likewise, simply to inflict minimal suffering on a fellow human being. Why, it almost resembled a schoolboy prank, the sort of thing a child might do to wreak revenge on a strict adult who was proving annoyingly troublesome! If only she could believe that it was some petty-minded, childish revenge! She shook her head, deeply troubled. No, there was some definite purpose in that attack on his lordship, and she very much feared that, if whoever was behind it wasn't wholly satisfied with the outcome this time, he or she might well resort to something else, the outcome of which might prove a deal more harmful.

'Didn't you quite like the way I played that piece?' Louise enquired, rising from the stool at the pianoforte and quickly noticing Annis's troubled expression.

Annis didn't hesitate to assure her that this was not so. 'I'm not in the habit of offering insincere praise. I've told you already that you play quite beautifully. Your mama must be very proud of you.'

'I shouldn't imagine so,' Louise responded, sounding a little peeved. 'Unlike you, who does everything so well, I can only play the pianoforte.'

Annis raised one fine brow in a sceptical arch. 'I cannot imagine why you should have drawn that grossly inaccurate conclusion. Certainly not from anything I might have said, at any rate! The only thing I've ever admitted to within your hearing,' she reminded her, 'is enjoying a wide variety of pastimes.'

'You can play the pianoforte well too,' Louise pointed out.

'But not nearly so well as you,' was Annis's prompt rejoinder.

'Well, at least you can ride a horse.'

'True,' Annis acknowledged. 'But don't run away with the notion that I'm some superb horsewoman. I am reasonably competent, and can generally keep my seat, that is all.'

'Well, you cannot deny you're very skilled with a needle,' Louise persisted, determined, seemingly, not to lose her side of the argument. 'Even Sarah, who's considered the best seamstress in the whole family, said that you'd need to go a long way to find anyone who can set a finer stitch than you.'

'You seem determined to put me to the blush, young Louise,' Annis quizzed gently, before finally relenting. 'Very well, I'll concede, I've some skill with a needle. But, if the truth be known, it doesn't stem from spending hours trying to perfect the art. It's simply that sewing aids my concentration. More often than not, I'll reach for my tambour frame when I'm troubled by something.'

'Like today, you mean?' Louise asked, looking suddenly worried herself. 'You're not thinking of changing your mind and leaving, are you?'

'Not at this precise moment, no,' Annis assured her, smiling. It really was most flattering to have one's company so earnestly sought. All the same, she had no intention of misleading the girl. 'I've accepted his lordship's invitation to remain here a few more days, mainly for my servant's sake. Dear old Disher isn't getting any younger, and I cannot expect her to go careering about the country at a moment's notice.' She smiled and shook her head. 'It's quite amusing really. She's employed to take care of me. Yet I sometimes think it's the other way round.'

Louise frankly laughed. 'It's exactly the same with Sarah and Nanny Berry. At least it was before the old lady was finally persuaded to retire a year or so ago. Sarah mentioned visiting again tomorrow to see how she goes on. Why not come with us?' she suggested. 'It's really quite funny to see Sarah go bright red. Nanny Berry still treats her as though she were a child. There isn't anything she doesn't know about my cousins, and she isn't afraid to tell you all their secrets.'

Annis checked for a moment before setting another perfect stitch. 'Is that so?' she murmured. 'Yes, I rather think I shall accompany you, Louise. The visit might prove enlightening.'

Although the unexpected entry of Sarah, closely followed by his lordship, into the small parlour induced Louise to relapse into silence, she was now not so daunted by his presence as not to enquire precisely what he had meant when he unexpectedly addressed the young woman seated beside her on the sofa as Cousin.

'On discovering something this morning, I thought it incumbent upon me to check our family tree,' his lordship explained, 'and lo and behold I find that Miss Milbank and I share the same great-great-great-great-grandparents.'

'Ah! A close connection, I perceive,' Annis quipped, slanting a look of comical dismay in his direction. His lordship, however, refused to be discouraged by this blatant show of flippancy on his guest's part.

'Close enough to dispense with formality, I think, Cousin Annis,' he returned, the challenging gleam in his eyes unmistakable.

'Oh, is she my cousin too?' Louise put in, thereby denying Annis the opportunity to give voice to any protest.

'No, dear. The connection comes on the Greythorpe side,' Sarah explained. 'But unless Cousin Annis objects, I see no reason why there is the need for continued formality.'

Did she object? More importantly, should she object? Annis silently asked herself, once again plagued by annoying indecision.

She couldn't deny that during recent years it had occasionally irked her because she had been denied the opportunity to mix freely with the majority of her mother's class. Yet here she was being openly invited to do so, to be treated on an equal footing. Just because she was fairly sure the privilege was being bestowed upon her at his lordship's instigation oughtn't to matter one way or the other. Given the reason for her presence in the house, he had treated her with the utmost respect from the first. Apart from that initial and quite natural wariness at the start, his behaviour towards her had been exemplary, and she had no reason to suppose that this might change, simply because he was now wishful to address her by her given name.

Furthermore, as his sister too seemed only too pleased to recognise the connection, distant though it was, Annis came to the conclusion that it would be churlish, indeed, to raise any objection, though she would have preferred a little time in which to grow accustomed to the new informality.

Unfortunately this was denied her, for Dunster entered to announce the arrival of two guests, and his lordship immediately presented her as his cousin to the unexpected visitors.

Annis found herself being surveyed with no small degree of surprise by two pairs of blue eyes of exactly the same hue. Here, however, every outward similarity between Miss Caroline Fanhope and her twin brother Charles ended.

Caroline Fanhope, fair, slender, and undeniably strikingly handsome, betrayed a marked degree of intelligence in her level, if not wholly friendly, gaze; while her brother, at the age of only four-and-twenty, was already betraying definite signs of what would develop into a very portly figure by middle age, unless he took drastic steps to prevent it. There was absolutely nothing remotely appealing or even noteworthy in his weak-chinned, fleshy face. Yet Annis could not rid herself of the suspicion that beneath the unmistakable air of inane joviality lurked an altogether different character.

'We heard only today of the accident that befell you, my lord,' Caroline revealed the instant pleasantries had been exchanged. 'And even though Dr Prentiss assured us that you were none the worse for the ordeal, Charles and I simply couldn't be easy until we'd come over to see for ourselves.'

While Miss Fanhope had been speaking, Annis had attempted to assess the household's reaction to the visit. His lordship, seated closest to his guests, stared fixedly at a certain area of the carpet, his expression, as usual, giving little away; while Sarah, ever the well-bred lady, listened politely to what was being said. Most interesting of all had been young Louise's reaction. She seemed all at once to have disappeared completely behind that barrier of hers, and had definitely edged a little closer to Annis, as though seeking that extra protection from one or both of the new arrivals.

'We understand too that it was none other than Miss Milbank who played the good Samaritan, and conveyed you home, Grey-thorpe,' the other twin continued when Miss Fanhope, having said her piece, began silently to survey the complete stranger on the sofa opposite. 'Had it not been for Mama feeling obliged to exchange a few words with Colonel and Mrs Hastie in town that day, we might have come upon you first and saved Miss Milbank the trouble of seeing you home.'

'Oh, she did a great deal more than just that, Fanhope,' his lordship wasn't slow to reveal, while maintaining his impassive countenance. 'She ensured, personally, that I received the very best treatment for my injuries. Even Prentiss wasn't slow to remark upon the fact that he could have done nothing more, even had he been able to reach the Manor. So, as you might suppose, I feel im-mensely lucky that Cousin Annis did happen along, though whether or not what occurred a short time before her arrival was an accident is now very much in doubt.'

'Oh, but, my lord…!' Even though her gaze had been fixed on Annis, Miss Fanhope had evidently digested every word the Viscount had uttered. 'Who on earth would wish to harm you? I'm sure you haven't an enemy in the world!'

'It's a rare gentleman indeed who's universally liked,' Annis pointed out gently. 'It is quite amazing how the pettiest of griev-ances can, without much provocation, assume alarming propor-tions. Not that I would attempt to suggest that—er—Cousin Deverel would deliberately go out of his way to put anyone's nose out of joint,' she added, after quickly identifying the twinkle of unholy amusement in a certain pair of violet eyes. 'But human

nature being what it is, some of us can harbour the most amazing
jealousies and ill feelings towards our fellow man.'

Caroline Fanhope, however, remained adamant. 'Had you come
from around these parts, Miss Milbank, you would know how
highly respected his lordship is. Why, you'll never hear an ill word
said against him.'

'But that is the whole point, Caroline,' his lordship pointed out.
'My cousin is not from around these parts, and is therefore able to
view what has occurred a little more objectively than perhaps we
can. She has a most refreshing, down-to-earth outlook on life, and
I value her opinion. Both Sarah and I are hoping that we can
persuade her to extend her visit with us.'

'Really?' There was precious little warmth in the smile Caroline
directed at either occupant of the sofa opposite. 'Is this your first
visit to Greythorpe Manor, Miss Milbank? I believe I'm correct in
thinking that we have never met before.'

'It is. And we haven't,' Annis assured her, determined to make
the situation quite clear, before his lordship, no matter his reasons,
could give rise to further unnecessary speculation. 'My connection
to the Greythorpe family is so distant that I never mention the relationship. However, I am well acquainted with Helen Greythorpe
and came here to see his lordship on his half-sister's behalf, not
for any reason of my own.'

This appeared to capture Caroline's interest in a big way, and
she began to ask what on the surface at least seemed a string of
quite innocent questions. 'Heralding from the Shires, then, Miss
Milbank, you must do a deal of hunting,' she continued, her curiosity seemingly endless.

'None whatsoever,' Annis quickly enlightened her, and was
quick to note too the catlike smile her response engendered.

'Oh, dear.' Caroline pulled a face of dismay. 'Please do not say that you too have developed an aversion to horses and partake in no equestrian activities.'

'On the contrary. I love horses and very much enjoy riding them. But you did not ask me that,' Annis pointed out, much to the female visitor's apparent annoyance.

She seemed to collect herself within seconds, and was once again smiling, even if it was hardly genuine. 'I have been attempting to persuade Louise to get back into the saddle since she arrived here, and come out with me, but to no avail. Unless she masters her childish fear, she will never be considered truly accomplished, don't you agree, Miss Milbank?'

'No, I do not,' Annis answered, inducing more than one brow to rise at the abruptness of her response. 'Overcoming one's particular *bête noire* is never easy. And I should know. I've retained a dread of enclosed, dark places throughout my life. It has been my experience that forcing people to face their particular fears, more often than not, does more harm than good. If Louise ever attempts to get into the saddle again, I'm sure there will be those only too willing to help her. If not, she has nothing of which she need feel ashamed. Quite the contrary, in fact! She may never be seen to advantage on the hunting field. But she would outshine the vast majority in any fashionable drawing-room, if called upon to play the pianoforte. Personally, I would far rather be considered gifted in one of the so-called feminine accomplishments than thought merely adequate in them all.'

By the reaction of the twins to this differing opinion, Annis gained the distinct impression that Miss Caroline Fanhope wasn't accustomed to having her viewpoint challenged. For several moments she appeared more put out than previously, not to say slightly annoyed; while her brother's flabby jaw had dropped perceptively. Sarah, too, appeared to be finding the pattern in the carpet of extreme interest now. A definite sparkle had returned to Louise's eyes, but was quite dimmed when compared to his lordship's look of unholy amusement.

It was he who broke the ensuing silence by revealing that he too considered his young cousin a very gifted player. 'Perhaps you might delight us all by playing at Grandmama's birthday celebration, Louise?' he suggested, before hurriedly adding, as he observed her new-found sparkle fading, 'But do not feel obliged to do so. We all know how much Grandmama enjoys finding fault. The rest of us, however, would be very appreciative.'

'As too would our mama if you were to entertain us at our party next week,' Caroline said, appearing to have mastered her pique. 'Perhaps Miss Milbank too would honour the event, should she still be in the locale?'

'Oh, I think I can safely promise you that she will be,' his lordship answered before Annis could give voice to the polite refusal forming swiftly in her mind, 'though whether she might be persuaded to reveal her not inconsiderable talent on the keys is a different matter entirely.'

Annis didn't know whether to feel flattered or annoyed. He'd witnessed her playing a duet with Louise on one occasion, and had heard her perform a particular favourite piece of her own on another, and was sure his appreciation had been genuine. Notwithstanding, having almost attained the age of four-and-twenty herself, she had long since grown accustomed to making her own decisions, and choosing with whom she wished to spend her time. Viscount Greythorpe, it seemed, was not above taking a good deal upon himself when it suited his purposes, though what his purpose could possibly be for wanting her to remain to attend a neighbour's party, she couldn't imagine.

'We look forward to your gracing the event, Miss Milbank,' Mr

Fanhope said, when his sister couldn't or wouldn't bring herself to utter such an untruth, for Annis felt sure that Caroline at least would be happy never to set eyes upon her again.

Notwithstanding, she managed to utter a polite farewell when she followed her brother's example by rising to her feet. The Viscount wasn't slow to offer his personal escort to the stables, a gallant gesture for which Louise at least seemed grateful, for she didn't hesitate to vent her spleen the instant the door had closed behind them, something that Annis felt the girl would not have done had his lordship remained in the room.

'Oh, that female!' she hissed between clenched teeth.

'Evidently not a particular favourite of yours,' Annis remarked a trifle unsteadily, after watching small hands ball themselves into fists.

'She's hateful! She never misses the opportunity to try to make me seem an absolute widgeon, simply because I no longer ride.'

'Oh, I'm sure that isn't her intention, dear,' Sarah countered, though not very convincingly. 'I think it has more to do with her upbringing. Lady Fanhope has tended to be indulgent where her sons are concerned, with Charles in particular, so I've been led to believe. She spoilt him dreadfully, still does for that matter. But with Caroline she is quite different. She ensured that her only daughter practised hard until she lacked no feminine skills, and insisted on her correct behaviour on all occasions.'

Annis reached for her embroidery again. 'If she's as accomplished as you say, Sarah, I wonder that she isn't married. Whether one may like her or not, it cannot be denied she's very handsome, strikingly so.'

'Unlike myself, who had two completely wasted Seasons in town, Caroline received several proposals of marriage in her one and only Season, all of which she refused. Sadly Lord Fanhope made some very unwise investments years ago that, I believe, resulted in his losing a vast amount of money and his having to mortgage the Hall. The family was forced to practise strict economies. So, as you can imagine, a second Season for Caroline was out of the question, though I do not think they are nearly so badly off now. I cannot see how they can be. Charles drives himself about in a bang-up-to-date high-perch phaeton and pair, and has his own travelling carriage and personal groom.'

Annis took a moment to consider what Sarah had told her before saying, 'Caroline, I judge, is no fool. She would have known she'd only be granted one opportunity to make a suitable match, so why on earth did she not accept one of her suitors? Were none of them to her taste?'

When she received no reply, Annis raised her eyes to discover Sarah staring at the same portion of carpet that had so captured her interest a short time before. The answer then was so crystal-clear that Annis could only wonder at herself for asking the question in the first place, though why her understanding of the situation should have resulted in a sudden uncomfortable feeling in the pit of her stomach she couldn't imagine.

'So, she's hoping for a proposal from a gentleman a little closer to home, is she?'

This softly spoken remark drew a frown of puzzlement across Louise's young brow, and brought a becoming touch of colour to Sarah's thin cheeks.

'Papa never made any secret of the fact that he would have approved the match. Lord Fanhope and he had been friends since boyhood, you see. Deverel has never once discussed the matter with me, so I do not know what his views may be, although I do happen to know that he much prefers Caroline to her brother Charles.'

'Hardly reason enough to contemplate matrimony, though,

surely?' Annis responded drily, the result of which had Louise gaping in astonished disbelief.

'You do not mean to say that Cousin Deverel is seriously thinking of proposing to *that* female? Oh, no, Sarah!' Louise now looked merely appalled. 'Your life wouldn't be worth living if she were to become the next Viscountess Greythorpe. Why, only look what happened the other week when she inflicted her presence on us—telling you how you should insist Cook dresses lamb so it went further, and criticising you for being far too easygoing with the servants.'

Sarah's half-hearted attempt at a protest in Miss Fanhope's defence fell on deaf ears as far as Louise was concerned.

'You may think she is very suitable for the wife of a Viscount, but I do not,' she argued, revealing how Annis's presence in the house had made her far less reticent to speak her mind these days. 'Why, I wager she'd treat you little better than a servant yourself as soon as she became mistress here.'

Surprisingly enough, Sarah too was determined to air her views. 'No, she wouldn't,' she countered. 'Her presence will have no effect upon me whatsoever. You see, I decided some time ago that I would leave the Manor when Deverel brought his bride home. Aunt Beatrice once suggested that I might like to make my home with her in London.'

By Louise's comical look of dismay, Annis gained the distinct impression that Aunt Beatrice wasn't exactly a firm favourite of the girl's either.

She didn't suppose for a moment that Sarah shared her cousin's opinion of good Aunt Beatrice. Diffident Sarah could be on occasions, but Annis couldn't imagine that she would ever consider making her home with a relative of whom she wasn't sincerely fond, or with whom she didn't rub along exceedingly well. Nevertheless, Annis wasn't at all certain that residing permanently in the capital was perhaps the wisest choice for someone who appeared very content with the peace and quiet and easy pace of life to be had in the country.

Furthermore, although Sarah had attained the age of eight-and-twenty, and undoubtedly had few romantic notions left in her head, Annis did not consider that she had gone beyond the age of forming a lasting attachment to a member of the opposite sex. Nor did Annis suppose for a moment that, even though she had endured a dismal existence at the beck and call of someone who neither cared about her nor appreciated her worth, Sarah herself was set against the idea of ever being tied to another gentleman.

The wonder of it was that she did not appear to have developed a hatred of men, Annis mused. In fact, the opposite seemed to be the case. She clearly adored her brother, and it had been equally evident that she held Dr Prentiss in high regard too. It was perhaps a pity that the good doctor was already married—happily so, by all accounts—for he, or someone very like him, would have suited Sarah very well. And where better to meet someone of that ilk than the city where Lady Pelham resided? Bath seemed to attract its fair share of widowers and gentleman who, not in their first flush of youth, preferred a quieter existence than could be found in the bustling metropolis.

'Forgive me for saying this, Sarah, but I cannot imagine that residing in the capital would altogether suit you,' Annis remarked, not reticent to give voice to her thoughts. 'Have you never considered settling in one of the watering places, Tunbridge Wells, or, better still, Bath? I think once you and your sister Helen become acquainted, you'll rub along together remarkably well. And I cannot think of anyone who has ever taken my godmother, Lady Pelham, in dislike. So it isn't as though you will know no one there. I too am seriously considering setting up house there.'

Although Sarah appeared much struck by the notion, it was

Louise who betrayed real enthusiasm. 'Oh, it would be wonderful if you both went to live in Bath!' she declared, clapping her hands like an excited child. 'Mama plans to take me there next year in order to prepare me for my first Season in the capital.'

'In which case it's no bad thing that you have been invited to the Fanhope party next week, or that you've been asked to play there. The sooner you accustom yourself to exhibiting your no little skill in front of an audience, Louise, the more comfortable you'll be when called upon to do so in the capital,' Sarah told her.

'Yes, I suppose you're right,' she agreed grudgingly. 'I just wish I wasn't playing in front of Caroline. She will be listening out for any slight fault.'

'I think that's highly likely, Louise,' Annis agreed. 'But look on the bright side. You're not being asked to do anything you actively dislike, like riding a horse, though I have to say that Caroline is right about one thing. I might deplore the methods she might choose to adopt, but the only way you'll ever conquer your fear is by attempting to get back into the saddle.'

'Yes, I suppose you're right,' Louise reluctantly agreed, before brightening once more. 'And at least I shall have you at the party to offer encouragement.'

Annis did not find the prospect wholly pleasing and wasn't afraid to say so. 'I have no objection whatsoever to offering you my support, Louise. But I very much resent having my life ordered about for me.' She transferred her steady gaze to the other lady present. 'Your brother might be master here, Sarah, but if he thinks for a moment that I shall permit him to dictate to me, he has a thing or two to learn... As he will discover for himself the next time I see him.'

Sarah and Louise exchanged startled glances, for it was a well-known fact that the Master of Greythorpe Manor wasn't accustomed to having his decisions questioned by anyone.

Chapter Six

The visit to Nanny Berry's cottage the following morning turned out to be both enjoyable and enlightening as far as Annis was concerned. She and the old lady rubbed along together remarkably well from the first, a circumstance that wouldn't have surprised his lordship in the least had he been there to witness their first encounter. So engrossed in each other's company did they become that Sarah betrayed no reluctance whatsoever in leaving them alone together, while she took her old nurse's active young dog for a walk, and paid a brief call at the vicarage, where Louise might enjoy, for a short while, the company of the clergyman's eldest daughter, a girl of similar age.

'Young Miss Marshal seems a deal more cheerful than last time she were here,' the old nurse disclosed from her chair conveniently positioned by the window, from where she regularly monitored the comings and goings of her neighbours. 'Still, it must be dull for the girl up at the Manor. It were never what you'd call a cheerful place at the best of times—leastways, not during the time I worked there. Might be different now…. Should be different now that Master Deverel's in charge. Much will depend on who he marries, I suppose. But he's sure to choose someone who'll suit him. He's a mind of his own, has the young master. He was the only one that'd ever stand up to the old Viscount when he were in one of his mean moods, even though it got the poor boy into such trouble more than once.

'I mind the time, as though it were only yesterday,' she went on, having swiftly fallen into a reminiscent mood, 'when the old Viscount, 'stead of reaching for the birch-rod, had Master Deverel locked up in the icehouse for talking back to him. Wicked, it were. Downright cruel! Deep in December, with the snow lying as thick on the ground as t'were t'other day. Why, the boy could easily have caught a chill that might have taken him off!' She gave vent to a wheezy chuckle, which quickly turned into a cough. 'But we gets word to the stables, and Wilks lets him out and hides him in the barn. None of the servants breathed a word, not even Dunster, and him only second footman at the time and keen to get on. The old master were never any the wiser.'

Seemingly still firmly locked in the past, Nanny Berry shook her head. 'I mind it were just about that time that young Master Deverel began to change. Began to grow more like his father—cold and distant, some said. But I don't reckon he ever did, not really. I think he began to realise his clashes with his father made things worse for poor Miss Sarah, so he made a real effort not to go out of his way to anger the old curmudgeon, and kept himself to himself much of the time. But I don't reckon his spirit were ever truly broken. It might be that I wants to see it…but I fancy, on one or two occasions, when he's come here to visit me of late, I've glimpsed that old twinkle he had when he were a young boy. It were true enough his own mother weren't given to showing much love and affection towards her children, but at least you'd hear laughter in the nursery when she were alive.'

As what the old lady had revealed had only confirmed a deal of what she had already suspected was the truth of the matter, Annis wasn't slow to assure the old nurse on one particular point. 'I'm as one with you, Nanny. Undoubtedly his father's behaviour did have an effect upon him. But he didn't succeed in crushing his son's spirit, or at least not damaging it beyond repair, of that you may be sure. Like his father before him, he possibly values periods of solitude. None the less, the present Lord Greythorpe is neither cold nor remote. Far from it, in fact! Moreover, he surprisingly possesses a most wickedly teasing sense of humour. I have observed it myself on several occasions, the last time being only yesterday afternoon when I had occasion to remonstrate with him over a— er—certain matter.'

Nanny Berry gazed at her visitor in dawning wonder, but whatever she had been about to utter in response was held in check, when frantic scratching and a succession of loud yaps suddenly issued from the other side of the street door.

'Well, would you look at that now!' she exclaimed, after Annis had risen to enable the young spaniel to regain entry and show its appreciation by pawing at her skirts. 'Loves a walk, does Rosie, but she's clearly broken free from the leash this day. Seems she didn't want to leave you behind, Miss Milbank. Taken to you in a big way, so she 'as, and no mistake!'

It took Annis a minute or two before she had the excitable young dog sitting by her chair, and peering up at her as though she were some kind of goddess whose protection had become Rosie's prime concern.

Reaching down a hand, she began to stroke one silky ear absently. 'Nanny, forgive me for saying this, because it really is none of my business, but don't you think…well…that you are the wrong sort of person to have such a lively young dog as this? She needs lots of exercise, and you cannot possibly take her for long walks, especially not in this cold weather, and while you're suffering so badly with your chest, not to mention recovering from the recent injury to your ankle.'

'Of course I'm too old to look after her,' Nanny answered promptly, not appearing in the least offended. 'But a promise is a promise, miss. And I swore to old Ben Turner, afore he died, that I'd look after Rosie until I could find someone more suitable to take care of her. Ben and I had been friends since we were children, miss, and I know how much he loved this little dog. Said she were the best of the litter and would be just like her mother, who could smell out a rose in a pit of slurry.'

The old lady released her breath in a sigh. 'Well, I knew his lordship wouldn't want Rosie. His gamekeeper's got his lordship's two hounds at his place on the edge of the wood. Great hairy beasts they are. They'd eat poor Rosie for breakfast as soon as look at her. There hasn't been a dog kept up at the big house, not since the Viscount's own mother passed on, so it were no good asking Miss Sarah to take her. Besides which, I don't think she's too fond of dogs herself. Old Ben could never take to the gamekeeper over at Fanhope Hall, and so didn't want Rosie to go there. That just left old Colonel Hastie. But his eyes aren't what they were, and he don't go out shooting much any more, so it t'were not a mite o' good asking him.'

Although Annis mentally prepared herself for the question she sensed would soon follow, it did not make voicing the answer one iota easier. 'I'm sorry, Nanny, I'm simply not in a position to take her. If I had a place of my own, I wouldn't need to give the matter a second thought, because I love dogs, and think Rosie's a darling. But I live with my aunt and uncle, and my aunt, like Sarah, isn't so very keen on them, and won't have them in the house. And I couldn't risk leaving Rosie free to wander. Like as not, she'd take to worrying my uncle's sheep, or chase the ducks and chickens in the farmyard.'

All at once an idea occurred to her. 'I do happen to know that Helen Greythorpe has a particular fondness for dogs, and has often spoken of having one of her own. Lady Pelham would raise no objection, I'm sure. I intended to write to them today, so I'll explain about Rosie. One never knows, we might find the darling girl a new home yet!'

Although the dog's future well-being remained firmly at the forefront of Annis's mind, it had surprisingly faded from the old lady's at the mention of Helen Greythorpe. Up until that moment she hadn't realised just how well her visitor was acquainted with the youngest member of the Greythorpe family, and wished to discover all she could about the last baby who had been in her charge, albeit for all too brief a period.

Although she was happy to satisfy the old lady's curiosity, for it was clear that Nanny Berry retained fond memories of both Helen and the last Viscountess to grace the Manor, whom she considered had been shamefully treated by the late Master of Greythorpe, Annis wasn't unduly sorry when the visit came to an end. Rosie, evidently determined to forge a closer bond, had jumped up onto her lap, and had there remained, because her goddess simply hadn't the heart to return her to the floor.

Thankfully sense prevailed the instant Sarah re-entered the small, though comfortable, abode. Looking less than impeccably groomed, with her hat now askew, she darted the little dog a decidedly unfriendly look, before suggesting they make their way back to the Manor in good time for luncheon, which forced Annis to part with her new-found friend while she still retained sufficient will to do so.

Sarah, on the other hand, retained no amicable feelings towards the animal who had had her peering through hedgerows for the past half an hour in a futile attempt to locate her whereabouts.

'Wretched little creature!' she exclaimed the instant she had closed the door behind them, and they had set off up the lane towards the vicarage in Greythorpe Magna. 'That's the very last time I offer to take it for a walk!'

'Yes, very annoying for you, I'm sure,' Annis responded, exhibiting praiseworthy control by not grinning wickedly, 'especially since, as a result of your exhausting and quite futile attempt to find her, your bonnet is now crookedly positioned.'

She refrained from mentioning anything further, and might have succeeded in pushing the little dog's plight to the back of her mind completely had not the sound of frantic yaps reached her ears just as they arrived at the garden gate leading to the vicarage.

'Oh, so you succeeded in finding her then, Sarah,' Louise said ingenuously, as she came skipping down the path to meet them.

Annis quickly intervened, before the normally very placid Miss Greythorpe gave way to a rare display of ill humour. 'Don't worry, I'll return her and ensure she's secure.'

'Oh, I'll come too,' Louise said hurriedly. 'There's something I particularly wished to ask you. Don't worry, Sarah. You carry on walking back to the Manor. We'll catch you up.'

'What on earth can you have to say to me that you didn't wish Sarah to overhear?' Annis demanded to know. Then promptly wished she hadn't asked when Louise revealed the answer.

She stared down at the little dog, now happily padding along at her heels, and couldn't help thinking that, if she had any sense at all, she wouldn't hesitate to leave that very day, before she became further embroiled in the affairs of those associated with Greythorpe Manor! That was out of the question now that she had been obliged to attend the Fanhopes' party. But she must make it clear to his lordship at the first opportunity that she would be leaving the Manor the following week!

* * *

His lordship, having spent most of the morning riding over the estate in the company of his steward, was looking forward, yet again, to a relaxed luncheon in the company of the ladies of the house. And one in particular! Not once in his life before could he recall having looked forward to getting back to the Manor. He had that morning, however, and had detected that almost tangible change in atmosphere the instant he had set foot indoors.

No, it wasn't just his imagination, he swiftly decided, dismissing the possibility from his mind, as he emerged from his bedchamber, having discarded his riding garb for more suitable apparel. What was it that Caroline had said, when he had escorted her and that unctuous brother of hers back to the stables the previous afternoon? Ah yes, that was it! he mused, suddenly recalling her precise words:

'After these past days of being forced to remain indoors, it's a real pleasure to get out and about again in the fresh air. Everything seems to benefit from a few hours of sunshine at this time of year. The air indoors is so much fresher too, when the need for continually burning fires is no longer so necessary. I expect you've observed changes at your house, too? I most certainly did.'

Well, Caroline might have been remarking only on the fresher air at the Manor compared to that at the Hall. And it had to be said that the chimneys at the Hall were prone to billowing out smoke, most especially when there was an east wind, as there had been in recent days. But his lordship was inclined to suspect that Caroline, ever perceptive and so like dear Lady Fanhope, always eager to offer advice on the running of a household should she detect some slight flaw, had quickly perceived the beginning of a transformation. Whether she wholeheartedly approved, however, was an entirely different matter.

Unexpectedly coming upon the person instrumental in bringing about the change induced his lordship to come to an abrupt halt at the entrance to the picture gallery. So engrossed was she in scrutinising a portrait of his late father, painted soon after his sire had come into the title, that she did not immediately perceive him, and he was therefore able to study her more thoroughly than he might otherwise have done.

She was undeniably most appealing in both face and form, and, although some might find her manners a trifle unusual on occasions, and her complete lack of inhibitions downright shocking, no one could fail to admire the natural grace of a carriage that was truly without flaw.

Yet it couldn't be denied that, had he caught his very first glimpse of her in some fashionable London salon, he might never have given her a second thought or glance; and most definitely would never have singled her out for particular attention, simply because she was the very antithesis of the type of female he had foolishly imagined would suit him best: those dazzling, ornamental fair-haired beauties who, it had to be admitted, more often than not, had had a deal more hair than wit, but who had truly possessed sweet natures and loving hearts. Which just went to prove how damnably blinkered he had been all these years in seeming to suppose that a kind and considerate mother for his children was all that he required in a future wife, and not the perfect helpmate for himself.

He found himself smiling, something he was increasingly prone to do these days without quite knowing why. Yes, amazing though it was, and after so ridiculously short an acquaintance, he, a gentleman who had earned himself the reputation for serious thought and extreme caution, was seriously contemplating Miss Annis Milbank as a future wife, simply because she was someone so much after his own heart—a female, little more than a slip of a girl, whose upbringing had been so vastly contrasting to his own.

The truth of the matter was, of course, he would never have been blessed to meet her at some fashionable London party, so he would ever be grateful to *Providence*, or whatever entity had ensured that their paths had eventually crossed, and in such a manner that had obliged him to pay her more attention than he might otherwise have done in the normal course of his life.

Yet from this point in time, experience advocated the use of extreme caution where Miss Annis Milbank was concerned, simply because she was so vastly different from most other members of her sex. He considered it highly unlikely, for instance, that she would succumb to flattery or be tempted into matrimony merely by the prospect of a title. Furthermore, unless he was much mistaken, money and social position meant little to her either. If the truth were known, it possibly hadn't even occurred to her to suppose that the partiality he had betrayed for her company stemmed from anything other than a determination on his part to play the gracious host, and therefore she wouldn't think to look upon him as a prospective husband. No, hers could be no ordinary wooing, that was for sure. Yet successfully woo her he must, or face a future that could never hope to be totally fulfilled.

Having every confidence that it would not be too long before her acute senses alerted her to his presence, he moved slowly forward. 'What a pleasant surprise coming upon you like this, Cousin! Did you have an enjoyable morning, or haven't you recovered sufficiently from your huff to indulge in an exchange of pleasantries quite yet?'

'Huff?' she repeated, withdrawing her gaze from the object of her attention long enough to cast him a suspicious look. 'I'm in no huff, nor have I been. It would take a deal more than a slight difference of opinion, a trifling skirmish, to have any effect upon me, my lord. When I'm in a huff, believe me, you'll be left in no doubt about it whatsoever!'

For answer his lordship threw back his head and roared with laughter, the result of which had her smiling up at him in whole-hearted approval before returning her attention to the painting of his father. 'What is it about my oh, so loving late sire that has captured your interest?'

'I was just thinking it is somewhat ironic that the child he could never bring himself to recognise as his own in his lifetime should have turned out to be the one who resembles him most strongly in looks.'

This was news to his lordship. 'Is that so?'

'Yes. But please do not run away with the notion that Helen is his image, because she most certainly is not. Nevertheless, there's a definite resemblance about the eyes and mouth, as you'll see for yourself when she visits here.' She took a step away the better to study the portrait hanging alongside. 'Now you, sir, if you'll forgive my saying so, bear a keener likeness to this young gentleman, here, whose name escapes me for the present, although Sarah, I'm sure, did enlighten me when she was kind enough to show me round the house the day after my arrival here.'

'That is none other than our late, lamented Uncle Henry, who had been destined to follow in Grandpapa's footsteps, but who sadly engaged in a little horseplay when up at Oxford which resulted in his untimely demise, and the younger and nowhere near so popular son coming into the title.

'Your father?'

'Quite so, Cousin,' his lordship speedily affirmed. 'From birth he was always unfavourably compared with his elder brother. Henry was taller, more handsome and infinitely more likeable, if

common report is to be believed. I suppose it was inevitable that
Father should have become increasingly resentful, especially
after fulfilling everyone's expectations, even going so far as to
wed the female who had been destined to marry his brother. Surprisingly, even though neither of my parents had much regard for
the other, the marriage wasn't altogether a disaster, but hardly
what one might describe as wedded bliss. I suppose it isn't hard
to understand why, after my mother's untimely demise, he was
determined that his second wife would be entirely of his own
choosing. And quite understandable too why he should have
become further embittered when he believed the wife of his
choice had played him false.'

'I can sympathise up to a point,' Annis admitted. 'But for the life
of me I cannot understand why he was so determined to believe
Helen wasn't his own child. He may have been embittered, but I've
never heard it said that he was lacking intelligence. He must have
known red hair has run in his second wife's family for generations.
Why was he so determined to believe Helen was the offspring of
that artist, even when his wife swore it was not so?'

'Who can say?' His lordship shrugged, straining the material of
his impeccably tailored jacket across his broad shoulders. 'I was
never close to my father, and so never attempted to understand him
better. I do know that he always put duty before the pursuit of his
own happiness. And I will say this for him—he never shirked his
responsibilities, as far as the estate was concerned, and left everything in good order.

'But as far as his personal relationships were concerned...'
His lordship shook his head, at a loss to understand. 'Perhaps
the marriage did not turn out to be the overwhelming success for
which he had hoped. After all, my stepmother was more than
twenty years his junior. I doubt they had much in common, and

maybe he just grasped the first opportunity to be rid of the female who had swiftly become nothing more than a tiresome young wife.'

He shrugged again. 'I was away at school, so didn't witness much of what went on at that time. Sarah might have a better notion. What I have always felt, though, is that he possibly served Helen and her mother a good turn by adopting the attitude he did. At least Helen wasn't forced to contend with the caprices of a gentleman who seemed hellbent on being miserable and making the lives of those around him wretched also. That's what I find hardest to forgive, Annis—the way he treated Sarah, who saw to his every comfort during his declining years; and the way he almost succeeded in making me resent my birthright, almost brought me to a point where I began to think of this place as a prison, not a home. Well, I'm pleased to say he didn't succeed. The shadowy corners of unhappy memories are at last beginning to see the light of reason after so many years. I'm determined that Greythorpe Manor will be the happy home it once was in my grandfather's day.'

All at once his lordship became aware that a pair of lovely grey-green eyes were regarding him with a certain amount of speculation and respect, and smiled wryly. 'You're a witch, Annis Milbank. You persuade a fellow to reveal far more about himself than he had any intention of doing, though I don't suppose I've told you any more than you discovered at Nanny Berry's this morning.'

'If you suppose that you're quite wrong,' Annis countered, having easily caught the accusing thread in his voice. 'Your old nanny was far more interested in finding out about your sister Helen than talking about you. All the same,' she continued, as the gong announcing luncheon reached their ears, 'I should like to talk with you this afternoon, if you can spare me the time. There's something I particularly wished to discuss.'

'Come and see me whenever you like,' his lordship responded, urbanity itself. 'I shall be in my library for most of the afternoon.'

This turned out to be true. Unfortunately Annis chose to write two letters before seeking that all-important interview to discuss arrangements for her return to Leicestershire the following week, and afterwards discovered from Dunster that his lordship was now entertaining a visitor. So she decided to occupy herself until the caller's departure by accepting the invitation she had received the previous day.

The early March afternoon was so surprisingly warm that she didn't even trouble to collect her cloak before stepping out of doors, and found her woollen shawl provided sufficient protection during the short walk round to the stables. Wilks greeted her arrival with delighted surprise, which gave her every reason to suppose that he hadn't expected her to take him up on his offer, or at least not so soon. Nevertheless, he seemed disposed to showing her round his domain himself, while revealing his extensive knowledge by remarking on the excellent points of each and every animal under his care, with one exception, which he accorded a loud sniff before passing it by.

Annis preserved her countenance with an effort. 'Would I be correct in assuming that that saddled hack is not one of his lordship's mounts, Wilks, but perhaps belongs to his visitor?'

'If his lordship were ever mutton-headed enough to be tempted to purchase a showy animal like this, miss, I'd disown him in a trice, so I would, and take myself off to work for the old Colonel down the road! He's tried to get me to leave the master often enough in the past, so he 'as. Never visits without 'is asking if I've changed my mind.'

'Evidently Colonel Hastie is not the guilty party, then,' Annis remarked, somehow managing to maintain her praiseworthy control. 'Not that I ever supposed for a moment that he was. Dare I ask who is the offender?'

'Only one round these parts, miss, daft enough to part with his brass for a creature like that—Mr Charles Fanhope. One can't help but feel sorry for that new groom of 'is, Jack Fletcher. Gets ribbed summat cruel when he goes into the local tavern of an evening. But he's a good lad and takes it in good part. Pity he can't find nothing better. Served his country during the war. Were in one of those new-fangled regiments. Mighty handy with a gun. Make a good game-keeper, so 'ee would,' Wilks added, causing a grating sound as he scratched the bristles on his chin. 'Been meaning to have a word with the master about young Jack, not that I think it would do much good. Master wouldn't want to be accused of taking Fanhope people away on top of everything else that's gone on afore, now would he, miss?'

'No, I don't suppose so,' Annis answered, after momentarily wondering to what the faithful groom had been alluding in partic-ular, but deciding it wouldn't be fair to ask him, especially as he appeared suddenly a little shamefaced, as though he had said more than he had intended. As she had already been accused of inducing people to do precisely that earlier in the day, she quickly changed the subject by asking instead which, in Wilks's opinion, was the most placid, well-behaved animal in the stables, suitable for a young lady of a highly nervous disposition to ride.

'Lord, bless you, miss! You wouldn't be meaning yourself now, I'm thinking.'

'And you would be perfectly correct, Wilks. I'm thinking of a suitable mount for Miss Louise.'

The experienced head groom's immediate look of surprise came as none to Annis. Servants eventually got to know most everything about those for whom they worked, especially the higher-ranking ones and those who, for whatever reason, had managed to forge a closer bond with either master or mistress, as evidently Wilks had done over the years. He would have known everything concerning the riding accident two years before, which had resulted in poor Louise breaking her collar bone, and which had eventually led to her very natural fear of anything to do with those four-legged creatures most likely to be found in the stables of the privileged classes.

'Well, miss, she could do no better than to begin again on Miss Sarah's grey mare. She don't ride much herself any more. And a more placid mount you'd be hard pressed to find.'

'And what about me, Mr Wilks…? Yes, I'm afraid Louise insists that I accompany her, otherwise she'll not even entertain the notion. So nothing with much spirit. Not that I would object myself, you understand? But we don't wish to alarm Miss Louise. So, no twitcher or kicker—a veritable lamb is what I'm after.'

'I've the very animal, miss,' he assured her. 'And you'll be wanting one of my lads along, I expect, just to be extra safe. In fact, I've a mind to perform the duty myself, miss. Happen the master would expect it.'

Annis wasn't sure whether this was true or not, but had absolutely no objection to his bearing them company, even though she had no intention of riding off the estate, until she was certain that a surfeit of nerves wouldn't induce Louise to experience a further tumble. So she told him she'd send word to the stables the following morning in good time for him to prepare the mounts, and then set off on an exploratory stroll of the shrubbery, as there was no sign yet of his lordship's visitor departing, and so little point in returning to the house.

Unfortunately she quickly discovered there was little point in lingering near the shrubbery either, for it was too early in the year and little worth viewing. So she merely continued along the path until she came to a fork and took the narrower path, which skirted the higher ground and which, she was confident, would eventually lead her back to the house.

Some detached part of her brain registered the sound of a twig cracking behind her, somewhere in the depths of the shrubbery, but her attention had been well and truly captured by a series of stone steps that led down to a subterranean construction, which had been sited with a particular purpose in mind in the upward sloping land at the back of the Manor.

The icehouse! The very place where poor Deverel had been dragged when a young boy, no doubt kicking and screaming, and incarcerated as a form of punishment. Children might require discipline, but that had been needlessly cruel. Wicked! Thank heavens he had had people about him who wouldn't stand idly by and allow their young master to endure unnecessary suffering and perhaps risk permanent damage. Little wonder his lordship had formed such a close bond with the, now, head groom, who had risked nothing short of his livelihood in order to help his young master all those years ago.

For a moment she hovered, then, curiosity having got the better of her, she descended the steps, slid back the sturdy iron bolt, and very slowly raised the catch. The wooden door was stiff, but with a little persuasion eventually opened to allow a sudden whoosh of ice-cold air to escape.

It was like walking into a frozen wall and equally unpleasant, Annis decided, forcing herself to take those first tentative steps inside. It was a test she always set herself nowadays in an attempt to conquer the fear she had carried through from her own childhood. She had always detested confined spaces, and doubted she would ever change. She could well imagine how poor Deverel must have felt during that short time he had been locked in the freezing prison before his blessed release—the icy-cold air nipping at his fingers and toes, like some ferocious dog, the blackness wrapping itself about him like a shroud, while the cruel, almost manic laughter of his father rang in his ears, as the bolt was slid across, ensuring confinement.

And now she was experiencing it too. And it was all too real! Somehow the door had slammed closed behind her. She felt those icy fingers of hysteria gripping her throat, constricting her breathing. Yet somehow she managed to reach out a trembling hand and locate the green slime-covered wall, then the door, and then blessedly the latch. She raised it and pushed, naturally expecting to attain instant freedom. But nothing happened. The door was merely stuck, she assured herself over and over again. It just required that extra effort on her part.

After all, who would play such a cruel and senseless trick? Who on earth would want to lock her in the icehouse? Of course someone was bound to hear her if she called. Someone must surely hear her...

Chapter Seven

The unexpected high-pitched scream, quickly followed by the ominous chink, chink of breaking china didn't precisely induce his lordship to start. All the same, the commotion was loud enough to break his concentration, and persuade him to rise from behind the desk to investigate.

'What the deuce...?' he muttered, entering the hall to discover nothing short of mayhem.

A footman, rising gingerly from the floor by the open front door, was favouring his left buttock, a maid, in a similar position at the foot of the stairs, was surrounded by broken china and making the most fearful din imaginable, somewhere between a succession of screams and high-pitched wails, while Dunster, for the first time in living memory appearing less than his sedate and capable self, was doing his level best to capture the transgressor responsible for all the disorder, who had just collided with the hat stand, sending it and its contents rolling across the hall floor, adding to the disorder.

The parlour door opened, momentarily capturing his lordship's attention, and Sarah came into the hall, uttering a murmur of dismay as her eyes quickly fell on the shatterer of the peace. 'Oh dear, not Rosie!'

'You recognise this misbegotten cur, Sarah?' his lordship demanded to know with less than his customary aplomb.

'Why, yes! She's Nanny Berry's dog.'

'I wager she's looking for Annis!' Louise exclaimed, having emerged in Sarah's wake, and clearly finding the situation highly diverting. 'She's taken to our cousin in a big way. She's already tried to follow us back here once today. What a clever little dog she is to have found out where Annis resides!'

His lordship was nowhere near so impressed and favoured the miscreant with one of his most disapproving frowns before she whipped herself between Dunster's legs and made a quick getaway up the staircase, sniffing the ground at frequent intervals as she went.

'For the love of heaven, go and get some help, Dunster!' he ordered, just as his loyal retainer was about to set off in hot pursuit. 'You'll never catch the wretched creature by yourself. Or, better still, let it locate Miss Milbank's whereabouts and leave her to deal with it,' he added with a certain grim satisfaction, 'as it would seem it is her society the wretched animal is intent on obtaining.'

His lordship favoured the hysterical maidservant with a similar look to the one he had bestowed upon the spaniel, which had the same effect, and sent the girl scurrying away to seek solace below stairs. He then turned to his sister. 'Where, by the by, is our cousin? I haven't seen her since luncheon.'

'Neither have we,' Sarah revealed. 'She mentioned something about wishing to write a couple of letters.'

'Yes, but that was ages ago,' Louise pointed out. 'It isn't like Annis to remain cooped up in her bedchamber. I wonder if she isn't feeling quite the thing?'

'Begging your pardon, my lord,' Dunster put in, having unashamedly listened to what had been said. 'But Miss Milbank isn't in her room. At least,' he amended, 'I do not believe she's returned to the house. I saw her about an hour ago, or perhaps a little more. She wished to speak with you, sir, but as Mr Fanhope was with you, Miss Milbank went outside. I do not suppose she intended to venture far. She didn't have her cloak with her, only a shawl.'

Without uttering anything further, his lordship bounded up the staircase, not liking what he had discovered. Annis was a sensible young woman. She wouldn't have ventured out with only a shawl, if it had been her intention to remain out of doors for any length of time, especially as the wind had increasingly grown in strength during the past half an hour or so.

As he approached the green bedchamber he heard a series of mild oaths and threats from within. The spaniel, it seemed, had managed to gain entry easily enough, but its unexpected arrival hadn't been altogether appreciated by Annis's middle-aged maid, who was now doing her level best to shoo the creature back across to the door.

'It's Disher, isn't it?' his lordship enquired, thereby instantly capturing the maid's attention. 'Have you seen your mistress within the past hour?'

'Why, no, sir. After she'd finished writing her letters, she said as how she was going downstairs to speak with you, my lord.' All at once an arresting look flitted across the maid's face as she watched the unwelcome four-legged visitor showing a particular interest in the carpet directly in front of the wardrobe door. 'I wonder, now, if that's not the little dog Miss Annis mentioned earlier, the one she was so concerned about, and hoped to find a home?'

'I wouldn't be at all surprised,' his lordship responded drily. 'I think the best thing to do is ask her without delay, don't you? And I believe I know just how to locate her whereabouts without too much trouble, if you would be good enough to assist me by handing me your mistress's cloak.'

Disher collected the requested item of clothing from the wardrobe without further ado, handed it across, and then watched as his lordship held the garment down to the dog who frisked about it excitedly, alternately sniffing at it and yapping, before eagerly following his lordship from the room.

Unlike his sister, the Viscount had always had a great fondness for dogs, especially those who, down the years, had accompanied him out hunting. He was experienced enough to be able to judge an animal that showed great promise as a prospective gun dog, and, unless he was very much mistaken, the little spaniel definitely belonged in this category. She might still be in need of training, but to have found her way to the Manor, a distance of some two miles from the cottages on the estate, was no mean feat, his lordship decided, a moment before the dog, as though to confirm his lordship's assessment of her ability, was quick to pick up the scent the instant they were out of doors.

Rosie set off down the path in the direction of the stables at a brisk pace. Fortunately for her his lordship wasn't so far behind, and, although somewhat breathless, succeeded in reaching the stable-yard in time to stop his head groom from hurling a sturdy piece of wood in Rosie's direction.

'It's all right, Wilks. She's with me. She's looking for Miss Milbank. I take it she has been here?'

'Aye, sir. But that were some little time ago.' The groom ran his fingers through his grizzled hair. I mind she went—' He broke off as the dog came hurtling from the stables to set off down the path leading to the shrubbery. 'That way, sir. Do you want I should go with you?'

His lordship nodded before following in hot pursuit. His confidence in Rosie's abilities as a prospective gun dog had increased with every passing minute, though they did receive something of a setback when he discovered her a few minutes later frantically scratching at the base of the icehouse door. At first he was inclined to believe she had located the scent of, perhaps, a rodent, and was on the point of coaxing her away, when he thought better of it, and decided to investigate further.

The sudden pain that shot through her head as her prop was unexpectedly withdrawn, as she seemed unable to stop herself from flopping backwards on to the hard cobblestone ground, was sufficient to rouse her, but it wasn't until Annis found herself airborne, wrapped in her cloak and held against a stone-hard chest that any substantial feeling began to return.

It started with a tingling sensation in both fingers and toes that quickly gave way to a surge of pain in and around the palms of her hands and wrists. Grimacing, she risked opening the eye that was not pressed against the warmth of a woollen jacket, and peered up to see the line of a masculine jaw and a mouth set in a grim straight line.

Reality then returned with a vengeance. 'Whatever are you thinking of? I'm sure I can walk. Oh, sir, put me down at once, do!' she demanded in a voice now decidedly hoarse after all the shouting she had done in those futile attempts to gain someone's attention during her confinement in her temporary freezing-cold jail.

She didn't quite catch the muttered response, but felt sure it was neither polite nor a promise of compliance, as he merely continued striding purposefully towards the house.

Once indoors, Annis didn't waste her breath in further attempts to remonstrate with him. Nor did she wish him to waste his, as he seemed intent on carrying her the full distance back to her bedchamber.

Although it had been some little time since she had been carried in a gentleman's arms, she remembered the occasion quite well. What she couldn't recall experiencing, however, when she had foolishly gone and twisted her ankle all those years ago, and her father had performed the same feat, was the peculiar sensations she was feeling now. There had been no odd fluttering sensations in the pit of her stomach or beneath her ribcage during that one previous occurrence, she felt sure. And why there should be that pulsating heat in the area directly below her cheekbones when the rest of her was still experiencing the lingering effects of the atmosphere in the icehouse she simply couldn't imagine.

When at last she felt herself being lowered carefully on to her bed, and those strong arms were no longer providing their support, Annis didn't know whether to feel relieved or disappointed. She didn't know either whether to feel annoyed or amused when, against her specific wishes, the doctor was summoned, and she was forced to undergo what she considered to be a completely unnecessary examination. Moreover, she didn't know whether to accept with a good grace or deliberately ignore his lordship's command to remain in bed for the remainder of the day. She only knew that when he favoured her with a visit, bringing her rescuer with him, shortly after the tray containing the remains of her evening meal had been taken away, she experienced nothing but untold gratitude towards the being who had done everything humanly possible to ensure a rapid recovery after her unpleasant ordeal.

'If you thank me again, you will become a bore,' his lordship warned, holding up his hand to check further heartfelt expressions of gratitude. 'Besides which, it's your four-legged friend here you should be thanking, not me.'

Up until that moment Annis had deliberately refrained from making eye contact with the little bobtailed dog, but the instant she did so Rosie seemed to suppose it was an invitation to jump up on the bed, and promptly settled herself beside her chosen mistress. Annis did not object. How on earth could she?

Although she had known almost from the moment she had been

released from her prison that Rosie was at the Manor, she had since discovered from Disher that it had been none other than the spaniel's unexpected arrival that had induced his lordship to set out in search of her; and even though she was well aware that Rosie's presence at the mansion had not been greeted with unanimous delight, Annis could not find it within herself to feel in the least bit sorry that her four-legged friend had dared to cross the mansion's hallowed portal.

'What to do with you now, though?' she murmured, absently stroking one silky brown ear, and completely unaware that she had spoken the thought aloud until she glanced up to discover the look of amused resignation flit over his lordship's features as he settled himself in the chair by the bed. 'Oh, no, sir! I wouldn't dream of inflicting her upon you,' Annis assured him, with a look of abject apology. 'You've done more than enough already. And I know you don't care for dogs.'

His expression changed instantly to one of mild surprise. 'You are labouring under several misapprehensions, child. I have done nothing. Wilks gave her a bath, Cook fed her, and the footman she did her best to injure has since forgiven her and taken her out for a walk. And why you should suppose I do not like dogs I cannot imagine.'

'Oh, no, that's right. I'm becoming confused. It's Sarah who doesn't care overmuch for them.'

'She prefers cats, certainly,' he agreed. 'But even she is of the opinion that the dog cannot be returned to Nanny Berry who, by the by, has already been apprised of the animal's whereabouts.' He smiled wryly. 'Your visit to her cottage this morning, my dear cousin, has not been without—er—how shall I phrase it, certain repercussions.'

Annis didn't pretend to misunderstand. 'You are referring to my inspection of the icehouse... Yes, I admit it. Discovering that you had been locked in there as a child did succeed in inducing me to allow curiosity to override sound good sense, and experience what it was like for myself.' The mere thought made her shudder. 'I must have been mad to have made the attempt!'

'I'm certainly astonished that you did so, given that you have a fear of confined spaces,' he remarked, which induced her to reveal surprise this time. 'You admitted to that particular *bête noire* the other day,' he reminded her, before adding with a slight thread of censure in his voice, 'What defeats me is why you didn't just open the door again and come out. Were you gripped by panic?'

Annis was so shocked she almost found herself gaping. 'What on earth are you talking about, Dev? The door was locked.'

Black brows rose sharply, though whether as a result of what she had just revealed, or because she had made free use of his given name for the very first time was impossible to judge.

'What's wrong…? The door was locked, wasn't it? Yes, it must have been. I couldn't open it, at least not from the inside. It was pounding on the door to attract someone's attention that bruised and grazed my hands so badly.'

Had it been anyone else his lordship would have been inclined to dismiss the notion that the door had ever been locked, and merely attribute the staunch belief to the result of panic. But not with Annis. She paid far too much attention to detail, and something was certainly troubling her now, something was niggling at the back of her mind.

'A mystery, wouldn't you say? Put it from your mind for the present,' he ordered gently. 'But tomorrow, if you feel brave enough, we'll return to the scene of the enigma, and see if we cannot discover the reason why an unlocked door wouldn't open, and you were unable to release yourself.'

As Rosie seemed to have little trouble in returning to the green bedchamber, after she had been taken down to the bowels of the house on three separate occasions during the latter part of the evening, Annis finally decided that the wisest course would be to allow her to remain. As far as she was aware, the little dog then passed a contented first night in her new home, curled up at the bottom of the bed, asleep by her chosen mistress's feet.

Despite her sore hands, Annis herself passed an equally restful night, except for one occasion, when she had woken after a particularly vivid and disturbing dream, which had resulted in her becoming increasingly sure that the icehouse door had been locked, if only for a brief period during the time she had been inside the cavernous structure; and which had made her more determined than ever to make a return visit to the site of her enforced incarceration early the following morning.

'There, what did I tell you?' she announced, experiencing a degree of satisfaction, and relief too when, in the cold light of day, the door had opened after a little extra persuasion on her part.

It had been entirely different this time, of course, knowing full well that his lordship was there on the other side of the sturdy wooden barrier, ready to offer immediate assistance should the need arise. All the same, that didn't alter the fact that she had managed to release herself easily enough, after the door had been closed.

'I know what you're thinking, Dev,' she added, having had little difficulty in guessing the reason behind his slightly sceptical look. 'It's true I don't feel in the least nervous now because you're here. But the point is, I just managed to release myself by lifting the latch and stepping outside, even though the wood is warped and the door does brush against the cobblestones near the entrance. And I could easily have done so yesterday, even in an anxious state, had someone not slid across the bolt... That same someone who must have followed me here, concealed himself in the shrubbery, and then laughed gleefully just as he deliberately threw the bolt. After a time he must have unlocked it again, without my knowing, possibly when I had become too exhausted to keep hammering on the door, and had decided there was no purpose in bruising my hands further.'

When his expression turned thoughtful, Annis knew he was beginning to give her the benefit of the doubt, and so unashamedly pressed home her advantage. 'The wind didn't start to get up until some time after I had entered the icehouse. The wind didn't have anything to do with that door slamming shut, Dev. Look,' she added, pointing to the scuff marks clearly visible on the stone floor. 'It takes real force to close it, a deal more than the wind had yesterday.'

He tried it for himself, decided almost immediately that she was right, and as a result was obliged to come to terms with the fact that her imprisonment had been no accident, or merely the result of blind panic on her part.

'But who would do such a thing, child?' he asked, with unwonted gentleness. 'Surely you don't suspect one of the servants...? Sarah...? Louise...myself?'

'Of course not!' she answered without so much as taking the trouble to mull over the possibilities. 'No servant who values his position would lend himself to such a start, and run the risk of being turned off without a reference. Since the end of the war with France, situations are not so easily come by, with so many people vying for so few jobs. Besides which, from what Sarah was saying the other day, I understand most all the people who work for you have been here for some time. They're obviously contented, and I certainly haven't done anything to change that situation. Quite the opposite, in fact!'

She shook her head, at a complete loss to explain the reason behind what she would have undoubtedly viewed as a very puerile act on someone's part, had it not been for what had happened to the Viscount the week before. 'Like the one perpetrated against you, it seems a senseless act, with so little purpose to it that one is tempted to dismiss it as nothing more than a childish prank. Which I must confess I find a trifle worrying in itself, because I don't suppose for a moment that a child was responsible for perpetrating these acts.'

'Quite so!' his lordship agreed. 'But hardly the actions of a rational adult, either. So one cannot help wondering just how malicious the guilty party might become if...'

'Perhaps we should concentrate on the why for now,' Annis suggested. 'Which, with any luck, might lead us to uncovering who is behind what thankfully remains for the time being at least as nothing more than tiresome foolishness.'

As though by some mutual understanding, they turned as one and began to retrace their steps as far as the stable-yard. Louise's simultaneous arrival dissuaded his lordship from discussing the matter further. Unlike the resolute young woman beside him, whose company he valued more highly with each passing day, Louise's disposition was undoubtedly on the nervous side, and it was much to the girl's credit that she was prepared to at least attempt to get back into the saddle. So it would not do for her to discover that Annis's incarceration in the icehouse had not been purely accidental, and that not too far away there was someone with a perverse sense of humour, prepared to select an unsuspecting victim at a moment's notice.

He might not be altogether happy that Annis had decided not to postpone this first venture out with Louise. Nevertheless, given that, except for a few cuts and bruises to her hands, she was none the worse for her ordeal, and Wilks himself was to accompany them on this occasion, he decided it might be for the best, at least for the present, to go on as though nothing untoward had occurred.

Consequently he was intent only on keeping the promise he had made earlier in a moment's madness to ensure the latest inhabitant of the Manor did not slip her leash and chase after her young mistress. Surprisingly enough, after testing the restraint a time or two, and voicing a few token protests as Annis, leaving her behind, led the way out of the stable-yard, Rosie seemed content enough to remain with his lordship. She padded alongside him so happily that he forgot his resolve to hand her over to a servant the instant he set foot back inside the house, and allowed her to bear him company in his sanctum.

After a thorough inspection of the unfamiliar surroundings, when she went about sniffing in various corners, Rosie settled herself down on the mat in front of the hearth, and would in all probability have been happy to remain there until her mistress's return, had it not been for Dunster's entry with the intelligence that Mr and Miss Fanhope had called.

His lordship was almost tempted to leave it to Sarah to entertain the visitors, but then decided not to be unsociable. So, after calling Rosie to heel, a command that she surprisingly obeyed, he went along to the parlour to be greeted with raised brows.

He reciprocated with a completely false look of astonishment of his own. 'Good gracious! Three visits from you in as many days, Fanhope. We are truly honoured!'

'Oh, we have come purely on my account. Mama was given an excellent recipe for a lamb stew and I thought Sarah might like a copy,' Caroline hurriedly explained, her attention fixed on the four-legged creature that had just had the temerity to growl in a most unfriendly fashion up at her favourite brother and was now sniffing about her skirts in an over-familiar fashion. 'I was under the impression you didn't care for dogs, and didn't approve of them in the house.'

'I cannot imagine from where people manage to acquire these totally false assertions,' his lordship responded with a sublime disregard for the truth, for he knew perfectly well where Caroline, at least, had obtained hers.

He had never made the least attempt to conceal his dislike of Lady Fanhope's overweight, pampered pug. It rarely bestirred itself from the most comfortable seat in the drawing-room which, in turn, never failed to earn it one of his lordship's severest frowns whenever he paid a visit to the Hall. 'I wouldn't go so far as to permit my two Irish wolfhounds free rein in the house, but I see nothing wrong in this little lady's presence under the roof.'

'It is I who have inherited Papa's dislike of dogs, not Deverel,' Sarah explained, 'although I have no objection to Rosie's presence, especially not in the circumstances. She's Miss Milbank's dog, and newly acquired.'

'And is Miss Milbank not willing to favour us with her company today? I trust she is not indisposed?'

The Viscount favoured the enquirer with a searching stare. Had it been his imagination or had there been just a touch of smugness in the male twin's seemingly innocent enquiry?

'Permit me to set your mind at rest, Fanhope. She is quite well, and is at this precise moment accompanying Miss Marshal out riding.'

Unlike her brother, Caroline appeared more gratified than surprised. 'Oh, that is excellent news! I'm so pleased your cousin has at last taken my advice and attempted to get back into the saddle. It was the only way to overcome her foolish fear.'

His lordship couldn't help smiling to himself. Caroline, he felt sure, had meant well. Nevertheless, if she thought for a moment that Louise had been influenced by anything she might have said, she was labouring under a gross misapprehension. Oh, no, unless he much mistook the matter, quite another person was responsible for what he considered a long-overdue show of determination on young Louise's part.

After fulfilling his duties as host and dispensing refreshments, the Viscount made himself comfortable in one of the chairs and surveyed his visitors over the rim of his glass, and Caroline in particular.

He had never made any secret of the fact that in a good many respects he admired her. She had been a pretty child who had lost none of her good looks during the passage of time. She was not lacking intelligence either, and had never been afraid to voice her own opinion, which, in turn, had led to some lively and interesting discussions between them over the years. Sadly, though, she had been too long influenced by a foolish and self-centred mother who had bestowed upon her an unshakeable belief in her own importance, which had sadly resulted in Caroline becoming increasingly conceited herself.

Was this flaw he had witnessed developing in her character the underlying reason why he had been unable to bring himself to fulfil a great many people's expectations by asking her to marry him? he wondered. Even taking into account this failing, she would undoubtedly make the ideal wife for a peer of the realm, and he had known for a fact that his own father would have approved the match. That in itself had, he supposed, subconsciously acted as a disincentive, fuelling a stubborn resolve on his part never to go out of his way to win his sire's approval. Moreover, he had been doggedly determined not to be considered a kind of compensation for the ill advice his father had once given Lord Fanhope, which had almost resulted in the Baron's financial ruin. Not that Lord Fanhope, a gentleman of the highest principles, had ever blamed anyone but himself for the near-ruinous investment he had chosen to make.

Absently the Viscount began to stroke the silky brown and white head that had suddenly appeared on his left leg, while he silently owned that there had been a time when he had given serious consideration to marrying Caroline. This, however, was no longer the case, and the sooner he made known this fact the better. Not that he supposed for a moment that this decision on his part would cause any heartache. Nothing so vulgar as loving feelings would ever be involved where Caroline's selection of a suitable mate was concerned. Social position and family duty would always remain her goals. Undoubtedly she numbered among those who believed that tender emotions were considerations best left to those who could afford them, and the lower orders that knew no better than to consider such trifling sentiments.

None the less, his long-standing friendship and regard for her were such that he couldn't with a clear conscience allow her to continue to imagine that she would ever be likely to receive a proposal of marriage from him. This might then induce her to take the action necessary to find another suitable candidate for her hand. After all, there seemed sufficient funds in the family's coffers nowadays to finance Charles Fanhope's expensive tastes and frequent excursions from home. So why couldn't a second Season for Caroline be funded before age began to detract from her worthiness as a prospective bride?

His lordship forced his mind back to the present, but his interest in the polite exchanges soon began to wane, and he found his thoughts increasingly turning to the owner of the creature who had had the impudence to use his leg as a prop, and wishing that she were present to add some much-needed leaven to lift the heavy monotony of the stilted conversation.

He found himself smiling, as he so often did these days. How quickly he had grown to appreciate that no-nonsense honesty of hers, and slightly satirical humour! How rapidly he had come to enjoy those spontaneous exchanges of swift repartee during the evenings. By no stretch of the imagination could she ever be described as a conventional young woman. Life with her under one's roof, however, was unlikely ever to be dull. Oh, how he wished she would return soon and free him from these manacles of boredom that increasingly bedevilled him when parted from her for any length of time!

Although he was blissfully unaware of the fact, his lordship was destined not to have his fondest hope granted. His young cousin, having caught sight of Mr Fanhope's high-perch phaeton heading down the yew drive in the direction of the house, had taken prompt action, inducing her two companions to exchange surprised glances, by turning her mount and setting off towards the home wood at a praiseworthy canter.

'Well done!' Annis announced, once they were safely out of sight among the trees. 'Just goes to prove what one is capable of achieving in a short time when one sets aside one's fears.'

Louise frankly laughed. 'If it's a choice between risking a further tumble, and having to suffer my hand being fondled by Mr Fanhope, I'll risk a tumble every time.'

'Can't say I blame you. He isn't to my taste either,' Annis admitted. 'Remind me to teach you how to perfect a withering look. I've found it an indispensable weapon over the years when dealing with a gentleman's unwelcome attentions. Not that I think I shall ever be called upon to suppress Mr Fanhope's ardour. Unless I much mistake the matter, he would never prove a nuisance, at least not in that particular way. I doubt very much that I am the type of female he finds alluring.'

Turning her head on one side, Louise cast her perfect companion a considering look. 'Suppressing any gentleman's advances, Annis—is that how you've managed to remain single all these years? I did wonder. At your age, you must have received several offers for your hand.'

'And how am I supposed to take that, you abominable girl!' Annis managed to scold, before she gave way to amusement at this perfect example of a backhanded compliment. 'I haven't received so many,' she admitted, after suggesting that it was possibly time to turn their mounts back towards the house. 'I have tended to eschew the company of younger men in recent years in an attempt to avoid inflicting bruised hearts or egos. Older men tend to be, in general, more worldly-wise and not so susceptible to fall victim to the more tender emotions. Besides which, I rather fancy I prefer the company of older men.'

'Is that why you favour his lordship's society?' Louise asked, unknowingly catching Annis quite off-guard by the ingenuous observation. 'It's clear he enjoys yours. Even Sarah said that she has never seen her brother so completely relaxed in a female's company before, not even hers.'

Could that possibly be true? Annis wondered. And why should it bring such a rush of satisfaction to think it just might be so? It was certainly not exaggerating to suggest there had been an ever-increasing bond of camaraderie developing between them since the understandable wary start to their acquaintance that she, at least, had not experienced the least desire to check. Considering they were both cautious by nature, the speed of their developing friendship had been quite amazing. Furthermore, it would not be delving into the realms of fantasy to suggest that their relationship had moved on to a slightly more intimate level since her unfortunate experience at the icehouse.

For several moments Annis felt the same peculiar sensations deep inside as she had experienced the day before, when she had found herself being carried back to the house in a pair of strong, masculine arms. Then common sense at last prevailed, persuading her to curtail foolish speculation regarding herself and Viscount Greythorpe before it could lead to silly misunderstandings and embarrassment to either of them, and ruin what had been for her a wonderful and most natural rapport with an honourable gentleman.

All the same, innate honesty forced her to admit, 'Yes, you are quite right, Louise. I do very much enjoy his lordship's society. I cannot perceive how anyone could not. He's a sensible gentleman and a most amiable one for the most part. But please do not run away with the foolish notion that there is anything more in our friendship than that. I would never be so idiotic as to look upon his lordship as a prospective suitor. Nor would he ever look upon me in the light of a suitable wife.' Even as she spoke, she would have given much to believe that it was quite otherwise, but she was far too down to earth to attempt to delude herself. 'I might be the daughter of a gentleman, and stem from good yeoman stock. But I'm not of your cousin's class.'

For several moments Louise appeared both puzzled and disappointed. Then she merely appeared chagrined, as she stared directly ahead at the Manor. 'Oh, bother! The Fanhopes are still there.'

As Annis couldn't imagine Caroline would remain for longer than the socially acceptable visiting time, she followed the direction of Louise's gaze to discover a vehicle on the driveway in front of the house, and did not hesitate to assure her, 'That isn't a high-perched phaeton, you goose! It's a gig. I don't know who that might be now alighting, but it certainly isn't Charles Fanhope.'

Eyes narrowing, Louise peered again at the vehicle, only more closely this time. 'Why, yes, it is! It's my brother Tom!' she squealed in absolute delight, before astonishing Annis once more by racing ahead, almost at a gallop this time.

Chapter Eight

Surprisingly enough, like the Viscount, Thomas Marshal was also destined to become one of those people about whom Annis was quick to make up her mind. She liked him on sight, finding his easy manners and boyish, good-humoured charm a refreshing change from the studied politeness most young gentlemen of his age and class attempted to perfect.

It swiftly became apparent that he had a genuine affection for his young sister, which Annis found a delight to witness and which, of course, was wholly reciprocated. It quickly became clear too that he was quite happy to spend most of his time keeping his sibling amused, acting as escort wherever she wished to go and willingly accompanying her out on her frequent rides. It soon became clear also, to Annis at least, that all was not well with the engaging young man. For the most part he was as cheerful as could be. A little too cheerful, Annis felt, and so found herself paying him more attention than she might otherwise have done, and in so doing caught him during several unguarded moments staring fixedly at a blank wall, a decidedly troubled frown creasing his young brow.

Enjoy his company though she did, Annis had no intention of

becoming involved in matters that were absolutely none of her concern, and most likely outside her experience too. What did she know, after all, about the personal affairs of young, unmarried gentlemen of fashion? Absolutely nothing, she quickly decided. Ergo, she would have been more than content to remain in blissful ignorance throughout his stay at the Manor, had Tom not chanced to enter the library on that particular morning when she just happened to be there and, more importantly, quite alone, writing a letter to her aunt and uncle.

'If you're looking for your cousin your luck is out,' she informed him, quickly falling into the casual, almost elder-sisterly manner she had adopted towards him from the start of their acquaintance. 'He's taken himself off to town, but intends to be back before luncheon.'

'Oh, it was nothing important,' he assured her, and Annis might have been totally convinced by the devil-may-care manner he was attempting to affect had she not witnessed those rare moments of despondency.

Her left brow was all at once a perfect, sceptical arch. 'Are you sure?'

He appeared momentarily taken aback, his boyish grin disappearing before her very eyes. 'Yes, of course I'm sure. Why—why should you suppose otherwise?'

Now is precisely the right moment to raise a shoulder in a dismissive kind of shrug, a tiny warning voice in her head strongly urged. Now is the time to accept unquestioningly what he has just said, and not attempt to probe further, common sense advised.

What is more, haven't you just written a letter to your aunt and uncle to say that, although you don't know precisely when you shall be arriving back in Leicestershire, they might expect to see you in the not-too-distant future? Sorting out the problems of those associated with Greythorpe Manor wasn't the reason for coming here, she reminded herself. And it mustn't become an excuse to remain either! So the sooner you make arrangements to depart the better!

Yet, when everything warned her to let well alone, she found herself saying, 'Because I sense all is not well with you, Thomas Marshal…that you're possibly in a spot of bother over a…female, perhaps, or—'

'Dash it all, Annis!' he interrupted, tugging at his cravat as though it had suddenly grown uncomfortably tight. 'It ain't anything of the kind! I'm not some dashed loose screw, you know!'

'In that case, your pockets are to let,' she returned in that no-nonsense manner that could still on occasion surprise even his lordship, and which had endeared her to Tom from the first.

'Deuced good sort is Annis Milbank,' he had said to his sister, soon after his arrival at the Manor, which Louise had considered high praise indeed. 'A fellow doesn't need to mind his P's and Q's all the time when she's about,' he had gone on to explain, 'which makes a chap feel dashed comfortable in her company.'

'Well, I dare say Dev will be able to sort things out for you without too much trouble.'

The instant Annis had made the suggestion she realised she had said quite the wrong thing, for it was clear that Tom was appalled by the mere idea of approaching the Viscount, even before he said,

'Confound it all, Annis! I can't go asking his lordship to bail me out. He's a Greythorpe, not a Marshal. Besides which, he's… well…well, it just ain't the done thing, that's all!'

'Isn't it?' Annis was most surprised to learn this. 'How odd! If he happened to be a close relative of mine, he'd be the very first person I'd turn to if I were in a spot of bother.'

'Well, that's just it,' Tom blurted out, suddenly appearing much younger than his one-and-twenty years. 'It isn't just a spot of trou-

ble…I've been playing a dashed sight too deep of late. I'm pretty
heavily in debt.'

Annis might not have had much experience in dealing with
troubled young gentlemen, and none whatsoever in dealing with
young brothers, as she'd never been blessed to have one. Nevertheless, she knew enough to be sure that nothing could be gained
by delivering a homily on the evils of excessive gambling. According to her late grandfather, a gentleman whose advice and opinions
she had valued highly, it was rare for a member of his sex not to
indulge from time to time. The sensible gamester, of course, win
or lose, knew when to stop and never ventured beyond his means,
for any gentleman worthy of the title always honoured his gaming
debts, even if he was obliged to leave his tailor's bills unpaid.

'Are you not even in a position to pay the debt at next quarter-
day?' she asked gently, but guessed what the answer would be even
before he shook his head.

'Between you and me, Annis, that's the reason I'm here. I wished
to ask for more time. Of course I've written to Father. But the Lord
only knows how long it will take for the letter to reach him. He
and Mama are travelling extensively throughout Italy, and have no
very fixed plans on how long they intend to remain in any one particular place. But it hardly matters, anyway, now. I must raise the
blunt by the end of this month.'

Annis frowned at this, because it seemed as though he had
received the ultimatum since his arrival at the Manor. 'To whom
do you owe the debt, Tom?'

'Charles Fanhope.'

'But he isn't still up at Oxford, surely?'

'Oh, no, he left a couple of years back. But he still owns a house
there… Well, part-owns it, along with a friend of his who resides
there with his mother. All very genteel on the surface—select little

card parties and the like.' He grew a little red in the face again. 'Other rooms have been set aside for quite a different purpose.'

Once again Annis found herself drawing upon those snippets of information gleaned from a worldly-wise grandsire, who had been a deal more open with her than perhaps most of his generation would have been when dealing with a gently nurtured member of the family.

'Yes, I see,' she murmured. 'Illegal gaming establishments. I'm not totally ignorant of the existence of such places.' Leaning back in his lordship's handsome, leather-bound chair, she felt quite smugly satisfied, having just had a niggling curiosity satisfied. 'Well, well, well! So, that's how Charles Fanhope manages to satisfy his expensive tastes. I must confess I had wondered about that.'

'He has the devil's own luck with cards, you know, and that's a fact!' Tom disclosed, sounding decidedly disgruntled. Then he shrugged. 'But I've no one to blame but myself for my present troubles. When I won, the amounts were always small, mere trifles; when I lost, I lost heavily. Before I knew it, I was in debt to the tune of...'

After a moment Tom, shamefaced, disclosed the precise amount, and Annis tried her level best not to appear shocked or dismayed, nor even remotely disapproving. After all, it wasn't for her, a relative stranger, to preach a sermon. Like as not, he'd receive plenty of those from 'well-meaning' family members when the truth came out, as become known it surely must in time.

'So, what do you propose to do, Tom? Is there some way you can raise the money?'

'There is just one member of my family I could have approached. Great-uncle Cedric might have told me I'd been a dashed fool, but he wouldn't have rung a peal over my head. Trouble is, he's over in Ireland at the present time, visiting various friends. It would take some time to track him down, and Fanhope, as I've

already mentioned, wants what's owed him by the end of the
month. And I can't say as I blame him either. He's already given
me ample time to raise the blunt,' Tom disclosed, further endear-
ing himself to his sympathetic listener, had he but known it, by
showing a generosity of spirit that in the circumstances she thought
very commendable. 'So, I really came here to tell Greythorpe that
I'd urgent business in town and would need to leave for the capital
without delay. I know Louise is going to be disappointed, because
I promised I'd be there at the Fanhopes' party tomorrow evening.
But what can I do, Annis? I must raise the money, and there's only
one way I can do so now.'

Alarm bells instantly began to chime in her head. 'You aren't
thinking of allowing yourself to fall into the clutches of some
back-street moneylender, by any chance?' She did not need to wait
for a verbal response. 'Oh, Tom, no! You mustn't! Once they have
you in their avaricious grasp, you'll never be free!'

'I know,' he muttered burying his face in his hands. 'But what
other choice have I? I won't go about attempting to raise it from
family and friends, I simply won't! I got myself into this mess, so
it's up to me to get myself out of it.'

It took Annis a moment only to decide. 'Well, if you're so set
against seeking his lordship's help, and I personally think you
ought to do precisely that, there is one other option open to you...I
shall loan you the money.'

It seemed at first that he had been deaf to the generous offer, then
very slowly he raised his head. 'You, Annis...but...?' Clearly he
was having a little difficulty in understanding precisely what she
had said. 'Can you lay your hands on that sort of blunt?'

'Well, of course I can!' she answered, hoping she had not
sounded waspish, but very much fearing she had. 'Why otherwise
do you suppose I would have suggested doing so in the first place?'

'Good heavens! I never thought…I mean, I—er—never supposed for a moment that you… Good gad!'

'Quite so!' Annis responded promptly in the hope that it wouldn't be too long before his mental faculties returned and he would be able then to communicate intelligibly once again. Although this thankfully turned out to be the case, she discovered that the young gentleman who sat opposite her, whose expression had changed in a matter of seconds from despair and quaint disbelief to hopeful expectation, suffered from a surfeit of integrity and misplaced chivalry.

Finally he looked wistfully across the desk at her before shaking his head. 'It's good of you, Annis. Dashed good, in fact! But I simply couldn't bring myself to take such flagrant advantage of someone I'd known for such a short time, especially not a female.'

'My dear Thomas, you're labouring under a misapprehension if you suppose for a moment that I intend to approach my bankers and make arrangements for them to issue a promissory note.' She smiled as he began to regard her with interest once more. 'Oh, dear me, no. What I propose to do is loan you the money at a moderate rate of interest over a fixed period of time. It will all be done through my man of business in Leicester, whom I shall contact the instant I return to the Shire, and who in turn shall produce a contract that is mutually agreeable to us both. All I shall need from you for the present is your precise direction in Oxford. And all that need concern you for the present is keeping your sister amused during the remainder of your stay here.'

Later that morning Annis came upon his lordship in the picture gallery, staring up at the very same portrait of his father that had captured her interest only days before. From his expression, which could best be described as pensive, it was impossible to judge what might be passing through his mind. His intended destination was a little easier to gauge, as he was dressed in his riding garb. Therefore he had merely paused on his way to his private apartments in the west wing and would undoubtedly be attending to the task of changing his attire in due course.

While his attention was fixed on his late sire, and he remained oblivious to her presence, she took a leaf out of his very own book and took the opportunity to study him closely, concentrating on each sharply defined feature in turn.

From the first moment she had set eyes on him she had never considered him a handsome man, and her increasing regard had in no way induced her to change this opinion.

At best, he could be described as attractive in a ruggedly masculine way. No one, however, could dispute the fact that he had been blessed with a superb physique, which was definitely seen to advantage in his present attire. A bootmaker would have been hard put to it to find a finer pair of straight, muscular legs on which to display his wares, and any master tailor would have been proud to see the fruits of his labours draped about such a fine pair of shoulders. No, she mused, moving forward, any female who did not instantly appreciate that Viscount Greythorpe was a fine figure of man would either be afflicted by grossly impaired eyesight, or be at her last prayers.

'Ah, Annis, my dear!' he announced, catching sight of her at last. 'Just the person I wished to see.' Delving into his jacket, he drew out a letter, which he had personally collected from the receiving office a little earlier in the day. 'Just to prove that I do take note of what you say,' he added, handing the missive over to her, the direction on which had undoubtedly been written in Lady Pelham's unmistakably stylish hand, 'and carried out my business in town today, and not on Tuesday as is my custom.'

'And I assume by your cheerful demeanour that no further attempt was made to inflict bodily harm upon your person,' she quipped.

'None whatsoever,' he confirmed. 'But I cannot deny I remained extra-vigilant throughout the ride back to the Manor.' He became serious. 'And thoughtful too. You see, I have been racking my brain, trying to think of something I have done that might arouse sufficient resentment for someone to want to put a period to my existence. And the truth of the matter is, Annis, my angel, I can think of nothing.'

She did her utmost to ignore the endearment as she stared up at the portrait directly in front of her. 'But you cannot say the same for your sire, is that it? And you cannot help wondering if…the sins of the fathers…'

'Shall we say, rather, that it was a possibility that crossed my mind,' he murmured with an appreciative half-smile at her unfailing perspicacity. 'The problem besetting me is, of course, that my father and I became more and more estranged as the years passed and so remained virtual strangers. Apart from the fact that he counted few his friends, and that he became increasingly cynical as the years passed and more and more reclusive, I know next to nothing about his life. In his defence, however, I am forced to own that I never heard anything to his discredit, except perhaps that on one particular occasion he could have been accused, and with some justification, I might add, of giving shoddy advice.'

As always that steady, intelligent gaze of hers assured him that he held her full attention. 'My father might have had his failings. But his judgement in matters of business was second to none. He was quite remarkably astute. One might almost say that he had the Midas touch where the selecting of sound investments was concerned. Staking a small fortune on the mere turn of a card never held the least appeal for him; taking a gamble on a business venture most definitely did.

'It was only to be expected that this supposedly unfailingly good judgement in commercial matters would become increasingly recognised, and his advice more frequently sought. But as far as I'm aware he made a point of never attempting to influence others where to place their funds, not even members of his immediate family. Perhaps it was because he was once persuaded to do so, and it was on this occasion his judgement proved to be flawed that dissuaded him from repeating the error. Personally, though, I have always believed he acted in good faith when he offered advice to none other than our close neighbour, Lord Fanhope.

'Evidently believing, as so many did, that my father's shrewdness in matters of business was second to none, Lord Fanhope made the mistake of borrowing heavily in the hope, belief, that the investment would provide him with a quick return. My father too was prepared to invest a considerable amount in this particular venture, though nowhere near as much as our neighbour. Then Fate intervened. A matter of a few days before he was due to sign on the dotted line, as it were, he learned of the plight of a particular friend whom he had known at university, and who was being housed at His Majesty's pleasure in the debtors' prison.'

His lordship smiled grimly. 'Surprising though it may seem, my father was once capable of the occasional altruistic gesture, at least in those early years of his life before he became totally soured and discontented. The money he had intended to invest in the trading venture was used to settle his friend's debts. The gentleman in question then repaid him by leaving the country, without so much as offering a word of thanks to the man who had been instrumental in releasing him from prison, and without leaving a clue as to where he was bound. A very bad investment, one might be forgiven for supposing.

'As things turned out, Lord Fanhope fared no better. Within

months the shipping venture, which he had expected to provide him with a very healthy return on his capital, collapsed, and he lost every penny he had invested. Ten years later, while he was still suffering the consequences of his bad investment by being forced to practise strict economies, a stranger turned up at Greythorpe Manor, acting on behalf of the gentleman who had disappeared off the face of the earth shortly after being released from the debtors' prison.

'The envoy presented my father with several items of exquisite jewellery, which now form the main part of the family jewels, and a banker's draft which in itself repaid many, many times over the money my father had disbursed on behalf of his friend all those years before. The friend, it transpired, had travelled to South America, where he had had the great good fortune to stumble upon an emerald mine, which had ultimately made him a very wealthy gentleman indeed. Hardly fair that one man should come close to losing most everything he held most dear, because of what at one time had seemed a very sound investment; while another should reap untold riches for what on the surface had seemed such an ill-judged decision.'

'One could well understand if Lord Fanhope harboured resentment,' Annis remarked, after turning over in her mind what she had learned. 'But if he did hold your father in any way to blame for the hardship he subsequently suffered, he waited a very long time before seeking revenge.'

'Quite so!' his lordship readily agreed. 'And I for one do not suppose for a moment that he is responsible for what happened to me. He has never once betrayed the least animosity towards me or any other member of my family. In fact, the opposite is true. He actively encouraged a closer association between our two households by ensuring that Sarah and I visited the Hall frequently when children. Furthermore, he remained one of the few people always welcomed here throughout my father's life. So you see, I related that story primarily to illustrate how difficult it would be to uncover the identity of the miscreant. I would be the first to own that my father was not a likeable fellow. He made few friends throughout his life. But he did not go out of his way to make enemies. For the most part he kept himself very much to himself. So I think we can discount revenge for anything he might have done as a possible motive for the attack upon me.'

'And we have agreed, have we not, to discount robbery also?'

His lordship nodded before asking, 'So what does that leave?'

'It leaves me with the strong suspicion that I was the unexpected, the imponderable, if you like. Someone had not taken into account the possibility of a complete stranger happening along at that season of the year and coming upon you lying in the road. Which leads me to wonder whether the incident was planned with the intention of a definite person discovering you.'

'And your temporary incarceration in the icehouse was the plotter's way of achieving a petty form of revenge on you for thwarting his plans,' his lordship suggested, his brows drawn together in deep thought as he turned, and walked slowly down the gallery in the direction of his apartments in the west wing.

'It's a possibility worthy of some consideration, certainly,' Annis conceded, falling into step beside him without conscious thought. 'The most obvious flaw, of course, is that no one could possibly have known that I intended to explore the icehouse that day. I didn't myself. Like the visit to the stables, it was a spur-of-the-moment decision on my part. So, either someone has been avidly observing my movements since my arrival at the Manor, awaiting his chance, which I very much doubt, as one of your people would surely have noticed if there was someone lurking about the place who had no right to be here. Or the two incidents are totally unconnected.'

'Or it was someone who wouldn't have been considered suspicious seen about the place,' his lordship said, not reticent to put forward his own suggestion. 'If so, the culprit must surely be a member of the family or a servant.'

'I know you don't really consider that a possibility,' Annis responded, without a moment's hesitation. 'And neither do I! No, I think it much more likely that I was wrong, that there perhaps was the odd gust of wind that afternoon strong enough to blow the icehouse door closed, and in blind panic I simply wasn't able to free myself.'

His lordship, however, was not so sure. A thought unexpectedly occurred to him. 'Fanhope was here that day, of course. On the surface, at least, he doesn't seem a likely suspect,' he continued, after further consideration. 'If his own father doesn't bear a grudge against me, why should he, given that he above any of the Fanhopes doesn't appear to have suffered as a result of my father's ill advice?'

'True,' Annis acknowledged, dwelling for a moment on the reason why this should be before returning her thoughts to the incident involving the Viscount. 'If I am on the right track, and a definite person was supposed to find you, we are left to puzzle over why…for what reason. More disturbing still—is the reason sufficiently important for the perpetrator to risk a further attempt? Most disturbing of all is the possibility that the marksman who pinked you so nicely, without hitting any vital spot, might not be so accurate next time.'

'A cheerful prospect!' his lordship remarked drily. 'You are nothing if not brutally frank, my angel.'

He took a moment to watch the colour, very becoming in one of her fair and flawless complexion, highlight the delicate cheekbones at his unexpected endearment, and experienced enormous satisfaction.

'Although I do not consider you're being unduly pessimistic, or that your uneasiness of mind is merely foolish fancy, I cannot go about fearing that every hedgerow, or every ditch, might conceal a possible attacker. On the other hand, though, it would be sensible for a while not to travel about unarmed. You too would do well to remain extra-vigilant,' he added, 'and not go off on your own.'

Even though Annis wasn't prepared to dismiss the warning any more readily than he had dismissed hers, she wasn't unduly concerned for her own safety, as her stay at Greythorpe Manor was now fast drawing to a close.

'So, I cannot persuade you to remain a few weeks longer so that I might have the pleasure of making my fair, good Samaritan known to several of my relations, at least those on my mother's side?' he asked, the instant after she had revealed her intention of leaving early the following week.

'Sadly, sir, I am unable to remain longer. There is a matter requiring my urgent attention back in Leicestershire.'

Although he appeared to accept this decision, betraying neither surprise nor disappointment, Annis gained the distinct impression that he didn't quite believe there could be any real necessity for her to leave so urgently. She could hardly say she blamed him either. After all, for some obscure reason, since her incarceration in the icehouse, she hadn't broached the subject of her leaving the Manor. Yet she could hardly say more without revealing Tom's present financial difficulties. And that she would never do! Before they had parted, she had given her word that the money she was prepared to lend him would remain a business transaction known only to themselves, and she had no intention of going back on her word.

All the same, she felt obliged to add, as it seemed the Viscount had no intention of commenting, 'Naturally I'll be disappointed not to be able to remain to see Helen and Godmama, as I'll have no time to make a detour and call in to see them on my homeward journey.' She drew out the missive from her pocket. 'Hopefully her letter will contain some better news from Bath.'

'Ah, yes! I quite forgot to mention there was a letter awaiting me at the Receiving Office from a certain friend of mine who resides in Exeter, and with whom I chose to make contact shortly after your arrival here, when you disclosed certain disturbing facts regarding my half-sister's involvement with an undesirable.'

His lordship's smile for once was not pleasant, and acted as a reminder that, for all the Viscount had turned out to be a most charming, well-adjusted gentleman, he did not lack strength of character, and would undoubtedly show determination if the need arose. 'It made interesting reading. Lady Pelham's suspicions were no mere foolish fancies. Draycot does indeed have something of an unsavoury reputation where the fair sex is concerned. In fact, he is well remembered by at least one well-to-do family residing at Okehampton, the members of which were only too happy to share vivid recollections of their unhappy association with a certain Mr Daniel Denby, as he was known then, to my friend.

'Seemingly Draycot, or Denby, paid the daughter of the house the same amount of attention as he has been bestowing upon Helen in recent weeks,' he continued, now appearing decidedly grim. 'I infer from my friend's missive that Draycot's progress with this particular young woman was somewhat swifter, for within a matter of a few weeks he had attained the girl's agreement to an elopement, and would undoubtedly have not delayed in making the dash for the Border had he not received sufficient financial inducement from the doting father not to do so. Needless to say his affection for the young lady dwindled rather rapidly after that, and he disappeared, instanter, from the area, uncaring of the broken heart he had left behind.'

'Are you certain that Draycot and Denby are one and the same person?' Annis asked, eager now to discover the contents of her own missive.

'Quite certain,' his lordship assured her. 'My friend took particular care to discover this, and travelled to Bath with the doting father in question in order to have this detail confirmed. Needless to say, he took every precaution to ensure the young rogue was not aware that he was being observed.'

Annis considered for a moment. 'I wonder if Lady Pelham discovered Draycot's past activities while she was in Devon, and that he might possibly have several aliases? Or indeed that he is content to settle for a meaty financial inducement in return for not attempting to whisk his hapless victims to the Border?'

His lordship shrugged. 'She'll know soon enough, for it's my intention to dash off a quick note today and enclose my friend's missive. Whether she chooses to act on the information by disclosing the truth to Helen is entirely her own decision. I have no intention of interfering. Her instincts have not played her false thus far…' he took a moment to smile down at her rather enigmatically '…on any matter.'

'And now, my dear Annis, unless there is anything else you wish to discuss of an urgent nature, you must excuse me. I need to change my attire.' All at once his expression changed again, and his eyes positively sparkled with a decidedly provocative gleam. 'Of course, you are quite at liberty to bear me company while I endeavour to make myself presentable for luncheon.'

His shout of wickedly taunting masculine laughter following her along the passageway, as she turned smartly on her heels, and hurriedly made off in the opposite direction towards the safety of her own room, acted as a timely reminder, had she needed one, that her being obliged to leave early the following week was definitely no bad thing.

Chapter Nine

The following evening, while journeying in his lordship's well-sprung carriage towards the Fanhopes' country residence, Annis had become increasingly convinced that returning to Leicestershire as soon as possible was the only sensible course of action left open to her.

Louise, sitting beside her, was chattering away like an excited child, yet Annis hadn't heard one word in a dozen of what her young companion had been saying. She was conscious only of his lordship seated opposite, but steadfastly refused to look in his direction lest his gaze retain the warmth that had sprung into his eyes when he had watched her descending the stairs, just prior to their leaving the Manor.

Although it had been necessary to depart from Leicestershire in some haste, Annis had not, thanks to the admirable Disher, set out on the wholly unplanned visit to Bath without an adequate wardrobe.

Having been a personal maid to the daughter of a peer of the realm, Disher had been well trained, and, with her usual efficiency, she had packed a variety of gowns, sufficient to cater for most every occasion. Consequently Annis had felt her appearance that evening had left nothing to be desired when she had descended the stairs to join his lordship and his family in the hall a short time earlier.

Her gown of turquoise silk was unmistakably the creation of an exceptional dressmaker, who clearly had an eye for the prevailing mode. Disher, whose plump fingers had lost none of their dexterity with the onset of middle age, had arranged Annis's hair in an elaborate cascade of silky brown ringlets, into which she had strategically placed a beautiful pearl slide that had formed part of the set presented to Annis's mother on the occasion of her come-out many years before. Annis had chosen to wear the three other matching pieces that made up the set, and had completed her ensemble by donning a new pair of long evening gloves and an ivory-coloured silk shawl.

Although well satisfied with the overall appearance of fashionable elegance she exuded, Annis could never be accused of the sin of vanity. If anything, she tended to underrate her looks, and had certainly never felt the smallest desire to be considered a beauty. Neither had she ever been susceptible to admiring masculine glances, of which she had experienced many since attaining the age of sixteen, nor was she susceptible to insincere flattery. Yet when she had joined his lordship in the hall, and had glimpsed the look of open admiration in those striking, deep blue eyes of his, something inside had stirred as never before.

It was utter madness to feel as she did, she told herself sternly, as she continued to stare resolutely through the rapidly fading light at the passing countryside. His lordship's approbation ought to mean nothing to her, and yet she couldn't deny the exact opposite was true. She couldn't deny either that she had liked him from the first, and, without having been really conscious of it, her regard had grown to such an extent that he now most definitely belonged among that small group of people whose judgement she admired and whose good opinion she valued.

If she could have been quite certain that the respect in which she now held him would not change into something quite different, she would not feel so uneasy about what she was experiencing now. The truth of the matter was, though, she was not at all sure she had sufficient control over her emotions any longer where Viscount Greythorpe was concerned. Furthermore, she lacked the courage to remain lest that iron self-control of which she had been proud in recent years proved to be insufficient protection against emotions she had begun to experience for the very first time.

'I'm sorry, I wasn't attending,' she admitted, after Sarah's voice had successfully penetrated the most unsettling reverie.

'My sister was merely admiring your pearls, and was asking from where they might have been purchased,' his lordship revealed, thereby forcing Annis to favour him with her full attention at last.

'Rundell and Bridge, I believe,' she answered. 'They once belonged to my mother.'

'They are indeed very fine,' he agreed, his eyes fixed on the adornment about her throat. 'I strongly suspect that, with your colouring, you could carry most any gemstone,' he continued, almost meditatively. 'Possibly emeralds, though, would suit you best... Mmm, yes, rather a pity, that.'

Annis hoped the dimness hid the crimson hue she could feel spreading up from beneath the pearls about her throat, but, from the sudden flash of white, masculine teeth, she suspected his lordship's sharp-eyed gaze had not been slow to note her embarrassment.

For the first time in a long time she seemed unable to think clearly, and was at a loss to comprehend precisely what the Viscount had been attempting to convey. Was it simply that he had made an innocent observation? Or had there been some underlying reason for the remark, a subtle hint perhaps?

If he had been trying to convey that the Greythorpe family jewels would never adorn her neck, there was absolutely no need for him to have done so, she thought bitterly, her confusion having given way to a rare and rapid feeling of high dudgeon. If he supposed for a moment that she hadn't discovered long ago that her mother's behaviour had been exceptional and that the majority of the top ten thousand would never consider choosing a partner outside their social class, she would swiftly disabuse him!

'It may have escaped your notice, my lord, but I'm not one to deck myself out in an array of gauds,' she announced, just as the carriage came to a halt outside the imposing front entrance to the Hall. 'My tastes are simple. I covet neither the trappings of wealth, nor social position, and I cannot foresee my attitude changing to any significant degree.'

Although his lordship's eyes narrowed perceptively and his gaze became markedly sharper, just prior to his alighting from the carriage, Sarah nodded her head in agreement as she led the way into the house, declaring that she had always considered moderation in the donning of personal adornments a mark of good taste.

Which made Annis wonder what was Sarah's opinion of their hostess, whose upper chest was hardly visible beneath the weight of diamonds and rubies cascading from the decoration fastened about her throat. Whether genuine or paste was perhaps open to conjecture, given the strained financial situation suffered by the family in the past years. Annis, however wasn't sufficiently interested to discover, and so refrained from staring at the adornment closely.

It proved far more diverting attempting to assess Lady Fanhope's opinion of each member of the Greythorpe party, and so Annis concentrated her thoughts on doing precisely that. Towards his lordship the Baroness was so fulsomely welcoming that she was in grave danger of being considered a sycophant by any disinterested party. Towards his sister her greeting was considerably less enthusiastic, and towards poor Louise she was, in Annis's opinion, downright patronising. The greeting she herself received could best be described as bordering on the icily polite, though there was a marginal thaw when their hostess discovered that the Greythorpes' house guest had every intention of departing the locale early the following week.

Had Annis still not been feeling slightly miffed over what she considered his lordship's unnecessary comments during the carriage ride, she might have lingered with the Greythorpe party for a while longer, after she had made the acquaintance of their gracious host, whose greeting, though not profuse, had been genuinely welcoming. As it was, she did not hesitate to avail herself of the opportunity to slip away from his lordship's side the instant she glimpsed a familiar, rosy-cheeked gentleman sprawled at his ease in one of the comfortable chairs.

Her late grandfather's good friend Colonel Hastie could not have been more delighted to see her. He positively beamed with pleasure the instant he caught sight of her approaching, and even went so far as to make the effort to rise to his feet when she reached him.

'Been suffering from the old trouble again in recent weeks, m'dear,' he explained, not hesitating to reseat himself the instant Annis had obligingly lowered herself into the chair beside his own. 'Much improved, but still get the odd painful twinge if I attempt to stand for too long, otherwise I'd have called at the Manor to see you long before now to confirm that it was indeed you staying with the family.'

After commiserating on his recurring gout and receiving, in return, his condolences on the loss of her grandfather, Annis satisfied his curiosity by explaining briefly the reason behind her presence in the locale.

'I did wonder what might have brought you into these parts,' he confessed in an undertone. 'Said to old Sophie, only the other day, that I couldn't recall your knowing anyone hereabouts except ourselves.'

Mention of his charming, long-suffering wife induced Annis to enquire into the lady's whereabouts, as she had failed to see any sign of her in the elegant salon.

'She's at present in the card-room enjoying a game of whist with some friends, m'dear,' he enlightened her. 'She discovered a short time ago that you'd be here tonight, and is looking forward to seeing you again. I dare say she'll be along presently.'

For all that he could be abrupt on occasions, one might even say downright rude, and was definitely prone to a degree of testiness when suffering from his old complaint, the old Colonel possessed a good sense of humour, and so Annis didn't hesitate to tease him a little by saying, 'I'm rather surprised not to find you trying your luck at the tables, Colonel. I clearly recall Grandpapa saying that, next to your beloved horses, games of chance were your ruling passion.'

'Wicked girl to remind me of my shortcomings!' he chided, good naturedly. 'Still, I can't deny you have the right of it there. But age, thankfully, has brought a little self-control where gaming is concerned, if in nothing else, and I no longer indulge as I once did. Besides which, I've never had much luck when playing under this roof, or rarely so, especially when I'm at young Fanhope's table. Has the devil's own good fortune, that young man!'

Annis checked for a moment before sampling the champagne, pressed upon her by a passing footman a few moments before. 'Does he indeed? You don't happen to know if young Thomas Marshal is in the card-room at the present time, do you, Colonel? He set out before the rest of us on one of Greythorpe's hacks, as there wasn't room for him in the carriage, and he said he'd much prefer to ride.'

'Now you come to mention it, m'dear, I do seem to recall the boy wandering in whilst I was there,' he revealed after a moment's thought. 'But, if my memory serves me correctly, he's merely watching the play.'

Thank heaven for that! Annis exclaimed under her breath. It wasn't that she was having second thoughts about lending Tom the money to clear his debts. Nothing could have been further from her mind. Nevertheless, she had no intention of allowing herself to become a bottomless purse for someone who had insufficient self-control to mend his ways, or simply had no intention of attempting to do so. It seemed, though, that her fears were unjustified.

'I may well chance my own luck in the card-room presently, Colonel,' she happily divulged. 'Is there any other table, besides young Fanhope's, I would do well to avoid?'

He chuckled at this. 'The gentleman who must surely be grateful for your timely arrival in the neighbourhood is no mean player, although I expect you've discovered this for yourself by now. Not that you need harbour any fears. I seem to remember your grandfather mentioning once you could hold your own in the most skilled company. Not that I'm surprised. You received the very best instruction, I dare swear.'

'I certainly did,' Annis wholeheartedly agreed, with simple pride and many fond memories. 'Grandpapa was something quite out of the common way in his skill at cards.'

'Well, if you take my advice, child, you'll avoid partnering our hostess at whist. Unlike her son, she has no skill whatsoever!'

Annis smiled wryly. 'I think it highly unlikely I'll be invited to do so. She wasn't particularly overjoyed at having to welcome the Greythorpes' unexpected guest to her party.'

The Colonel revealed no undue surprise at learning this. 'Ahh well, the reason for it is not so difficult to understand,' he responded, after staring at the delicately featured profile beside him. 'Given the appalling weather we've been suffering of late, your putting up at the Manor wouldn't have been considered strange. Your remaining, on the other hand, when travel again became no real hardship, would naturally give rise to a deal of speculation, and might well be viewed by those with more than just a mild interest in the comings and goings of the inhabitants at the Manor with a certain amount of suspicion and resentment. There are those too who would be quick to consider you as something of a threat at a time when there has been an increasing expectation of a declaration of intent from the Master of Greythorpe Manor.'

Annis had little difficulty understanding the Colonel, even though she experienced a definite tightening of the vocal cords as she asked, 'You believe his lordship intends to declare publicly his intention of marrying Caroline Fanhope?'

'Well, let us put it this way, m'dear, I wouldn't be unduly surprised,' the Colonel admitted. 'Although it's common knowledge that Greythorpe and his father were never close, the boy does take after his late sire in so much as he's a stickler for the proprieties. So it came as no great surprise to me that he delayed in declaring himself and adhered to the period of mourning. His friendship with the Fanhope gel goes back a long way. He's had numerous Seasons in town, and yet he's never betrayed any real interest in any other filly, at least not to my knowledge. So I suppose it's only to be expected that hopes run high under this roof as to his eventual choice for a suitable wife.'

'Indeed, yes,' Annis was forced to agree, while experiencing a rapidly increasing hollowness within. 'But to suggest that I might be viewed as a threat to such a hopeful outcome... Surely not!' she added, dismissing the notion with a wave of one hand and a decidedly forced chuckle, both of which were witnessed by one of those very interested parties mentioned by the Colonel only moments before.

'Your house guest, my lord, is being well entertained by our neighbour, I see.'

The Viscount, having kept a discreet, yet watchful, eye on a certain party, wasn't so sure. 'It would certainly seem so, yes,' he was prepared to concede. 'I happen to know they've been acquainted for years, so I should imagine Hastie, who, as you are fully aware, is not always comfortable in female company, would feel contented in hers. Furthermore, Annis isn't easily shocked or in any way missish, which would immediately endear her to anyone of the Colonel's stamp. Indeed, to the majority of my sex.'

His lordship was not unduly surprised to find himself being regarded with no small degree of interest by the female whose intelligence he had always considered above the norm. Nor was he in the least disconcerted by the bluntness of the question she then directed at him.

'Do I infer correctly from that, my lord, that you yourself value her company highly?'

'You do indeed, Caroline,' he responded softly, and knew by the sudden lowering of delicate eyelids that he had no need to utter anything further, now or at any time in the future, with regard to his intentions.

He experienced neither pity nor remorse for having made his objective known to the female whose friendship he had valued over the years. If anything, he felt admiration for the dignified way Caroline was dealing with what must be a bitter pill to swallow.

Furthermore, nothing in her demeanour induced him to alter his former opinion and imagine that his declaration of intent, which had been both clearly yet subtly delivered, would be likely to induce the woman beside him to fall into a decline. Caroline, he knew, thought highly of him, but he would never be foolish enough to suppose that her feelings had ever gone deeper than a sincere regard, or that a desire to wed him had been induced by anything other than a wish to fulfil the aspirations of her family. He did not experience the smallest sense of guilt either, simply because not once, either by word or action, had he intimated that he had any intention of offering for her hand at any time in the future.

It was true that since coming into the title he had considered more seriously the prospect of marriage, and his thoughts had dwelt not infrequently on the type of woman that would suit him best. It would also be true to suggest that, failing to find a compliant, beautiful simpleton with a loving heart, he had considered that Caroline, or someone very like her, would suit him very well. That, of course, was before a certain very unusual young female had unexpectedly entered his private world, forcing him to take stock, to re-evaluate hopes and aspirations.

Not immediately, but soon after their first encounter his attitude had begun to change about many things. It still astonished him to reflect on the fact that her mere presence under his roof had brought about a dramatic change in his attitude towards his ancestral home. A dwelling from which throughout most of his life he had been happy to escape had, almost overnight, begun to turn into a place of blissful contentment, the most delightful home, simply because Miss Annis Milbank resided within its walls.

Most surprising of all was the affinity he had experienced from the beginning of their acquaintance. There had been few women in his life with whom he had developed a close and wholly platonic relationship, at least no young and desirable females. Throughout his adult life he had had little difficulty in consigning members of the gentler sex into clear-cut and definite slots. There had been those usually more mature ladies whose company he had sought for intellectual stimulation, or their razor-sharp wit. There had been those with whom he had enjoyed more intimate relations and a few who had for brief periods only succeeded in retaining his interest as a possible future wife.

Never before Annis had entered his life had he believed it possible for just one woman to encompass his every requirement. Physically desirable and mentally stimulating, Miss Annis Milbank was morally above reproach, even though it had to be said that she was a most unconventional young lady. This, however, only seemed to enhance the abundance of natural charm she exuded.

Yes, he could quite understand why Colonel Hastie—the lucky dog!—appeared so relaxed and contented in her company. He himself never grew weary of her presence and could never imagine he ever would, for the deep attraction he felt towards her was not merely physical.

Yet this evening he could not deny that perhaps for the first time he had appreciated fully those purely physical attributes. Even though he knew beyond a shadow of a doubt that Annis would make the most perfect wife for him, he was not so besotted, even now, as to consider her some ravishing beauty that should be set on a pedestal and admired for her sheer perfection. True enough, her looks were more than just highly pleasing and more than worthy of a second glance. It would also be true to say, in his opinion, that her womanly curves, wonderfully proportioned, would be difficult to better. What set her quite apart from all other women of his acquaintance, however, was that aura of natural charm she exuded.

When he had turned to see her descending the stairs at the Manor earlier, he had almost found himself gaping like a half-wit, so stunned was he by the perfect picture of graceful womanhood she presented. Almost at once he had found himself studying her intently, subconsciously determined, he supposed, to find some minor flaw. Yet when he had voiced that most insignificant suggestion about emeralds, there had been a definite flash of annoyance and wariness in those lovely eyes of hers.

That spontaneous reaction troubled him deeply, because he knew her well enough to be certain that she was not a female to take a pet over trifles, and would not take offence merely because he had considered her appearance might be slightly improved by the donning of a different jewel. It was almost as if she had instantly stepped behind a barrier in an attempt, he could only assume, to protect herself. But protect herself from what, for heaven's sake! And why should she have felt the immediate need to do so?

Concerned though he was, his lordship could not forget where he was or with whom. He succeeded in thrusting the conundrum to the back of his mind to puzzle over at a more appropriate time, and turned his attention to the female beside him who, it had to be said, was making a praiseworthy attempt to appear perfectly composed after the body blow he had dealt her.

'Would you do me the singular honour of partnering me in the set of country dances which, unless I much mistake the matter, is shortly to commence?'

Lady Fanhope, always mindful of her duties as hostess, had not overlooked the fact there would be a number of younger persons attending the party and, in consequence, had previously arranged for one of the more mature matrons present to play a selection of country dances.

Caroline watched her mother's particular friend seat herself before the fine instrument in the corner of the room, before returning her attention, a rather wistful expression flickering in her eyes, to his lordship. 'I'd be delighted, Deverel,' she assured him. 'But you're not obliged to do so if you truly have no desire to take to the floor.'

The fondness in the smile he cast down at her, as he entwined her arm through his and escorted her across to that area of the room set aside for dancing, was completely spontaneous and totally sincere. He had always had, and possibly always would have, a genuine fondness for her.

'Believe me, Caro, I can think of few things that would give me greater pleasure.'

He had spoken no less than the truth. Caroline was a graceful dancer and one who, moreover, never failed to perform her part in any set faultlessly. Unfortunately he wasn't so fortunate with his second partner who, either through nerves or general clumsiness, had little difficulty in finding his feet at frequent intervals. None the less, he risked further bruising by requesting yet another fair maid not long out of the schoolroom to partner him, before the lady doing sterling work at the pianoforte took pity on him by announcing her intention of playing a selection of waltzes.

The Viscount, then, wasted no time whatsoever in restoring his gauche young partner to the protection of her fond mama's side and making a beeline for the one young lady he was determined to swirl about the room in the dance that had become very popular with his generation, and which had won, increasingly, approval from the strictest of matrons.

Now standing among a group of older females, which included his own dear sister and Colonel Hastie's loquacious wife, Annis appeared on the surface at least much more her usual self. Indeed, apart from the raising of one of those perfectly arched brows of hers in evident surprise, she seemed happy enough to accompany him on to the dance floor; until, that is, he slid a hand about her waist and captured her fingers in readiness for the commencement of the dance. Then she was all delightful confusion.

No, his imagination was not playing tricks on him, he quickly decided. There had most definitely been a deepening in the healthy hue suffusing delicate cheekbones; grey-green eyes, staring fixedly in the region of his neckcloth, as though expecting to see at any moment something menacing peering out from between the folds, had almost doubled in size; and there remained a quickening in the frequency of rise and fall to the perfectly moulded bodice of her delightful gown.

Highly gratified by these revealing reactions, his lordship couldn't help smiling to himself. Calm and collected for the most part, she appeared so self-confident, so worldly-wise, that one tended to forget that in certain respects she was a complete inno-cent—untouched, merely awaiting the gentle guidance to enable her to enjoy more intimate experiences.

The huge satisfaction attained from his determination to be the guiding hand was tempered somewhat by the lingering, niggling suspicion that all was still not quite well with her that evening. He was forced to acknowledge too that it was hardly the most appropriate time or place to attempt to discover what was preying on her mind. Instead, he decided to divert her thoughts by assuring her that she need not feel in the least uncomfortable if she had not performed the waltz in public too many times in the past.

'Let me assure you that my poor toes have become inured to the sudden application of extra pressure, after the many previous assaults upon them this evening.'

Although she was not to know it, her spontaneous gurgle of laughter was a joy for him to hear, and went some way to lessen-ing his concern over her present state of mind.

'I would be less than truthful if I didn't admit to witnessing the efforts of your various partners, Dev,' she admitted, 'and cannot but admire your forbearance, especially in view of the fact that, accord-ing to Sarah, you rarely take to the floor, unless Miss Fanhope agrees to partner you, that is.'

'Ahh, yes, darling Caro! She can always be relied upon to

perform faultlessly. Would that every young lady possessed her easy grace on the dance floor!' he murmured with feeling.

It was then that Annis discovered for herself that there was a great deal of truth in the old adage that there was a first time for everything. Experiencing a surge of searing jealousy was entirely foreign to her. Yet thankfully in those moments that followed she retained at least sufficient control to say in level tones, 'Well, I might lack Miss Fanhope's expertise, Dev. But I assure you, I shan't add to your bruises. The waltz is performed even in the Shires, and happens to be one of my favourite dances.'

She proved this by an exemplary performance. But at no small cost. So determined was she to demonstrate that Caroline Fanhope was by no means the only member of her sex with the innate ability to move gracefully about a dance floor that she concentrated fully on her feet, and virtually ignored her partner and the conversation he attempted to maintain.

Only afterwards, when he had restored her to his sister's protection, did she curse herself under her breath for allowing foolish pride to lessen considerably the pleasure she might otherwise have attained from dancing with the Viscount for the very first time. She might have eventually succeeded in controlling those shock waves that had rippled through her at his gentle, yet supremely provocative touch, while admirably proving that she too had not been cursed with two left feet. Yet his lordship must have felt as though he had been twirling a mannequin about the room. So she couldn't say she was altogether surprised when he wandered away soon afterwards, without securing a subsequent dance.

Her disappointment was tempered somewhat by Tom's sudden appearance. He requested her hand for the supper dance that was about to take place, and then continued the role of gallant by escorting her in to supper directly afterwards, where they were immediately joined by Sarah and her middle-aged escort, and Tom's sister, who was clearly enjoying the attention of a dashing young officer in smart regimentals.

There were no spare seats at their table for the Viscount, when he did eventually saunter into the room, squiring a lively young matron of about his own age. Annis experienced a twinge of disappointment at being deprived of his company, but was convinced she would have felt nothing more than this had his lordship, completely ignoring all the other available seats, not made directly for the vacant places at the table in the corner, where the daughter of the house held court.

Desperately striving not to succumb to a rare bout of self-pity born, she was firmly convinced, of an ever-increasing disappointment with the entire evening, she tried her utmost to ignore the evident sounds of enjoyment emanating from the corner of the room, and succeeded to a certain extent with the help of the immediate company.

Tom, with his usual youthful exuberance, succeeded in creating a cheerful mood, and many exchanges of light-hearted banter ensued, mainly at the expense of Louise, who appeared to take his constant teasing in good part. Whether this new-found maturity the girl was exhibiting was the direct result of the increasing confidence she had acquired after overcoming her fear of getting back into the saddle, or simply a desire to impress the red-coated swain now paying her such avid attention, was anybody's guess. All the same, Annis could not help but feel that this new-found assurance had come at precisely the right time, for no sooner had the guests begun to make their way back to the large salon than their hostess demanded that Louise fulfil her pledge by exhibiting her skill on the pianoforte, before the dancing recommenced.

After offering a brief word of encouragement, Annis seated

herself beside Sarah. Tom, exhibiting praiseworthy sibling support, positioned himself directly behind their chairs, as there were insufficient seats to cater for all those guests wishing to listen to the recital. Not everyone did, of course. A brief glance about was sufficient to reveal several noticeable absentees, the majority of whom, Annis suspected, had sought refuge in the card-room.

She was just beginning to think that Deverel himself numbered among those betraying a decided lack of musical appreciation, when she caught sight of him standing beside their distinguished, silver-haired host; noticed too several minutes later that he was not slow to join the rapturous appreciation of his young cousin's faultless performance.

Blushing delightedly, Louise appeared quite happy to remain at the instrument in order to accompany her friend, the vicar's eldest daughter, who entertained the guests equally well by singing a ballad in her lovely soprano voice. It then became the turn of a gentleman, quite unknown to Annis, to exhibit his skill on the fine instrument, before the daughter of the house rose from her chair and made her way towards the corner of the room.

It was at this auspicious moment that Annis became aware that Tom was no longer standing sentinel-like behind her chair, and for a few moments looked about the room for him in vain. After excusing herself to Sarah, she did her utmost to convince herself that it had absolutely nothing to do with those uncharitable feelings she was experiencing towards Miss Fanhope that had persuaded her not to remain, but a need to dispel the niggling suspicion that Tom might well have succumbed to temptation and taken refuge in the card-room.

As things turned out she was right to feel suspicious, for she indeed discovered him seated at one of the gaming-tables. What was patently clear also, by the pained look he cast her as she approached, was that he wasn't particularly enjoying the experience of partnering their hostess in a game of whist, and in all probability had been coerced into doing so.

Offering a little moral support, Annis patted his shoulder, as she came to stand behind his chair. It wasn't long before she realised that Colonel Hastie's assessment of their hostess's skill at cards was accurate. Lady Fanhope's play could best be described as indifferent, and of little help to her young partner. It was clearly a one-sided contest, and Annis's attention soon wandered to the corner table, where one of the players was either the antithesis of their esteemed hostess, or was enjoying a spate of rare good fortune that evening, if the numerous piles of neatly stacked coins in front of him was any indication.

She continued to observe the one-sided play, her sharp gaze registering the contrasting facial expressions of both players, while noting their every movement. In consequence, it was not many minutes before a seed of suspicion rooted itself deep inside and grew at quite an alarming rate.

Without conscious thought she raised one hand to cover her mouth, and momentarily closed her eyes, thereby blotting out for a few brief moments what she felt certain she was witnessing. Oh, dear Lord, not that, she voiced in silent prayer. Please do not let it be that...

Chapter Ten

'Confound it, Fanhope!' his hapless opponent exclaimed, throwing down his cards in disgust and rising to his feet. 'I always have the most fiendish ill-luck when playing you!'

'I know the feeling,' Tom muttered for Annis's ears only, thereby inducing her to smile rather enigmatically.

She now strongly suspected that perhaps as many as half those who sat down to play with the Honourable Charles Fanhope, sooner or later, rose from the table unhampered by weighty purses. Furthermore, she believed she knew precisely why!

Although she was completely unaware of it, the decision she was about to make in those next few moments, as she watched Charles Fanhope's latest victim trudging, thoroughly disgruntled, from the room, would effectively change the course of her life. She was very tempted to let well alone, to keep her suspicions to herself, and leave Hampshire three days hence without revealing her misgivings to a single soul, not even to Greythorpe himself. Yet her passion for justice simply wouldn't permit her to ignore such a blatant disregard for fair play, even though the innocent along with the guilty might well suffer as a consequence of the exposure of this one person's reprehensible behaviour.

'Well, let us see if we can succeed in persuading Lady Luck, fickle jade that more often than not she is, to change her allegiance for at least part of this night,' Annis whispered in Tom's ear before strolling over to the corner of the room.

'Why, Miss Milbank!' Looking genuinely surprised by her sudden arrival at his table, Charles Fanhope at least attempted to affect the manners of a gentleman by rising at once to his feet. 'I was about to put in an appearance in the drawing-room. Promised Mama I wouldn't spend the entire evening gaming, and do my bit to entertain the guests. Will you permit me to adopt the role of escort, and perhaps secure your hand in the next set of country dances, which I believe is about to commence?'

Annis feigned acute disappointment. 'Naturally, I should be delighted to partner you, sir. To be truthful, though, I was hoping to enjoy a different form of entertainment for a while. I've already spent time on the dance-floor this evening. Still, if you'd prefer to—'

'Not at all! Not at all!' he hurriedly assured her, inviting her to sit herself with such alacrity that she might have been forgiven for supposing it was her company which he craved and not the contents of her purse. 'And what is your preference, ma'am...? Picquet, for, shall we say, a shilling a point?'

Once again Annis feigned disappointment. 'Well, if that is what you wish, sir. But won't you find it a little tame?' She fixed her gaze on the neat piles of gleaming golden coins at his elbow. 'After all, you appear to be enjoying no little success this evening. Wouldn't you prefer to continue with the same game as you were playing with your previous opponent?'

Once again he seemed surprised, but in no way suspicious. 'Are you familiar with French ruff, ma'am?'

'I believe I have played once or twice before, and am able to recall the rules. If my memory serves me correctly, it is a game not dissimilar to whist, is that not so?'

By the self-satisfied smirk that curled his full lips, Annis could only imagine that he viewed her as a prize fruit, just ripe for the picking. 'Quite correct, ma'am,' he confirmed, his unpleasant smile clearly widening as she delved into her reticule and drew out the purse she invariably carried.

'A lady of means, I perceive,' he remarked, eyes sparkling with easily discernible greed, as they remained firmly focused on the well-filled leather pouch.

Annis was very much hoping that a belief that he was being offered a golden opportunity to acquire some easy money would silence any cautionary little voice advocating circumspection in Charles Fanhope's head. All the same, she was well aware that it would be a grave mistake to stigmatise him as nothing more than an avaricious cheat who would do almost anything to line his own pockets. His success at concealing his wrongdoing thus far was proof enough that he practised discretion when the need arose. Nevertheless, it wouldn't hurt to offer him a little incentive on this occasion, especially as such an egoist as he would never suppose for a moment that a mere female might outwit him.

'I'm no pauper, sir, so you need have no fear that I will not honour any debt I might incur.'

'The thought never so much as crossed my mind, my dear Miss Milbank,' he assured her promptly. 'Besides which, I had no intention of playing for high stakes. Dear me, no.' To Annis's ears his unexpected shout of laughter held a distinctly false ring. 'Greythorpe might become slightly miffed if I were to attempt to fleece one of his womenfolk, and that would never do, now would it?'

Her smile could not have been sweeter. 'Let me remind you, sir, that the connection between Greythorpe and myself is remote, to say the least. Consequently his lordship would never attempt to question my behaviour. He would receive short shrift if he did. Besides which,' she added, when he appeared distinctly unimpressed by this assurance, 'as it is my intention to depart the locale early next week, my estimable cousin isn't likely to consider objecting to any aspect of my behaviour worthwhile for the short period I remain under his roof.'

Annis suspected that the flicker of smug satisfaction she glimpsed in his insipid blue eyes possibly had more to do with her revealing her intention of returning to the Shires in the near future than any sudden decision on his part to change his tactics and attempt to make her his next victim. The play that immediately followed tended to substantiate this, for it was fairly even and remained so until she had won five games in quick succession. She then decided, as anyone might, to up the stakes.

Until that point Annis was certain in her own mind that everything had been completely above board, and that no attempt had been made to cheat her. Then everything changed. His knocking his half-filled glass of wine over the table did not fool her for a moment; it was no mere accident. Nor was she lulled into a false sense of security by the seal he appeared to break on the fresh pack of cards taken from the drawer on his side of the table.

Marked to be sure, the poxy cheat! she mused, mentally resorting to her late grandfather's colourful idioms, as she watched the expert shuffling.

It went without saying that it was impossible to examine the pack too closely without arousing suspicion. A moment later she didn't feel the least need to do so, for his right hand had sought his quizzing glass. To the unsuspecting it might have appeared as if he had developed the habit of innocently toying with his quizzing-glass's black ribbon. Annis, however, had already detected those extra slight movements. So it came as no great surprise when he took the next three games in quick succession, and with them every coin she had in her possession that evening.

Just as Fanhope eagerly scraped the winnings across the table, Annis glimpsed the tall figure meandering his way ever closer round the tables towards her. As far as she was concerned, Greythorpe's arrival could not have come at a more opportune moment. Yet she very much doubted her opponent shared this viewpoint. Alert now to his every twitch, his slightest movement, she did not miss that watchful, almost wary flicker in his eyes. All at once she was convinced that much of his success wasn't due to an expert sleight of hand, but to a strong sense of self-preservation that necessitated the practising of caution on all occasions.

Indeed, it had crossed her mind to wonder, when she had first learned of the existence of a certain house in Oxford, why Fanhope had not chosen to set himself up in the capital. After what she had discovered this night, of course, the reason had become crystal-clear. London would undoubtedly have offered much richer pickings, but it would also pose the real danger of a much higher risk of being discovered.

A hardened gamester would never become one of his victims. Nor would an intelligent man with a vast experience of the ways of the world, like Greythorpe. Undoubtedly a desire to maintain the ability to command the finer things of life, after years of enforced economies, had proved sufficient inducement thus far for Fanhope to veer on the side of caution. He had therefore selected his prey from the aristocratic fledglings who flocked into the university city every year, and whose fathers were quite able to clear outstanding debts when called upon to do so.

Unless she was much mistaken, he considered the majority of women fair game too. It wouldn't surprise her to discover that, with the exception of his sister, and possibly his mother, he didn't hold her sex in high esteem. Consequently he hadn't thought twice about indulging in his fraudulent practises with her on this occasion. That he evidently considered her birdwitted might not be precisely complimentary, but it was certainly to her advantage that he evidently hadn't judged her to be a bluestocking. She was under no illusion, though. Attempting to act out of character in front of Greythorpe would not be easy, and she could only hope that his lordship, astute demon that he was, would quickly grasp that something was amiss, appreciate that she might need his support, and wouldn't be slow to follow her lead.

She need not have doubted him for a second. Her dazzling smile and much fluttering of eyelashes by way of an initial greeting was sufficient to ignite a clear flicker of puzzlement.

'Darling Dev, now you must not scold,' she quickly added, sickly sweet, and fawning.

Her eyes, as she glanced up at him, conveyed quite a different message, and she instinctively knew that he had not misunderstood the flashing look of mingled warning and entreaty in their depths, before he turned his own, very briefly, on the substantial pile of coins at the other end of the table.

'Yes, darling Cousin. I'm having the most monstrous ill luck! And you know how I do so hate to lose.'

Yet a further blatant untruth, had he needed one, to confirm his suspicion that all was not as it should be, for he was well aware, after so many evenings of pitting his skill against hers at cards, that her self-control was second to none. She could not be enticed to prolong a winning streak, nor could she be tempted to try to turn a run of ill luck by remaining at the table.

'I want you to assure Fanhope, here, that he need have no qualms about accepting my IOUs.'

'Oh, I believe I can do better than that, Annis, my darling,' his lordship responded, cutting across Fanhope's spluttering assurance that he would never dream of questioning a lady's integrity.

Briefly grinning at the genuine look of surprise she flashed him at his unexpected endearment, he delved into his pocket and dropped a weighty purse directly in front of her. 'I came prepared to risk a hand or two myself this evening. But in view of the fact that I might be called upon to stand your banker, I shall refrain. Just promise me that you will at least leave me with my shirt.'

'Oh, I think I can safely promise you that, Cousin,' she returned in the same flirtatious tone. 'But now go away, do! I cannot have you hovering over me, frowning in disapproval. You will put me off my game.'

Annis, of course, was far more concerned that Fanhope was not put off his or, rather, discouraged by Greythorpe's presence to continue cheating as before. There was certainly a tense set about her opponent's fleshy shoulders now, as he watched his influential neighbour saunter across to the table at which poor Tom was still endeavouring to produce at least one half-decent game, having been cursed with such an abysmal partner. So his lordship's presence was certainly having an effect on Charles's behaviour, a fact that was borne out when she was permitted to win the next two games.

'Oh, joy, I've won again!' she chirruped, clapping her hands like an excitable child at the supposed return of her good fortune. 'I knew I ought to trust my intuition, and not abandon the game.'

Fanhope's smile, as he watched slender fingers gathering together the winnings, looked distinctly false. 'You should perhaps be thanking your cousin for his generosity. Not that I should have refused to accept your vowels,' he hurriedly added.

'I should think not!' she returned, sounding truly aggrieved. 'I'm not a pauper, Mr Fanhope, as my cousin well knows.'

She wasn't slow to observe the assessing glance he shot at the adornment about her throat. 'Why on earth do you suppose that Cousin Deverel didn't think twice about handing over his purse?'

He gathered together the cards and began to shuffle them in his surprisingly dextrous, podgy hands. 'I must confess that it did surprise me somewhat to see him do so so willingly. I should be the very last person to suggest that there is any trace of meanness in his character. But he has definitely earned himself the reputation of being very self-controlled where gaming is concerned, and betrays scant sympathy for those who are not.'

Annis shrugged. 'The very fact that I am a guest under his roof no doubt persuaded him to act as he did on this occasion,' she suggested, while observing the subject under discussion bending to whisper something in his young cousin's ear and receiving a nod in acknowledgement, a moment after Tom had shot a glance over in her direction. 'And you must remember that Greythorpe's nothing if not a gentleman. Added to which, my cousin knows well enough that my close relatives have ensured that I shall never be called upon to practise economies.'

This assurance was received with a condescending smile. 'Ahh, yes! I do recall Mama remarking only the other day something about being acquainted with your own mother many years ago...before your esteemed parent chose to disappear from the social scene, never to be seen again.'

'If Lady Fanhope said that, then she is guilty of grossly misleading you, sir,' Annis derived the utmost pleasure in countering, flatly refusing to become nettled by this childish piece of blatant provocation. 'My mother was seen frequently with those of her own class whom she held in high regard. Though it must be said that she considered very few of those belonging to the higher echelons as close friends, or worthy of her attention.'

Whether or not it was as a direct result of receiving this retaliatory swipe, or the fact that Greythorpe chose that moment to saunter from the room in that lazy, elegant way of his, Annis wasn't altogether sure. All the same, she wasn't unduly surprised when her opponent won the next game, and then the four that immediately followed in quick succession. As a result his lordship's purse was much depleted, with only sufficient, as she purposefully upped the stakes, for her to bet on one further game.

By this time the evening was well advanced, and a number of people had begun to seek the relative peace and quiet to be found in the card-room, well away from the high-spirited younger guests expending their energy on the dance-floor.

After watching Fanhope's grasping, fleshy fingers once again eagerly gathering together the winnings, Annis became aware that their table had begun to attract no little attention. Among those who had been avidly watching proceedings were Colonel Hastie and his wife, and Tom, who at some point had managed to persuade some poor, unsuspecting soul to take his place at the whist table.

Annis wasn't prepared to permit this unwanted attention to detract her from her goal. More importantly, her partner did not seem too perturbed by the little gathering of onlookers, either, for he appeared neither unhappy to accept her IOU, nor disinclined to continue with his former reprehensible play.

None the less, Annis was aware that time was against her, and that Fanhope's low opinion of her sex, or maybe her in particular, would not be sufficient inducement for him to continue indefinitely. Consequently she made the decision to attempt to expose him for the unprincipled wretch that he was in the very next game, tempting him with odds that he could not—or would not—refuse.

It might have been her imagination, but she felt sure that a hush spread throughout the room a moment after she had unfastened the clasp and dropped her treasured pearl necklace in the middle of the table. Her bracelet and matching dress ring quickly followed, much to the discomfiture of at least one of the onlookers avidly watching proceedings.

'Child, you can't!' Colonel Hastie urged, clearly appalled. 'They were your mother's, child…her very own! Do they mean so little to you?'

The shoulder she raised in a gesture of detachment might have fooled anyone into believing that she was completely indifferent to the loss of her pearls—anyone, that is, with one possible exception. And unless she much mistook the matter it was this very being of whom Tom had slipped away to go in search. Time now was very much against her!

'Well, Fanhope, what say you? Will you stake everything you've won tonight for those pearls…on this one final hand?'

The urgent tap his lordship received upon the shoulder induced him to break off what he was saying to their host, and raise a questioning brow as he turned to discover his cousin, his young face grave, standing directly behind him.

'You must come, sir!' Tom urged in a frantic undertone. 'She must be made to stop! It's all my fault. But I don't think she'll listen to me.'

That he was being summoned back to the gaming-room did not altogether surprise the Viscount. He had no way of knowing precisely what Annis had been about earlier. None the less, he had appreciated that she had been trying to convey something to him by those two or three meaningful, brief glances that had been at variance with the rest of her totally uncharacteristic, frivolous behaviour. She had not wished him to linger, of that he had felt sure. He felt equally certain that she had definitely had some specific purpose in behaving in that peculiar fashion, though just why Tom should imagine he had influenced her actions in some way was a complete mystery.

'You have the advantage of me, Cousin,' he said, deliberately keeping his tone light in an attempt to conceal his unease. 'Why should you suppose you could influence the fair Miss Milbank's actions?'

'Why else would she do it?' Tom demanded, thereby totally confounding the Viscount. 'She promised to help me...to loan me the money. But I never supposed for a moment she'd foolishly attempt this way first! I can't let her risk losing her pearls... I simply won't!'

Although completely at a loss to understand precisely to what his cousin was alluding, his lordship had grasped one salient point, and was instantly troubled by it.

He recalled clearly a conversation he had had with Annis one evening, when she had surprisingly revealed that her mother had retained very few mementoes of her former privileged existence after she had met, and subsequently married Arthur Milbank. The pearl set had numbered among the few belongings Lady Frances had chosen to take with her on that fateful night, when she had fled the ancestral home in order to marry the man she loved. Annis now treasured each and every one of those remembrances of her mother's former life, and none more so than her late mother's pearls.

Intrigued though he still was by much of what Tom had inadvertently revealed, his lordship made no attempt to discover more. He merely led the way back into the card-room, to all intents and purposes, appearing much as usual, suave and unhurried, a gentleman commanding attention merely by force of personality.

Annis, at least, was instantly aware that he now bore witness to the proceedings, even though she made no attempt to turn round and look at him. She sensed it in the sudden heightening of barely suppressed excitement in those about her; saw it in the guarded flicker in her opponent's eyes; and she could only hope that, now Fanhope had already uttered those fateful words, 'I accept', in response to her proposed stake, that sheer avarice would sustain his nerve sufficiently for him to make that one last fateful, fraudulent attempt to secure the game.

Each seeming like an aeon, the seconds ticked slowly by, adding considerably to the tension, while affording his lordship ample opportunity to study the pile of shimmering gold, with its crown of pearls in the centre of the table, and the two persons vying to rise from it with their purse and pockets considerably heavier.

How calm they both seemed. How sublimely unconcerned at the very real prospect of being the unfortunate one to leave substantially poorer. Annis he knew was remarkably controlled. This above any of her fine physical attributes had been what had first attracted him to her. The prospect of winning possibly did mean little enough to her. The loss of those pearls, on the other hand, was, he very much suspected, quite a different matter. So what had induced her to take the risk in the first place?

Out of the corner of his eye he saw Colonel Hastie sidle up beside him. His bushy, grey brows knitted together, he was clearly troubled by what he was witnessing.

'Dash it all, Greythorpe! Can't you do something to stop this tomfoolery?' he demanded, in what he no doubt considered to be undertone, but which in fact had carried to those standing nearby, all of whom turned an expectant gaze in the Viscount's direction. 'She's wagering her mother's pearls, for God's sake!'

'And she's every right to do so, if she so wishes, Colonel,' his lordship pointed out. 'I have no authority over her. Nor would I attempt to exercise it at this late stage even if I had. The wager has been accepted. It must stand.'

The finality in his lordship's softly spoken response was unmistakable, and the Colonel, wisely, made no attempt to remonstrate further. Instead, he sought solace in the contents of his snuffbox. His evident agitated state was possibly responsible for his taking an unwary pinch and then sneezing violently. The resulting cloud of fine brownish-yellow powder that rose in the air induced several of those nearby to move away, and even prompted Annis's opponent to delve in his pocket for a handkerchief.

It was then that Greythorpe knew. He was not deceived for a moment, even though Charles Fanhope made a great play of waving the piece of fine lawn in the air before returning it to his pocket. More importantly he was very, very certain that the other player involved was in no way duped either. Consequently what immediately followed came as no great surprise to him.

He watched Annis discard three cards, and clearly replace them from those at the top of the pile. He heard her opponent declare his intention of doing likewise, and saw him toss them down on the discard pile. He watched the fleshy fingers reach out for the replacements and the slender hand grasp the wrist, twisting it over before Fanhope could even think of taking evasive action. The three picture cards which subsequently slipped from his palm shocked some into immediate silence, while drawing gasps of horror and dismay from others.

It was Tom who finally gave voice to the accusation hanging in the air. 'You filthy cheat! You damnable cur, Fanhope! You didn't take those cards from off the pile. They came from your pocket.'

'No, not his pocket,' Annis corrected, surprising Tom somewhat. 'He drew those particular ones from his sleeve. And not for the first time. I am in no doubt that a careful examination of that fine example of the tailor's craft will reveal several cunningly positioned pockets, concealing many cards.'

Although he rose abruptly to his feet, scraping his chair noisily across the wooden floor as he did so, Fanhope appeared disdainful rather than discomposed, as he glared down at his accuser. 'I wouldn't expect someone of your station to appreciate the seriousness of the accusation you have just levelled, madam,' he told her, his tone evenly controlled, though clearly betraying contempt. 'But I should advise you to have a care and cease this folly, lest your sex fail to protect you.'

'But I will not fail to do so.'

Lord Greythorpe's softly spoken assurance generated a further wave of mutterings. Those who had been inclined to dismiss the charge made against the son of one of the most respected gentlemen in the neighbourhood as nothing more than the fanciful notion of an ill-bred young woman, and an excitable young man, were obliged to reconsider. His lordship was no stranger in their midst. He too was held in the highest esteem, a gentleman whose judgement and opinions were frequently sought. If he was prepared to support, unconditionally, the young woman's defamatory claim, then it must surely be true, must it not?

'There's one way to settle this here and now,' Tom announced, easily making himself heard above the general mumble of disagreement and lingering uncertainty.

He was round the table in a trice, tugging at the beautifully tailored jacket, while Fanhope manfully attempted to fend him off. It might quickly have degenerated into an undignified brawl had the gentleman whose place Annis had filled at the table not decided to lend Tom his support.

Fanhope proved no match for them both. Before the coat had even been pulled from his shoulders, the evidence of guilt had begun to cascade to the floor. A high-pitched squeal, largely ignored, from the general direction of the table where whist had been the chosen game, momentarily muffled the expressions of disgust uttered by those close enough to have witnessed the array of picture cards of every suit that had fluttered to the floor.

The miscreant, having abandoned his ineffectual struggle, had now adopted a different tack. No longer supercilious and defiant, he attempted to convince one and all that his behaviour that night had been nothing but a joke, a mere prearranged wager with a certain unnamed party to see if he could succeed in taking money by default, and that he had never had the slightest intention of re-taining so much as a single penny of the winnings. But his splut-tered protestations of innocence fell on deaf ears; and it was left to their host, evidently having been alerted to the distasteful episode taking place in the gaming-room, to restore a semblance of order to proceedings.

Lord Greythorpe, whose attention had remained fixed on the young woman seated in dignified silence at the table, numbered among the very first to notice their host's approach, and moved aside.

He had always held his neighbour in high regard, and never more so than in those moments as he watched the look of immediate un-derstanding flicker over the aristocratic features, as Lord Fanhope fixed his sombre gaze on the bedraggled figure of his son. The un-mistakable look of distaste that swiftly followed increased margin-ally as the world-weary eyes turned to view the spectacle of his wife slumped in a chair, her mouth gaping, seemingly oblivious to the well-meaning attention of her friends.

He raised one long-fingered hand and, as though from nowhere, Caroline appeared at his side. 'Your mother would seem to be in some distress, and in need of your assistance. Kindly have her conveyed to her room, and ensure that she is made comfortable.'

The Viscount continued to study their host avidly as Lord Fanhope turned his attention once more to his son. Perhaps the look of distaste had faded marginally from the grey eyes. The ice-cold edge in the refined, softly spoken voice could have escaped no one's notice, however, as the Baron said,

'Enlivening though your presence has evidently been, I think we can dispense with your company, also, for the remainder of the evening, Charles. That should afford you ample opportunity to consider long and hard your future, both immediate and long term, before presenting yourself in my library, after I have fulfilled my duties and seen the last of our guests on their way.'

The Viscount was not unduly surprised when Lord Fanhope turned to him, before finally returning to the drawing-room, requesting that he kindly remain to ensure that order was restored and to assure any one who had suffered a loss at his son's table that evening that he or she would be fully reimbursed.

Although his lordship would never have dreamt of suggesting he and Lord Fanhope were precisely close friends, he had always enjoyed an amicable relationship with his neighbour, and so was more than willing to lend his support at such a time. More importantly, he was determined to be seen to be doing so, especially as several of the guests were now announcing their intention of leaving.

He was not unduly surprised, either, when his own sister suddenly appeared at his side, requesting they too should not remain for too much longer. Sarah had a hatred of scenes that ultimately gave rise to strained atmospheres, and it could not be denied that more and more guests were openly voicing their disgust at what had taken place. None the less, he would have deterred her from leaving had it not been for his rapidly increasing concern for the young woman whose actions had resulted in the ill-natured remarks about their host's eldest son now flying about the room.

She had not uttered a single word since she had voiced her certainty that young Fanhope was a cheat. Nor had she attempted to retrieve those much-cherished adornments from the top of the pile, the whole of which remained still unclaimed in the centre of the table.

He didn't think for a moment that she now regretted what she had done. On the contrary, he didn't suppose that, even if it were possible, she would alter the decision she had made to attempt to expose Charles Fanhope. What he very much suspected, though, was that it had afforded her no personal satisfaction whatsoever in having been so successful in her endeavours.

This was neither the time nor the place to attempt to lift her spirits by words of comfort or expressions of total support for her actions. All he could do now was spare her the added mortification of having to satisfy the curiosity of the vulgarly inquisitive by answering a barrage of unnecessary questions, which would undoubtedly occur once the initial shock over the revelation had begun to dwindle, by ensuring that she was returned without delay to the Manor.

It was well past midnight when his lordship himself finally arrived back at his ancestral home. Although he had never encouraged his servants to wait up for him, he couldn't say he was unduly surprised to discover the conscientious Dunster undertaking the last of his duties—the extinguishing of candles in the hall. On the other hand, he was somewhat surprised to be informed that his young cousin, whose assistance he had sought in seeing the ladies safely home, had not yet retired, and had been awaiting his return in the library.

He discovered him in one of the comfortable chairs, half-empty glass in hand, staring thoughtfully down at the dying embers in the hearth.

As this engaging young man had not once shown the least inclination to bear him company, once the ladies had retired to their beds, Greythorpe could only assume that Tom must have a specific reason for altering his routine. He might have wished that he had refrained from doing so on this particular night, for he felt decidedly weary, and talking into the small hours would not have been his first choice. Given, however, that Tom had been of assistance by adopting the role of dependable escort on the return journey from the Hall, his lordship decided to forgo his own preferences at least until they had taken the time to enjoy a night-cap together.

'No, don't get up,' he ordered, when Tom made to rise. 'Drink up and I'll give you a refill.'

As Tom needed no further prompting, the Viscount, after pouring out two generous measures of fine brandy, settled himself in the chair on the opposite side of the hearth, ready to listen to whatever it was Tom evidently felt the need to impart before retiring to bed.

'Rum goings-on this evening, sir,' he began after a lengthy silence. 'I hope you didn't think I went too far grappling with Fanhope that way.' A further pause, then, 'The truth of the matter is, sir, it made me so angry because…well, because I strongly suspect I might number among those who've been victims of his cheating.'

'Yes, I rather thought that might possibly be the case,' his lordship admitted. 'And I'm not your guardian, you young stiff-rump,' he added lightly. 'There's no reason why you shouldn't address me by my given name. In fact, I should prefer it.'

A boyish grin quickly followed Tom's initial look of surprise. All at once he seemed infinitely more relaxed, settling himself comfortably in the chair, and swallowing a goodly measure of brandy.

'The fact is, sir…I mean, Deverel, I'm dashed if I know just how to proceed. I felt honour-bound to retrieve my IOUs from Charles Fanhope, and had matters in hand to enable me to do so. But after what I've discovered tonight I don't feel as though I'm under any obligation whatsoever. Fanhope's a dirty cheat, sir, and deserves no consideration.'

From one of his pockets, the Viscount drew out a playing card, and studied the back of it intently for several moments, before returning it to the safety of his coat. 'Oh, he's undeniably a cheat,' he readily confirmed. 'There isn't a doubt about that. I strongly suspect he's been indulging in the dishonourable practice for quite some time and has successfully duped a good many people. Lord Fanhope is determined that full reparation will be made as far as possible. But the precise number of his son's victim's will probably never be known.'

The look Tom shot across the hearth was openly admiring. 'But you do not number among them, sir?'

'I do not believe he ever attempted to cheat on the few occasions he played with me, no,' his lordship confirmed.

'Then what put you on to him in the first place?' He frowned now in puzzlement. 'You must have suspected something untoward was going on, surely? Why else would you have come over specifically to ask me to keep an eye on proceedings at Fanhope's table?'

The gentle smile that pulled at the corners of his mouth instantly transformed the harsh contours of his lordship's face. 'Because I was certain Miss Milbank was suspicious about something.' If possible, his smile grew increasingly tender. 'She's a very capable young woman who's enjoyed a very unconventional upbringing. The mistake young Fanhope made was to underestimate her. Miss Milbank's powers of perception on occasions are nothing short of formidable. And she's certainly nobody's fool.'

'She certainly is not,' Tom readily agreed. 'She has a remarkable head on her for business too. Though I must confess, when I saw her stake those pearls, it did cross my mind to wonder whether she might, in fact, have changed her mind about the loan, and was attempting to retrieve my IOUs for me in a different way. That's why I sought you out in such a hurry. I couldn't stand by and allow her to stake her pearls.'

If Tom had expected this disclosure to be met with a look of approval, he was doomed to disappointment. The Viscount's smile had disappeared completely, and his voice when he spoke was icy cold, equally rivalling that of Lord Fanhope when he had addressed his son late the previous evening.

'Do I infer correctly from that that you approached Miss Milbank for a loan in order to settle your gaming debts?'

'Good gad, no, sir! It wasn't like that at all,' Tom assured him, appalled. 'I didn't intend telling anyone... But Annis sensed there was something wrong, and sort of...well, sort of wheedled it out of me.'

Had he chanced to glance up at that moment, instead of keeping his eyes firmly fixed on the contents of his glass, he would have observed a look of wholehearted appreciation once again transform his lordship's features.

'The thing is, sir, I'd made up my mind to go to the moneylenders. But Annis wouldn't hear of it, said she would lend me the money, and would return to Leicester early next week to consult with her man of business.'

He did raise his eyes then, and saw at a glance that his lordship appeared far more approachable. 'It was all above board, sir. I was to pay her a fixed interest on the loan. The only thing I'm not certain about is whether I should still do so—borrow the money from her, I mean, given what we've discovered tonight.'

'If you are willing to leave matters from here on in my hands, Tom, I shall be more than happy to act on your behalf, as I do appreciate that it was your intention to return to Oxford early next week.'

'I would be so grateful if you would, sir.' Appearing as if the weight of the world had just been lifted from his shoulders, Tom finished off his brandy and went over to the door. 'Annis said at the outset that I ought to confide in you...said, too, that there was no one to whom she would sooner turn if she were ever in trouble. She was right about that also… Goodnight, sir.'

'Said that, did she?' his lordship murmured, after watching the door close quietly behind his cousin. A slow, smugly satisfied grin curled his mouth as he followed Tom's example and finished off the contents of his glass in one satisfying swallow. 'You were by no means the only one unsure of just how to proceed in certain matters, Cousin. I have been similarly afflicted… But, by gad, no longer!'

Chapter Eleven

Annis, at least, hadn't been unduly surprised to discover no member of the Fanhope family in attendance at the Sunday service two days later. She hadn't been unduly surprised either when no mention of the family's absence had been raised throughout the entire journey back from church a short time earlier, for everyone at Greythorpe Manor, including herself, had refrained from alluding to the unfortunate events that had taken place on the evening of the party. Everyone, she silently amended, with the exception of Tom, who had sought her out the previous afternoon for the sole purpose of apprising her of the return of his IOUs.

'It makes one feel so devilish uncomfortable, though,' he had gone on to explain. 'It wasn't Charles who cancelled the debt; it was his father. The only good thing about the whole unfortunate business is that I shan't now need to borrow from you. Greythorpe advised me to accept with a good grace, and merely send a note back to Lord Fanhope acknowledging receipt and including a brief word of thanks.'

Annis hadn't been unduly surprised by the actions Lord Fanhope had taken on his unscrupulous son's behalf. Common report strongly suggested that the Baron was no fool. Ergo, appalling though it might have been for him to do so, he would have swiftly accepted that it was unlikely that Charles's misdemeanours had been confined to that one night, but had possibly begun quite some time ago. What did rather startle her, though, was the revelation that Tom had clearly confided in his cousin at some point.

'In the circumstances I felt I must,' he had readily confessed in response to her eager question. He appeared absurdly young as he had cast her a sheepish grin. 'You were absolutely right, you know. Can't imagine why I was so reluctant to do so in the first place. Dev's the very best of good fellows! Never attempted to rip up at me. Nor did he so much as call me a dunderhead for getting myself into such a mess financially, though I don't think he was alto-gether pleased that I'd accepted help from you. Said I was to approach him if I ever found myself in high water in the future. Which I won't, of course. I've learnt my lesson.'

Returning to the present, Annis couldn't help smiling to herself as Tom's assurance to stay on the straight and narrow from now on passed through her mind. Whether he succeeded or not, perhaps only time would tell, even if the passing of time had singularly failed to reveal, at least thus far, Lord Greythorpe's state of mind about the unfortunate happening in recent days.

Absently folding another garment, she added it to the pile of clothes in the trunk. Some detached part of her brain registered the sound of wheels on gravel. Yet, apart from supposing that it must surely be the departure of the visitor who had arrived some little time earlier, she paid it no mind, and channelled her thoughts, once again, on the Viscount's puzzling behaviour in recent days, and her own perverse and wholly uncharacteristic reactions to it.

When she had informed him several days ago that a matter re-quiring her urgent attention necessitated her return to her home, she had been both relieved, because he had not attempted to discover the precise reason behind her sudden decision to leave the Manor, and much moved by his generosity in placing his own carriage, and servants, at her disposal for the homeward journey. Ashamed though she was to admit to it, alongside these positive reactions, she had also experienced an ever-increasing feeling of pique, simply because he had never once attempted to persuade her to change her mind and remain at the Manor.

Not that she would have done so, of course, she reminded herself, miffed perhaps, but still determined to leave on the morrow, even though the reason for her doing so no longer existed. What both surprised and—yes—now increasingly hurt her was his lordship's continuing attitude of seeming indifference. After all, he must surely appreciate now the reason why she had felt she must leave, and yet he still hadn't attempted to dissuade her from going.

It wasn't her imagination; his attitude towards her had most definitely changed in recent days, and she couldn't help wondering whether he disapproved of the way she had revealed Charles Fanhope's true character to the world at large. She wouldn't go so far as to say that, after the undeniable furore she had caused, she suspected he found her presence under his roof an embarrassment. All the same, he had certainly made a point of distancing himself from her, and reverting to his old practice of taking refuge in his library.

Disher's entry into the chamber forced Annis to put an end to the disquieting reverie, for the time being at least, and try to concentrate on the more mundane task of packing in readiness for her departure early the following day.

'I'll carry on with that, miss,' the maid suggested, setting aside the pile of freshly laundered linen that she had brought with her. 'I met Dunster in the hall. Apparently his lordship is wishful to see you in the library, as soon as you can spare him a moment. Sounded urgent.'

'Great heavens!' Annis was intrigued, not to say astounded,

after his behaviour towards her since the party. 'I wonder what he can want?'

'The butler didn't say, miss. I just hope Lord Greythorpe hasn't changed his mind about lending us his carriage tomorrow. I was looking forward to travelling back in fine style.'

'You're a snob, Dish,' Annis told her, and then whisked herself from the room, thereby denying her loyal retainer sufficient time to recover in order to refute the shocking suggestion.

Outwardly calm, though inwardly anything but, Annis didn't delay in answering the summons. Her lingering feeling of pique, and slight unease, swiftly turned to one of utter bewilderment when his lordship, quite without warning, captured her hands in his, firmly yet gently, within seconds of her entering his sanctum, and led her across to the fire. Hardly the actions of someone who was privately harbouring a grudge against her for disturbing the calm waters of peaceful neighbourly relations. Quite otherwise, in fact! she swiftly decided.

'Thank you for responding to my request so promptly, my dear,' he began, releasing his hold on her reluctantly, she felt, in order to allow her to make herself comfortable in one of the winged chairs. 'I've just received a visit from Lord Fanhope. The poor man's in a devil of a taking. Charles, it would seem, is unwilling to face up to his responsibilities and took it into his head to flee the ancestral home some time during the night. He has chosen to keep his destination a secret. Not even Caroline knows what his plans may be.'

'Oh, dear,' was all Annis could think of to say until after she had taken a sip of the Madeira his lordship had seen fit to press upon her, though it singularly failed to lift her spirits. 'Lord Fanhope no doubt holds me entirely responsible for the troubles besetting his family at present.'

'On the contrary, he blames himself,' his lordship didn't hesitate to enlighten her. 'And, I must add, with some justification, though I refrained from saying as much. He has known for some considerable time that the allowance he has made couldn't possibly have provided the expensive lifestyle his son has been enjoying in recent years. Yet he never once saw fit to query where the extra funds to finance Charles's excesses were coming from.'

His lordship paused while he quenched his thirst from his own glass. 'Again with some justification, he blames himself for permitting his wife to show a preference for their elder son, and allowing him his way in all things from an early age. Even though Charles is more than capable of throwing a tantrum if thwarted even now, he was, seemingly, made to see that if he stood the remotest chance of ever being accepted in polite society again he must be seen to repent the error of his ways and repay the money he has acquired by default.'

'Why, then, did he choose to run away if he is prepared to attempt to do the honourable thing and shoulder his responsibilities?' Annis asked, wondering what could have prompted such odd behaviour.

'Because he's an immature fool, that's why. He seems to suppose that repaying the money, or as much as he's able, will right him in the eyes of this censorious world of ours, and flatly refuses to be packed off to the West Indies for the foreseeable future to run the family's partly owned and, sadly, failing plantation out there.'

Annis never supposed for a moment that she would find herself experiencing any sympathy towards the Baron's graceless elder son, but she was wrong.

'So that's what Lord Fanhope plans for him!' She pursed her lips together in a silent whistle. 'I cannot say that I altogether blame Charles, accustomed as he is to a life of luxury here, for rebelling against such a decision.'

Annis knew by the dour expression that his lordship did not share her opinion, even before he said, 'As I've already said, Charles is a half-wit if he supposes for a moment that the return of his ill-gotten gains will set all to rights. Society might be shallow for the most part, and easily diverted by fresh rumours of salacious behaviour. But certain misdemeanours take far, far longer to be forgiven and forgotten, as you above anyone should know.'

He watched as delicate lids were partially lowered in silent acknowledgement of this. 'Unbelievably, in our world murder is considered a lesser crime than either non-payment of gaming debts or cheating at cards. Fanhope wishes his son well out of the way, not only for Charles's sake but for the rest of his family too. Mud sticks, my dear,' he reminded her, 'and the innocent along with the guilty become besmirched when the dirt starts to fly. If he can take steps to lessen what will inevitably be thrown about when society at large gets wind of the scandal, then he intends to do so.'

Sighing deeply, his lordship turned towards the hearth. 'God only knows I've no wish to embroil myself in this affair. Yet at the same time I feel I must and, indeed, am very willing to show my support for Fanhope and certain other members of his family at such a time. After all, its the very least I can do in the circumstances.'

As he kept his gaze firmly fixed on the glowing coals in the grate, his lordship failed to notice the probing look that sprang into grey-green eyes a moment before a decidedly unsteady hand raised a glass to lips that, like his own, bore no semblance of a smile now.

'As a consequence of Fanhope's visit this morning, I've been obliged to change my own plans for the immediate future,' he continued, and, although he had sounded very matter of fact, as though he were discussing a topic of no more concern than the weather, Annis thought she could detect the faintest thread of regret in his voice, and frustration too. 'Fanhope is no longer a young man, and deeply concerned as he is with the inevitable repercussions his son's behaviour will have upon the rest of the family, he's in no fit state to go careering about the country alone in an attempt to locate Charles's whereabouts. I could do no less than offer to accompany him, and place my own carriage at his disposal, as his own is somewhat antiquated and not the most comfortable conveyance on four wheels. And he's far too scrupulous a person to make free with his son's equipage at the present time.'

Annis raised her head at this. 'Did Charles not make use of his own carriage when he himself departed?' she asked, somewhat surprised.

'No, my dear. As I believe I've already mentioned, he chose to depart in the dead of night, and surprisingly elected to make use of that showy chestnut of his,' he informed her, displaying admirable self-control. 'One can only assume that he considered his fleeing the family home on horseback would meet with more success. Besides which, he could hardly leave in his own carriage, as he had already been obliged to dispense with the services of all his personal servants, including his newly appointed groom.'

Had she too not appreciated that Charles's latest selfish actions only added to the concerns of the other members of his family, she might not have been so successful in containing her mirth as his lordship had been. The thought of someone choosing a horse that was far more suitable for a high-stepping jaunt along Rotten Row than attempting a galloping cross-country getaway was somewhat comic.

A thought suddenly occurring to her obliged Annis to give Charles the benefit of the doubt. 'You don't suppose he might have sought refuge with someone close by?'

''You credit him with far too much intelligence if you suppose that, my dear,' his lordship returned at his most scathing. 'Remember, his ability to select inferior horseflesh is second to none. No, it's my belief it was his intention to travel much further afield. Possibly Oxford is the intended destination, though just how many miles he managed to cover before being obliged to seek a change of mount is anyone's guess.'

Annis somehow managed to keep her countenance, though it took a monumental effort. 'When do you propose to leave?'

'Within the hour. Tom is to accompany us, as he knows the precise whereabouts of this gaming-hell Charles, apparently, partly owns. If we should run him to earth there, all well and good. If not, then I'm afraid it will mean the far more difficult task of scouring the capital, for if it is his intention to hide himself away for the foreseeable future, he could select no better place than the metropolis. Which means that I shall need to absent myself for several days, possibly a week or more, as I shall take the opportunity, naturally, to stay at my London residence and see to one or two matters requiring my attention there.'

He took a further moment to finish the contents of his glass, while all the time staring intently down at her, his expression quite unreadable. 'It also means that I must go back on my word, and can no longer offer you the use of my travelling carriage.'

Whether this caused him any particular anguish was impossible to judge, for his voice was as inscrutable as his countenance. Nevertheless, it just wasn't in her nature to succumb to moods of selfish pique simply because things were not going according to plan, and Annis had no intention of doing so now. 'Do not give it another thought,' she urged him. 'It might take me a few days to organise a post-chaise. Which will mean, of course, that I must take advantage of your—'

'On the contrary...' his lordship interrupted.

Removing the half-finished glass from her fingers and setting it aside, he once again captured her hands and drew her gently to her feet. It was almost like having one's fingers encased in a pair of well-made gloves; except that Annis could never recall that the simple donning of a pair of warm mittens had resulted so promptly in a rapid increase of heat to rise up her arms or that the mere donning of any garment had ever sent a peculiar tingling sensation scudding its way down the length of her spine.

'It is I who am about to take advantage of yours by asking whether you would yet again oblige me by postponing your departure, at least until my return. I should, ordinarily, never have considered leaving the Manor at such a time, with my grandmother's party looming ever nearer, and so many arrangements to make. Sarah, as you are aware, is quite able to cope. Sadly, though, she does have a tendency to concern herself unnecessarily over trifles, and get herself into a state of confusion if things don't go quite to plan. You, thankfully, do not, and would therefore be a marvellously stabling influence upon her, as well as being on hand to offer sound advice, should she seek it. Then, too, there is the arrival of our first guests to consider. Your godmother, as you are fully aware, proposes to arrive here the week after next. It is my intention to return in good time. However, if things do not go according to plan and I am delayed for whatever reason, it would ease my mind considerably knowing that there is someone back here at the Manor more than capable of taking charge and making decisions in my absence.'

Perhaps not quite the sort of praise most females might wish to receive; more disturbing still, not even a compliment at all, if one should just happen to infer from it that one is considered managing! Nevertheless, Annis couldn't mistake the sincerity with which he had spoken, and found herself instantly complying with the request, the result of which had him releasing his comforting grasp on her hands and not delaying in voicing a hurried farewell.

The old adage about making decisions in haste, etcetera, did not occur to her at all during the time it took to retrace her steps to the upper floor. It wasn't until after Annis had entered the bedchamber and had instructed her maid to begin the unpacking that the seeds of doubt were well and truly sown.

'You're bamming me!' Disher announced in her usual forthright fashion. 'You've never gone and changed your mind about leaving yet again?' She shook her head, doubt clearly etched in her plump features. 'I'm not so certain sure his lordship is such a good influence on you, Miss Annis. I've always thought of you as a young lady who knew her own mind. But no longer! Why, his lordship can twist you round his little finger, so he can!'

'Rubbish!' Annis returned, unsure whether to feel offended at such an absurd notion, or amused by it. 'And I'd like to know why you might suppose it was the Viscount who made me alter my plans.'

'Well, who else could it have been?' Disher was at her laconic best. 'Truth to tell, miss, if I thought for a moment that you truly did know your own mind over a certain matter, I'd be dashed well pleased that you'd met your match at long last, not troubled by it.'

'I really haven't the faintest notion what you're talking about, Dish,' Annis responded with total sincerity. 'If you must have it, as a result of what took place on Friday last, Charles Fanhope has seen fit to take himself off in the dead of night, and his lordship has offered to assist the Baron in running his errant son to earth.'

'Well, what of it?'

'All things considered, his lordship thought it best to use his own travelling carriage.'

'Well, what of it?' Disher demanded again, much to her young mistress's increasing annoyance. 'We could easily make other arrangements, and hire a carriage.'

'True enough,' Annis was obliged to concede before revealing, 'Only he also asked if I'd remain until he returns in order to assist Miss Greythorpe with the preparations for the forthcoming party.

You know the sort of thing—be on hand to offer support, should the need arise.'

'And you believed him?' Disher struggled to rise from her kneeling position in front of the trunk, her expression one of total disbelief now. 'I don't know what's happened to your wits of late, Miss Annis, and that's a fact! Seems to me you've started to believe what suits you, and ignore the plain truth, even when it's staring you in the face.

'Now, I'm not saying that Miss Sarah's the most capable young woman who ever drew a breath,' she went on hurriedly, thereby denying her outraged young mistress the opportunity even to attempt to refute the accusations being levelled at her. 'But no one could ever say she's unable to run a household with reasonable efficiency. She may well trouble herself unduly over trifles and have a tendency to get herself into a right muddled state from time to time. But she knows well enough that she's got an army of servants on hand here at the Manor who know what's what. So I can't see as how there's any reason for her to trouble herself unduly if this party should turn out to be far larger than first planned, and held to celebrate something a deal more important than an old lady's birthday.'

Annis pricked up her ears at this. 'What's all this about a larger party, Dish?' she demanded, and was instantly subjected to a prolonged stare that was both probing and wary at one and the same time.

Then Disher turned her back, raising one plump shoulder in a shrug that was altogether dismissive, as she returned two dresses to the wardrobe. 'I've been told nothing official, miss. All I can tell you is there's been talk.'

'Servants' gossip, you mean,' Annis correctly interpreted, but the maid paid little heed to the belittling tone.

'More than just gossip, I should say,' Disher countered. 'Not that much is said in front of me, you understand, being an outsider. But what I do know for certain is that Viscount Greythorpe told Dunster to ensure that every single bedchamber in the house was made ready should the need for its use arise. And that he must be prepared to order a great many more provisions at a moment's notice. Furthermore, it was rumoured that his lordship inspected the cellars for himself only the other day. Which is something he's never done since coming into the title.'

'Well, they're his cellars, aren't they?' Annis pointed out, certain in her own mind that, having heard nothing herself, too much was being made over mere trifles. 'Surely he's at liberty to inspect his own stock of wines and spirits if he's a mind to do so? Just as he's entitled to hold a larger event to celebrate his grandmother's birthday if he so chooses.'

'Just as you say, miss,' was all Disher was prepared to respond, before whisking herself from the room, and leaving her young mistress to ponder over whether there was genuinely something going on at Greythorpe Manor that she knew absolutely nothing about.

The following morning Annis went down to the parlour as usual to break her fast, and was a little surprised to discover Louise already there. Except for those first few days at the Manor, when she had eaten breakfast in her bedchamber, Annis had more often than not opted to join his lordship downstairs, simply because, far from betraying resentment at her presence, the Viscount had offered every encouragement to bear him company for the first meal of the day. After her brother's arrival at the Manor, Louise too had joined them, and seemingly she was happy to continue to do so even though she no longer had her considerate sibling's support. Ordinarily Annis would have been delighted to have the girl to bear her company. But, as charming as Louise was, she was no substitute for his lordship.

God, how she missed him! He had been gone for less than twenty-four hours, and yet already she was feeling his absence keenly. It was like a huge part of her had been torn away, leaving a great, aching void.

'Well, this makes a pleasant change, having just female company at breakfast,' she lied, unblushingly, 'though I must confess I'd half-expected you to resume your practice of eating in your room, now that Tom's returned to Oxford.'

'Oh, no, I like company at meal times. As long as you're here I'm happy to come down. It's only Sarah who prefers breakfast alone in her room. Which is all to the good because it grants me the opportunity to talk to you about something in private.'

Louise could see at a glance that she had her personable companion's full attention. 'It was my intention to go out riding this morning, as usual. Only Sarah just happened to mention yesterday that she intends to pay a call on Lady Fanhope. By all accounts the Baroness is still keeping to her bedchamber for much of the time. And as I don't suppose for a moment that you would wish to visit, I wondered if I shouldn't offer to accompany my cousin?'

'It isn't a case of my not wishing to go along,' Annis corrected. 'But I think it would show a shocking want of tact on my part to do so, given that I'm indirectly responsible for the family's present troubles.'

Louise cast her a sideways glance. 'Do you feel so terribly upset over it all, Annis? His lordship seemed to think you did. Said on no account were any of us to mention anything about it within your hearing. He would not have you upset further.'

Did he now? Annis mused, pleased to have one little mystery solved. At least she now knew that it had been concern for her feelings that had been responsible for the lack of comments, and not, as she had very much feared, that she was being held entirely to blame for the whole unfortunate episode.

'I wouldn't go so far as to say that I was terribly upset, no,' Annis admitted, after giving the matter some thought. 'But it gave me no satisfaction in being the one to reveal Charles's dishonourable practices and cause such distress to the rest of his family.'

'Well, no one can blame you for what's happened since,' Louise pointed out, seemingly eager to voice her own opinions now that the Viscount was safely out of the way. 'Tom thinks you're a great gun, and so clever to have spotted what Charles was about. Even Sarah said that she couldn't help but admire the way you held your nerve and didn't shy away from causing a scene. And we all know Sarah will do almost anything to avoid confrontations.' Louise sighed. 'That's why I don't think she should go alone to the Hall. You know how easily upset she is by any cutting remark. And I wouldn't put it above Lady Fanhope to say something spiteful about you, even though she's supposed to keep to her bed for much of the time, with her nerves in complete disorder.'

Yes, indeed, it was quite surprising just how much Louise had altered, and for the better, during the past few weeks. She betrayed little shyness nowadays whenever in the Viscount's company, and none whatsoever when with Sarah who, in turn, no longer appeared to have the least difficulty in maintaining a conversation with her young cousin.

'Sarah, I should imagine, would welcome your company,' she said, echoing her thoughts aloud. 'In different circumstances, I shouldn't hesitate to join you. But, as I've already mentioned, I think it would be wrong to inflict my presence on the Fanhope family at the present time. I'm the very last person anyone residing at the Hall would wish to see.'

Although far too diplomatic to agree wholeheartedly with this viewpoint, Sarah made no attempt whatsoever to alter Annis's decision to remain at the Manor, when she emerged from her bed-chamber an hour later, having already donned her outdoor garments in readiness for the visit.

'How do you propose to entertain yourself during our absence? Not that I have any intention of remaining away for long. What with one thing and another, I've far too much to occupy me back here.'

'Don't concern yourself on my account, Sarah,' she urged her. 'Your brother's absence forces me to take full responsibility for Rosie again. Dev's been so good with her, taking her for long walks. She's going to miss him dreadfully.'

'No more than I am,' Sarah surprisingly divulged. 'His going away at such a time does make things a little awkward, especially with the party only three weeks away, and nothing official settled as yet.'

Because all at once Sarah seemed unable, or unwilling, to meet her gaze, Annis was immediately reminded of what she had surprisingly discovered the day before, and began to suspect that there had been a deal more in what her maid had divulged than she had first thought.

'I did hear tell that Dev might wish to hold a larger event than first planned. Is that true?'

If possible, Sarah's expression grew a deal more guarded. 'Well…yes, no…I mean, I'm not quite sure. I do not believe anything has been settled for definite quite yet. At least Deverel's said nothing to me…to—to anyone, I don't suppose. Or maybe, what with one thing and another, he feels it might be better to wait a while. It's just such a pity that he's been obliged to go away at such a time, otherwise everything might have been organised by now, and not just left hanging in the air, as it were… So difficult to know what to do for the best… Oh, good, here's Louise. We'd best be on our way.'

That, Annis mused, studying Miss Greythorpe's hasty progress outside to the antiquated landau that had once belonged to Sarah's own mother, was a prime example of Sarah at her confused best. A total stranger overhearing that garbled nonsense could be forgiven for supposing that a weakness of brain possibly ran in the Greythorpe family, she decided, calling Rosie to heel, and setting off at a sprightly pace across the park. She, of course, knew better and was firmly convinced that there was absolutely nothing amiss with Sarah mentally, and that these bouts of confusion and indecision were merely the sad legacy of having suffered too long the sole companionship of a taciturn father who had been quick to criticise and slow to praise. It was little wonder that the poor woman worked herself up into a state whenever things occurred that deviated from the norm and obliged her to make rapid adjustments to her daily routine, which in the past had undoubtedly received swift condemnation from the late master of the house.

There was more behind Sarah's priceless display of muddle-headedness that morning, though, Annis quickly decided. Unlike his father, Deverel was not super-critical, or in the least judgmental, come to that; not where his sister was concerned, at any rate. Clearly he had said something to suggest that he might wish to increase the size of the party, even if he perhaps hadn't taken her fully into his confidence. So why had Sarah seemed so unwilling to divulge at least what she did know? And why hadn't Deverel revealed his plans when he had once again issued that personal request for her to remain at the Manor? Was there perhaps some reason why he had not wished her to know what he intended? Or was it merely that recent events had forced him to rethink his own plans, and if so, why? Why should his involvement with the Fanhope family's concerns at the present time influence any decision to hold a larger party at the beginning of next month?

Her poor head beginning to whirl with the increasing number

of unanswered questions, Annis felt for the very first time that she quite understood just how poor Sarah felt on occasions—confused and at a loss to know in which direction to proceed first. Then, quite suddenly, her head was miraculously cleared by the one and only explanation that presented the answer to every jumbled thought— Deverel had at some point in the recent past decided that his grandmother's birthday party would offer the ideal opportunity to celebrate quite a different event.

Sudden enlightenment ought to have resulted in a rapid return to normality, whereas in fact the opposite was true. The landscape surrounding her began to whirl before her eyes and she was assailed by such a feeling of nausea that she didn't hesitate to take full advantage of the fallen tree, conveniently positioned a mere few yards away, while she still retained the full use of her lower limbs.

Never before had she experienced the consequences of having suffered a severe shock. It was several moments before she had regained sufficient control over herself to combat the unpleasant effects and had begun to acknowledge fully just why she had reacted in such an uncharacteristic fashion in the first place.

It simply wasn't in her nature not to face reality, no matter how cruel, no matter how painful. And she had no intention of not doing so now. She had fallen irrevocably in love with the man who, but for her, would have been announcing his engagement to Caroline Fanhope to the world at large in three weeks' time.

Briefly her thoughts returned to the evening of the party and images passed in rapid succession before her mind's eye: the way Deverel had appeared in Caroline's company—totally at ease, and gazing down at her with lazy affection; the way they had looked when dancing together—matching each other's movements precisely: two halves of a perfect whole.

Could it possibly be that it had been their intention to announce their betrothal that very night? Annis released her breath in a loud groan. If that was indeed so, then it was little wonder his lordship had seemed a little remote prior to his departure. Unwittingly though it had been, she had destroyed any hopes he and Caroline might have harboured for an immediate future of blissful contentment.

Of course, dear Disher had guessed the truth of it all, Annis continued to ruminate, recalling almost verbatim her faithful retainer's somewhat puzzling observations of the day before. Of course, what had been said made complete sense now! Darling Dish had evidently had no difficulty in recognising her mistress's ever-increasing regard for the Viscount, and had not been unduly disturbed by it. In fact, she had given the distinct impression that the opposite would have been true, providing she had been certain that Annis herself had kept a sensible control over her emotions and had accepted that a more binding relationship than a sincere friendship would never be forthcoming.

Well, if this were true, and some secret part of her had continued to refuse to acknowledge this in the past, it was no longer the case. Of course, her mother had been an exception! It was rare for a member of the aristocracy to choose a spouse from outside his or her social class. And perhaps it wasn't such a bad thing that this was the norm, for who knew better than she herself the difficulties that must be faced by the progeny of those rare alliances.

By selecting Caroline Fanhope as his future bride, Viscount Greythorpe would be considered to have made an ideal choice. It mattered not a whit that neither was in love with the other, and maybe his lordship preferred it that way. After all, his late father's first marriage, an arranged affair where love had played no part, had proved to be more successful than his second. Such an alliance would not do for her, but then she was no aristocratic pure blood. Yet there had been numerous occasions when she had proved to be very much her mother's daughter, and never more so than in those following moments when she comprehensively suppressed any thought of giving way to a display of emotion.

In fact, the tall figure who had come upon her quite by chance, and who had been unobtrusively watching her from the cover of the trees, would never have supposed for a moment that beneath that supremely calm exterior beat a heart that might well never recover fully from its thoroughly battered state. The only emotion she betrayed as she rose to her feet and turned to see him emerging from the home wood's undergrowth was, understandably, shock, not untouched by fear.

Chapter Twelve

The fact that there was no sign of Rosie didn't trouble Annis unduly. The dog, always quick to detect the scent of a rabbit or some other small creature, would often disappear into the wood, whenever they happened to wander this way, and had never failed to reappear after a short while. Nor was she disturbed to any great extent by the sight of a gun held fast in one large hand, for in no way was it being wielded in a threatening manner. What did concern her, however, was the fact that she didn't recognise the man at all. Not that she would ever dream of pretending that she was acquainted with all his lordship's employees. Nor would she attempt to suggest that she even knew most every one of them by sight. She had, none the less, already met the gamekeeper during her much extended stay at the Manor, and had seen both the men who worked under him. And this person was certainly neither of them!

So what was he doing here in the wood? He'd hardly be poaching at this time of day, she quickly decided, before asking outright if he was employed by the Viscount, and wasn't in the least surprised when she received an immediate shake of the head in response.

'Don't work for anyone now, miss…thanks to you.'

That simple declaration might have held an ominous ring had

his voice sounded in the least threatening, but it hadn't. If anything, there had been a touch of indifference in the tone, and a hint of wry amusement in his expression. 'I'm sorry...should I know you?' she asked when he continued to regard her in silence.

'No, miss, you don't know me.' He began to move slowly towards her, and yet strangely enough she no longer felt the least disturbed by his unexpected presence. 'But I've seen you afore. I mind the first time I ever clapped eyes on you. It were on the very day you arrived in these parts.' His smile was distinctly rueful now. 'I never thought, back then, that it would be you that 'ud go and lose me my job. But I can't say as how I'm overly troubled by it.'

More intrigued than anything else, Annis studied the handsome face closely and could detect not the least hint of resentment in his expression. Which was amazing in the circumstances, if she truly had been responsible for his losing his position.

Not quite knowing whether to believe him or not, she began by asking how she had succeeded in losing him his job, when she hadn't even been aware of his existence before that day.

'After you'd shown his lordship just how his precious son could afford his own servants, Lord Fanhope felt Mr Charles could well do without my services and his valet's.'

The stranger's tone had already suggested that he wasn't unduly concerned to find himself without employment, as did the raising of a brawny shoulder in a shrug, even before he confirmed it again by adding, 'Not that I mind. Not enjoyed working for Master Charles from the start. And Lord Fanhope was decent enough to see us paid until next quarter-day, and made sure we had good references too, making it clear to anyone who'd care to know that we lost our jobs through no fault of our own. The valet's already on his way back to London to find work there. And I'm thinking I might need to follow, 'cause there ain't much doing round these parts. I've been asking about for quite some time. But I just couldn't up and leave. There was something I'd to do first…something I've got to get off my chest before I go on my way.'

Although intrigued by the admission, Annis, prompted by her own pangs of conscience, concentrated on his present predicament. 'I do not know for certain, of course, but his lordship just might be interested in taking on an extra pair of hands. You could try his steward. He would be better able to tell you.'

Given that she had tried to be helpful, Annis felt slightly miffed when all he did in response to her display of concern was dissolve into whoops of laughter. 'Lord bless you, miss!' he exclaimed when he was able. 'I wouldn't have the brass-faced cheek to ask his lordship for work, not after what I done… No, miss, I came 'ere, 'oping to see someone, the 'ead groom, Jeremiah Wilks. Known 'im since I were a lad… Just wanted to 'ave a word, like…get something off my chest.'

Once again Annis subjected the man to a few moments' close scrutiny, quickly noting the way he held himself erect. 'Have I ever heard your name before?'

'Don't see why you should, miss. It's Jack Fletcher.'

'Then I have. Wilks spoke of you once. And, if I remember correctly, he said that you took the King's shilling, and were mighty handy with a pistol.' Her memory, always acute, didn't let her down on this occasion either. 'And you were in what Wilks described as one of those newfangled regiments out in the Peninsula, a Rifle Regiment.'

'Aye, miss, that I was.'

Annis was then assailed by a very real possibility. 'You mentioned you saw me on the day I arrived here. So I cannot help wondering why is it I have no recollection of seeing a big fellow like yourself.' Had she been a cat, one might have been forgiven for supposing she had just downed a large bowlful of cream. 'You see, I have the reputation of being something of a noticing person. Which leads me to suppose that you took great pains to ensure you were not observed.'

There was definitely a guarded flicker in his blue eyes before he smiled crookedly. 'Now, that would be telling, wouldn't it, miss?'

'It might be as well to tell me, as I strongly suspect I've guessed correctly already,' Annis advised him. 'Besides which, there's no possibility of your seeing Wilks today. Nor for the next few days, I don't suppose. He's taken his lordship to Oxford in search of your ex-master.'

Clearly this was news to Master Fletcher, whose eyebrows rose sharply, before he showed his contempt by spitting on the ground. 'Couldn't face it, eh? Well, I can't say as it surprises me none.' He regarded her in silence for a moment. 'But if it's all the same to you, miss, happen I won't linger myself.'

Annis might well have been sensible and veered on the side of caution, and not attempted to detain him further, had not Rosie chosen to make a reappearance at that moment.

Usually wary of strangers, and on occasions quite openly hostile, the dog behaved in a most uncharacteristic manner by wagging her bobtail frantically and jumping up Master Fletcher's legs in order to win his full attention. His response was immediate, and everything Rosie demanded. Kneeling and placing his rifle on the ground, he began to pet her in a way that both pleased and calmed her. Besides herself, Annis knew of only one other who had succeeded in winning the dog's affection and trust so easily.

As Rosie had shown impeccable judgement where his lordship was concerned, Annis saw no reason to doubt the animal's instincts now, especially as they were wholly in accord with her own.

'Clearly you have a way with animals, Master Fletcher,' she

remarked, once he had succeeded in suppressing Rosie's enthusiasm for his company and had brought her quietly to heel. 'Perhaps you are even one of those people who would do almost anything to avoid harming a living creature. Naturally your years in the army would have necessitated your adopting a different attitude, at least towards the two-legged variety, with whom no doubt you were obliged to put your skill with a rifle to the test on numerous occasions. But was it essential for you to do so where Viscount Greythorpe was concerned?'

Annis noted the wary expression return with a vengeance as he rose to his full height once more. 'Please do not insult my intelligence by attempting to deny it,' she added when she suspected he might do just that. 'I don't suppose for a moment that you'd have wished to unburden your soul to Wilks had you a personal grievance against the master he clearly worships. No, of course you would not. It is much more likely that old habits die hard. And after years in the army, you find it difficult to disobey a direct order. What I'm not so certain about,' she freely admitted when he continued to regard her in stony silence, 'is whose orders you carried out that day, when you shot Lord Greythorpe?'

A further moment's silence, then, 'Master Charles Fanhope's, ma'am.'

In truth, Annis would have been less surprised had he named Lord Fanhope himself. At least she could understand why he might harbour a grievance against Deverel. But she couldn't immediately perceive why his son might bear a grudge against the Viscount, and asked outright if this was so.

'Bless you no, miss! Master Charles don't bear his lordship no ill will,' Jack Fletcher assured her. 'Leastways he didn't. No saying how he might be feeling now, though, him sometimes being a bit odd in the top storey, like.'

Annis was only partially successful in suppressing a smile at this blunt assessment of Charles Fanhope's mental state. 'Why, then, did he order you to shoot him?'

'Because he had some daft notion it would bring his lordship to the sticking post a bit quicker.'

The look of utter bewilderment that quickly followed this pronouncement was sufficient to assure Jack that the pretty young woman keeping him talking hadn't understood a single word.

He grinned cheekily across at her. 'Master Charles believed that if Lord Greythorpe were obliged to spend some time up at the Hall, being gently cared for by Miss Caroline, he'd feel such gratitude towards her that he'd be more inclined to settle on a date for a wedding.'

Somehow Annis succeeded in not gaping in total disbelief. 'And was Miss Caroline herself a party to this idiotic plan of his, do you suppose?'

She was favoured by a further example of that wickedly attractive masculine smile that was almost as winning as his lordship's own. 'Not that I'm aware of, miss, no. It was wholly Mr Charles's notion.'

'Heavens above!' Annis shook her head. 'It beggars belief that he imagined for a moment that such an idiotic plan might be carried out successfully.'

'It does that, miss,' Jack agreed. 'What he really wanted was for me to wound his lordship bad enough to keep him laid up by the heels at the Hall for a week or two, but cause no lasting damage. But I've seen too many wounds turn mortal bad, those you'd expect to heal, no trouble.'

All at once he appeared earnestly concerned. 'May the good Lord forgive me, I ought never to have done it in the first place. But believe me when I tell you, miss, I never meant more than to deal a scratch, no matter what the master ordered. I would have stayed with his lordship too when the horse reared, unexpected like, and succeeded in throwing him, had it not begun to snow. I'd just reached the wood on old Hastie's land when your carriage came bowling round the bend. I was that relieved to see it. The master came along no more than five minutes after you'd gone. As mad as fire when I told him, he were. And mayhap it were a judgement on me that I lost my job in the end. But I ain't complaining.'

Annis glanced down at Rosie, who had by this time contentedly returned to her side, and smiled to herself. Having already managed to acquire one waif during her extended stay at the Manor, surely one more wouldn't make that much difference, given that she was to some extent responsible for his present unfortunate predicament?

She took note of his unkempt appearance—the creases in his rough clothes and the mass of long, untidy blond hair. 'By the looks of you, Master Fletcher, I would imagine you've had a rough time of it since leaving the Hall.'

He gestured behind him at the wood. 'At least it's been dry, miss. And I won't need to tarry longer, now I've spoken to you.'

'But you have no fixed destination in mind?'

Whether he was disinclined to reveal his intentions, or had genuinely no plans, Annis wasn't certain, but wasn't unduly surprised by his shrugged response. 'Would you have any objection to working for a woman...? I'm in earnest, Fletcher,' she assured him when he regarded her in evident surprise, laced with amusement. 'I should warn you, however, that your final destination might well be the city of Bath, and your duties many and varied. So, if you are not prepared to put up with some drastic changes in lifestyle, you'd best say so at the outset.'

Even though his tongue had evidently acquired a will of its own, preventing him from saying anything coherently, Annis had little difficulty in interpreting the half-formulated declarations of gratitude, interspersed with assurances that he could quite easily turn his hand to a variety of duties, as a definite acceptance of the offer.

'In that case, Master Fletcher, we had best find you somewhere to stay. I shan't be leaving the Manor until his lordship returns, and even though I know for certain that ordinarily he would be willing enough to house any servant of mine, you might well prove to stretch the Viscount's philanthropic tendencies a little too far, given that you did shoot him, acting under orders or no. I should add,' she went on, after he had manfully half-suppressed a chortle of laughter, 'that the lady in whose care I hope to place you remains touchingly devoted to his lordship, so I would advise you not to take her too far into your confidence.'

Jack didn't pretend to misunderstand. 'But you will tell his lordship, won't you, that it was me that shot 'im that day?'

'I'm not so certain I shall, no,' she answered, after giving the matter some thought. After all, she added silently, as she followed her new servant into the wood in order to collect the few meagre belongings he had safely stowed beneath the gnarled, exposed roots of a certain tree, why should Caroline and the rest of her family be made to suffer further humiliation because of her brother's ridiculous and totally unnecessary actions? In the circumstances it was perhaps best if Greythorpe was left in ignorance. Added to which, she reasoned, her spirits plummeting to an all-time low, he wasn't likely to be put into further danger now that Charles's hopes for his sister had all but been realised.

By the time they had reached Nanny Berry's cottage, Annis had discovered a deal more about her new servant. The most surprising thing of all was that he had learned to read and write a little, thanks to the efforts of a young captain in whose company Jack had spent a deal of time during a period of forced incarceration at the hands of the French.

Nanny Berry too had received a limited education early in her working life, when she had become a tirewoman to a kindly mistress, and seemed happy to further Jack's education, as far as she could, during his stay at her cottage, in return for his undertaking a few basic tasks.

'No, I don't mind a bit, miss,' the old lady reiterated, after Jack had disappeared into the garden to begin by chopping up a good supply of fire wood. 'I remember his father very well. Handsome young rogue he were, and a good worker. If nothing else, he'll be company for me. And he'll be comfortable enough, bedding down here on the floor by the kitchen fire, though I dare say the master wouldn't object none if you were to take him back to the house.'

'No, I don't suppose he would, Nanny. But I'd rather not take advantage. Jack's my responsibility. It was as a result of what I did that he lost his position up at the Hall.'

If Annis had expected the admission to cause any degree of astonishment, she was doomed to disappointment. Nanny Berry merely regarded her in silence for a moment before saying, 'Well, I wouldn't go so far as to say that, miss, though I must confess I'd already heard about the goings-on. Can't say as it came as much of a surprise, neither, to any living round these parts, leastways not to them that's known Master Charles all his life. Cunning, deceitful little boy he was, as I recall. And it's been my experience that spiteful children don't change that much as they grow older.'

'I infer from that that his present plight isn't likely to arouse much sympathy?' Annis remarked, after mulling over what had been said.

'Not to most of those working up at the Hall, no,' Nanny confirmed. 'Talk to any of the servants and they'll all say the same—young Giles is worth a dozen of his elder brother. Apart from Lady Fanhope, no one's got a good word to say about him.'

Annis wasn't slow to disagree. 'But what about Caroline…? She seems genuinely fond of her brother.'

'Ahh, well now, that's only to be expected, now ain't it, miss? There's most always a strong bond between twins. But I don't think even Miss Caroline's blind to his faults. She was the first born, and much the sharper. He were always slower to learn. Still…' Nanny Berry shrugged '…he weren't born easy, by all accounts. Too big a head was what their nurserymaid said at the time, I seem to remember.'

As Nanny Berry was betraying all the signs of falling into one of her reminiscent moods, Annis quickly decided not to delay too long in taking her leave. Jack, who had returned indoors with a pile of logs for the fire, took it upon himself to escort her back as far as the edge of the home wood, where he had come upon her earlier, by sheer good fortune, as far as he was concerned.

Annis too was not in the least unhappy about the unexpected encounter. Nevertheless, once they had parted company, her newly acquired servant faded so quickly from her mind that she didn't even think to mention him to either Sarah or Louise when she eventually reached the Manor.

During the following days Annis found time hung heavily. No matter how many varied tasks she found to occupy her, none could suppress the onset of those periods of lethargy that attacked her with increasing frequency. Even her daily rides across the estate with Louise were only partially successful in lifting her spirits, and then not for very long. Worst of all were those times spent with Sarah, when the Viscount's sister would wish to discuss some aspect of the forthcoming party. Only by digging deep into those thankfully bottomless reserves of self-control could Annis prevent herself from betraying the fact that she had lost completely any

interest she might once have had in an event that she had no intention of attending now at any cost, and one, moreover, she had
become increasingly convinced ought not to be taking place.

Lord Fanhope's return and subsequent visit to the Manor did
succeed in lifting the heavy tedium of life at the mansion, if only
for a brief period. He had little to impart, save that his elder son
and heir had indeed made a brief visit to Oxford from where he
had journeyed to the metropolis and had succeeded in covering his
tracks so well that no trace of his whereabouts could be unearthed.

'You'll forgive my saying so, my lord,' Annis remarked, after
she had complied with his surprising request to bear him company
back to the stables. 'You do not seem unduly troubled by the fact
that you have been unsuccessful in running your son to earth.'

His lordship gave vent to a heavy sigh, but his voice when he
spoke contained an unmistakable element of strength and determination. 'Ashamed in part though I am to admit to such a thing, Miss
Milbank, it would not trouble me unduly if I never set eyes upon
Charles again. Too long have I chosen not to face the truth about my
heir's character…and about my own also. Too long have I allowed
things to continue without taking a firmer stand. I have long suspected that Charles has been obtaining money by some nefarious
means or other. But I elected not to delve too deeply into his personal
concerns for fear of disturbing the calm waters of my own life.'

A further sigh escaped him. 'I should have adopted a firmer
stance years ago when he was a boy, and not permitted my wife to
spoil him to the point where his character was damaged beyond
repair. Instead of which, I attempted to compensate for her clear
preference by spending more time with our daughter and younger
son. Privately, I think young Giles is far more fitted to step into my
boots when the time comes. But that doesn't alter the fact that
Charles is my heir.' He shook his head sadly. 'Well, it might be too

late to instil any degree of honour in him, but I can at least force
him to face the consequences of his actions. And I shall not deviate
from that resolve, no matter how long it takes for him to find the
courage to return.'

Annis had always been sensible to the consequences of her
actions, and never more so than now. 'Believe me when I tell you,
my lord, that it has given me no satisfaction whatsoever to have
been the one responsible for the distress you and the members of
your family are suffering now.'

He reached out to take her hands briefly in his own. 'My dear
child, disabuse your mind of the notion that I hold you in any way
culpable. Greythorpe feared that you would continue to suffer
pangs of conscience. But truly you must not. Any blame rests
squarely on the shoulders of certain members of my family, and
with me in particular.'

She could not agree, but decided it would benefit neither of
them to discuss the matter further, and so changed the subject by
asking a question, the answer to which might possibly be of benefit
to her at least in her present state of mind.

'I'm afraid I don't know when Greythorpe means to return,
child,' the Baron disappointedly revealed. 'I gained the distinct
impression that he wasn't altogether certain himself. As you're
aware, he kindly ensured that I was conveyed back to my home in
his own travelling carriage. What I can tell you is, on the morning
I left London, it was his intention to leave the capital also in the
company of a close friend whose destination, I believe, was his
estate in Nottinghamshire.'

At her immediate expression of surprise, he added, 'I cannot tell
you what precisely induced Greythorpe to travel northwards,
although he does have a small estate in Derbyshire.'

'Yes, so I understand. All the same, it seems an odd time for him to take it into his head to pay a visit there, given that his grand-mother's party is but two weeks hence.'

'He's unlikely to forget that, child, in view of the fact that it's his intention to hold a very splendid affair, a far grander function from what was originally planned, so I understand. If nothing else, it can double as a celebration of his coming into the title,' his lordship beamed. 'We're all very much looking forward to it.'

It swiftly became apparent that Sarah shared this sentiment. Whether the new vigour she displayed for organising the event was a direct result of his lordship's letter, which was faithfully placed into her hand by the loyal Wilks on the very day he returned from London, was difficult to judge, as she chose not to reveal the contents, at least not to Annis, who continued to do her utmost to conceal her own vastly contrasting views.

Unfortunately, as the days continued to drag slowly past, she found it increasingly difficult to summon up the least enthusiasm whenever her advice was sought, and resorted in the end to avoiding Sarah as much as possible by taking Rosie for longer and longer walks, or, weather permitting, retreating to some secluded little spot in the garden.

She knew, of course, that it was no answer, and by the end of the week she was forced to acknowledge some very unpalatable truths. She might have been reasonably successful in avoiding Sarah; she could no longer avoid the truth about her own state of mind—she was consumed by jealousy at the mere thought of the Viscount becoming engaged to Caroline Fanhope. So how on earth did she suppose that she could attend the very event to celebrate what many would consider the perfect alliance, without revealing to a single soul that it was she who truly loved Deverel Greythorpe with every fibre of her being; that she alone would prove to be his ideal helpmeet, and lifelong friend?

The irony of it all was that his lordship would understand precisely how she felt. He would instantly appreciate that she simply couldn't, wouldn't be such a hypocrite as to remain and pretend to wish him happy.

And what better opportunity to tell him than now? she decided, automatically raising her head at the unmistakable sound of a footfall. Now that he was here, and drawing ever closer…

Like a sleepwalker locked in a kind of trance, she rose slowly to her feet and found herself moving down to meet him. She saw that brilliant smile pull at his lips a moment before he reached out his arms towards her. She instinctively raised her own, and her hands were captured and held fast in a brief reassuring clasp before strong arms stole about her and warm lips brushed down her cheeks to capture her own instantly responsive and very willing mouth.

Chapter Thirteen

His lordship arrived back at the Manor in good time to enjoy luncheon with his sister and cousin, and most especially with the young woman who had succeeded in occupying his thoughts to the exclusion of most everything else almost from the first moment they had met.

Changing out of his travel-stained garments was achieved in record time, primarily because, for once, he wouldn't permit his pernickety valet to have his way and delay him by attempting to correct trifling faults. He then returned downstairs to discover his butler arranging for the large trunk littering the hall to be carried up to Annis's room.

A brief glance at the long-case clock was sufficient to inform him where his sister, a female who rarely deviated from her daily routine, was to be found at this time. 'Are all the ladies in the parlour awaiting the luncheon gong?'

'Your sister and cousin are most certainly there, sir. But I believe Miss Milbank has yet to return to the house.' The butler coughed delicately. 'If it is her intention to maintain her current practice, she will not do so until the very last moment.'

His lordship, who had been on the point of paying a brief visit to his library in order to place there for safekeeping a very special item that for the present he wished to keep safely hidden, checked, and turned to look at his butler again. 'Something amiss, Dunster?'

'I wouldn't go as far as to say that, my lord, no. But Miss Milbank, I have observed, has acquired a distinct preference for her own company in recent days, and has spent a great deal of time out of doors. Well concealed, I should imagine, but certainly able to hear the village church clock chiming the half-hour.'

His lordship regarded his major-domo with blatant approval. 'Well done, Dunster! I knew I might rely on you to keep an eye on things here in my absence. Delay luncheon if need be. I'm for the shrubbery!'

The Viscount didn't trouble himself to await a response before striding out of the front entrance, simply because he knew he could depend upon that first-rate ruler of the household staff to ensure that no one attempted to seek him out. Not that he himself was altogether sure why he should suddenly feel the need for privacy. If Dunster was to be believed, all was not quite as it should be. This did not mean, of course, that there was something seriously amiss. Nevertheless, it didn't seem as though it was the most perfect time to declare himself, if something trifling was troubling the great love of his life.

But as he rounded the bend in the path and caught his first glimpse of that supremely special lady nestling among the foliage of a particularly vigorous rhododendron, all his carefully considered stratagems, all those mentally rehearsed declarations of intent, were abandoned in an instant of time.

He watched her head turn the moment after she had detected his footfall, saw the look of unalloyed joy spring in the clear grey-green eyes, and noted too the spontaneous curl of those perfectly moulded lips that quickly followed a second before she rose to her feet, and moved in that naturally graceful way of hers towards him. He found himself automatically stretching his arms out towards her in welcome, and saw the slender hands being raised instantly in response, demanding capture.

What possible need could there be for declarations now that the woman he loved beyond words was in his arms, her slender curves pliant against a body over which he was desperately striving to retain mastery, while her mouth openly invited those first more intimate tokens of a sincere regard that he had been forced to suppress for far, far too long? For days he had hoped, prayed that his return would ignite some visible sign of pleasure in the female whose refinement and self-control he so admired. Never had he supposed that in a few moments of sweet spontaneity she would reveal so comprehensively that her feelings for him went every bit as deep as his did for her.

Reciprocated love and unfulfilled desires made for a heady brew, and he might well have been tempted to drink too deeply from the cup had not his sharp ears detected the strange little sound, somewhere between a sob and a gasp, that rose in her throat the moment before she attempted to break free.

He released her at once and took a precautionary step or two away, lest temptation test his self-control too severely, and looked down into the sweet face that betrayed mortification and confusion in equal measures.

'Oh dear.' She raised slender fingers to a cheekbone that now flamed with the telltale crimson hue of maidenly embarrassment. 'How dreadful! I never meant that this should happen... What must you think of me?'

'I think, my sweet life, that you have just revealed far more than you ever had any intention of doing,' he responded sagely, before guiding her back the few paces to that conveniently sited bench and gently drawing her down beside him. 'Notwithstanding, I think I ought to warn you that any attempt on your part to deny your true feelings would, now, be rather futile.'

'Oh, don't! Please don't,' she urged in a voice made unsteady by a half-chuckle and a renewed threat of tears. 'I would not have had that happen for the world. My only excuse is that I had no notion that you meant to return today. Your arrival caught me completely off guard.'

'Is that so?' The gleam in his eye was proof enough that he was rapidly losing the battle not to tease her. 'In that case, my sweet life, I must endeavour always to maintain the element of surprise, especially if the outcome is always to be so satisfactory.'

Mortification faded behind the glance of reproof she shot him. 'How can you jest so? I have been reliably informed that gentlemen have a tendency to think differently about such matters, but even so your surprisingly light-minded attitude borders on the distasteful. Furthermore, it only strengthens my belief that you are on the brink of committing a grave error of judgement.'

As her mien had changed dramatically and now resembled nothing so much as a prim governess chastising an errant charge, he found his self-control sorely tested, but somehow managed not to laugh outright as he said, 'You find me positively agog with curiosity, my precious scold. Precisely what judgement on my part do you deem erroneous?'

Alerted by the faint gasp of outrage, he reached out to capture her wrists, thereby thwarting any attempt on her part to effect an immediate departure.

'Unhand me at once, Greythorpe!'

The demand fell on deaf ears. 'Come down from the boughs, my sweet life, and explain to me what is vexing you so.'

Annis regarded him in silence for a moment, seriously toying with the idea of ignoring the request, then common sense prevailed. Unless she was prepared to indulge in an undignified struggle in what would undoubtedly result in a futile attempt to thwart him, she had best relent and humour him, though why he was being so deliberately obtuse eluded her completely for the present.

'Very well, if you will have it so…. Are you or are you not proposing to announce your engagement at the forthcoming party?'

Black brows were raised in mock surprise. 'Given your recent behaviour, my darling girl, I would have thought that question superfluous! Or are you trying to suggest that I have been totally wrong in my assessment of your character, and that you are in the habit of openly encouraging a gentleman's advances? Not that I wholly object, you understand,' he continued, clearly having fallen into a rollicking mood, 'providing of course the advances are solely mine.'

'My behaviour…?' Unlike his, her astonished outrage was completely genuine. 'And what of your own, pray? Or is it your intention to continue to welcome the amorous advances of every female who crosses your path and offers the merest encouragement to gratify your baser instincts?'

'Now, now, I cannot permit that accusation to be levelled at me. I might not have lived the life of a monk, but no one can accuse me of not having been most selective.'

'How can you jest about such a matter, Greythorpe?' she chided gently, her sincere regard for him as a person having quickly mastered her pique at this surprising show of flippancy on his part. 'I fail to understand why you should risk your future happiness by tying yourself irrevocably to a female to whom deep down inside you must appreciate yourself you are manifestly ill suited?'

'On the contrary,' he countered, all amusement gone. 'I am determined to marry the lady who is so much after my own heart, simply because a life where she plays no part is now wholly unthinkable, most especially as she has in these past treasured minutes removed the last remaining doubt I might possibly have been harbouring that she isn't every bit as much in love with me as I am with her.'

During the silent moments that followed, his lordship very much feared that she had failed to understand, or perhaps did not wish to do so. Then, she raised her eyes to reveal a clear look of dawning wonder in those wonderful grey-green depths, before the delicate lids lowered in a futile attempt to check the veritable torrent of rising moisture.

Annis accepted with gratitude the handkerchief pressed between her trembling fingers and the support of a very comforting broad expanse of shoulder. The wonderful sense of relief she had experienced at being assured that the man she had grown to love so deeply had not been on the brink of committing an act of sheer folly, coupled with the surge of euphoria at discovering that her feelings were wholly reciprocated, had been too much even for her precious self-control.

'Oh, dear, what must you think of me,' she muttered, after successfully regaining a modicum of restraint, at least sufficient to put the square of fine lawn to good use.

'I think, my darling, you owe me an explanation,' he responded in a voice that was gentle, whilst at the same time edged with sufficient determination to leave her in no doubt that he was in earnest. 'Clearly you expected me to make a declaration at my grandmama's birthday celebration. But not, I think, regarding we two.'

'Well, of course not!' she freely admitted, seeing absolutely no reason to lie. 'I thought it was your intention to marry Miss Fanhope.'

'Caroline…but…?' He couldn't have sounded more surprised had he tried. 'Who on earth put such an absurd notion into your head? And don't you dare to suggest it was Sarah, because I simply won't believe it! I'll admit I did write during my time away, informing her that I had taken the opportunity whilst in London to look up some close friends and invite them to the party. But I know her well enough to be sure that, even if she believed I did have an underlying reason for inviting those friends, she would keep her own counsel until she had been officially informed.'

He held her away in time to catch the guilty expression that she found impossible to suppress. 'You surmised it yourself, didn't you?' he added accusingly.

'Yes…no… Oh well, I suppose so, yes,' she was finally obliged to concede. 'As soon as I discovered there was a strong possibility that you'd be inviting more guests to the party, I began to ponder on the reason for the change, and it seemed obvious to me that you possibly had something else to celebrate. And I was right about an engagement.'

'True,' he conceded. 'Just completely wrong about my choice of future wife.'

'Well, how on earth was I supposed to know that you'd fallen—?'

'Hopelessly in love with you,' he finished for her, when a further rush of maidenly embarrassment stilled her tongue. Gently raising her chin, he forced her to meet his gaze. 'How could you possibly not know when I have done everything humanly possible to keep you here since your arrival, short of locking you in your room? I was fast running out of excuses to induce you to stay.'

'It is far easier to view things dispassionately when one's feelings are not involved,' she reminded him primly, before becoming serious again, her mind plagued by an unpleasant reminder of that lifelong imputation. 'But have you considered, Dev, that perhaps not every member of your family, not all your friends, will approve your choice? Remember, I am not wholly of your world. My mother's actions have meant that—'

'Enough!' His voice, like a pistol's ear-piercing report, had her almost jumping out of her skin. 'Yes, well may you look startled, my girl! I shall not have you spouting such flummery at me! Unconventional you might be. But your mother raised you to be a lady, unquestionably so. And only a blind idiot might suppose otherwise. Every member of your family and mine will be invited to our wedding. If any choose not to accept, then so be it. I shall certainly lose no sleep over it. But I think you might be surprised just how many elect to attend.'

He had spoken with a deal of assurance, not to say sternness and resolve, leaving her in no doubt whatsoever that she had been completely wrong in her assessment. Her inferior social position was of no importance to him, and never had been, and he cared not a whit what anyone else might think.

'Clearly you have given the matter some thought,' she remarked, much moved by the stance he had adopted.

'Some,' he admitted. 'But not nearly so much as I gave to the selection of this.'

From the pocket of his coat he drew out the precious, glittering object that it had been his intention to retain for a short while longer, and had it adorning the appropriate finger on her left hand almost before she had time to focus on the perfection of the large, sparkling stone. 'My first thought was of emeralds, but then I remembered that you showed no real enthusiasm for the donning of that particular gemstone.'

She didn't pretend to misunderstand. Nor could she readily forget the occasion when she had foolishly misjudged his motives for raising the subject.

'You misunderstood my reaction, Dev,' she told him softly. 'Just as I misunderstood your reason for suggesting the donning of the gem in the first place. I shall endeavour to be more open from now on, so that such foolish misjudgements might be avoided in the future.' She stretched out her arm, the better to study the diamond's perfection. 'And shall begin now by saying that you couldn't possibly have made a better choice. It is beautiful. And such a perfect fit too!'

'That was easily achieved. I merely attained the size from the pearl ring you left on the gaming table on the night of the Fanhope's party, before returning the set to your maid for safekeeping.'

Easily detecting the faint shadow the memory of that particular occasion caused to flit across her face, he rose abruptly to his feet, and drew her up beside him. 'Come, let us return indoors, so I may attain the utmost satisfaction in commencing to announce our betrothal to the world at large.'

The following morning Annis was still cocooned in her bubble of sheer contentment, delighting in the heady sensations of floating somewhere between reality and that magical fairy-tale world where the heroine's happiness is assured now that she has attained the love and protection of her perfect prince.

'Oh, I do so enjoy being an affianced bride, Dish.'

'I can see that, Miss Annis,' was the prompt tongue-in-cheek response. 'I dare swear you haven't taken your eyes off that great gaud since it was slipped on your finger, though why you should feel the need to keep staring at it so intently, I can't imagine. You cannot possibly not see that it's there. The stone's as big as a hen's egg, so it is!'

Annis removed her contemplative gaze from the fingers of her left hand long enough to cast a disapproving one across the bedchamber. 'Anyone listening to you might be forgiven for supposing my most cherished possession is vulgarly ostentatious. Well, it isn't! It's just perfect. Just like the wonderful being who gave it to me.'

The maid raised her eyes ceilingwards. 'I've every faith that you'll come back down to earth presently. You've too much of your mother's sound good sense in you not to do so.'

'That's just what his lordship thinks,' Annis revealed. 'At least, he suspects that I'm more like dearest Mama than I realise, though it was my roguish charm that he strongly suspects I inherited from my incorrigible grandfather that first captivated him. Now, wasn't that a perfect thing to say?'

Disher's eyes rolled again. 'If you say so, miss.'

'I do.' Annis subjected her invaluable, lifelong companion to a thoughtful moment's contemplation. 'You knew, didn't you, Dish? You weren't in the least surprised when I rushed up here to tell you about the engagement yesterday.'

A suspicion of a smug smile appeared briefly about the maid's thin lips. 'No, I wasn't surprised, miss. I tried to drop you a hint, remember? I told you about the plans for a possible larger party.'

'Mmm. It would seem I've been remarkably obtuse where his lordship is concerned. Why, neither Sarah nor young Louise betrayed much surprise when they were told. They were both truly delighted. But not, I think, unduly surprised. And I never imagined for a moment that his trip up north was arranged for the sole purpose of meeting my aunt and uncle and inviting them to the party, although I'm not sorry he did so. Even though he was taking a great deal upon himself, assuming that I would accept his suit, he did have the foresight to collect a further trunkful of my clothes.'

She paused for a moment to draw her brows together in a slight frown of disapproval. 'I can see that I mustn't become too complacent, though. I cannot quite like the way he insisted that I had my breakfast in bed this morning.'

'Oh, Miss Annis, come down to earth, do!' Disher adjured. 'Why do you suppose he insisted I join the family in the parlour yesterday evening, and do the same today? He'll not have one breath of scandal attached to your fair name if he can help it. His sister was all very well to play the part of duenna before the engagement, but he knows how tongues wag. That's why he's so keen for Lady Pelham to arrive tomorrow.'

Annis considered for a moment before remarking, 'Well, given that Colonel Hastie paid that impromptu visit just before dinner yesterday, I suppose there is something in what you say, because I do not doubt that once he's informed Mrs Hastie about the engagement, which I expect he's done already, it will spread throughout the locale like wildfire. Before you know it, I'll be expected to take my own personal groom with me whenever I wish to go out—'

Annis sat up with a start, almost tipping the remains on the breakfast tray over the bedcovers. 'Heavens above! I clear forget to mention anything about Jack. Oh, Lord! Now, here's a dilemma.'

Disher took the precaution of removing the tray and setting it upon a conveniently positioned set of drawers for safety, before saying, 'I can't see why that should cause you such concern, Miss Annis.' She'd accompanied her young mistress on one of her walks to Nanny Berry's cottage a few days before and had thought Jack a very hardworking and obliging young fellow. 'His lordship might not choose to employ him himself. And if he's no need for an extra pair of hands, you can't hold that against him. But I can't imagine he'd just turn him off without allowing Jack to find himself another position.'

'That isn't what's concerning me,' Annis admitted, tossing the bedcovers aside and slipping her feet to the floor. 'There's something I failed to mention to you concerning our friend Jack Fletcher. But his lordship must be informed… Yes, decidedly he must be told. And without delay!'

'But not before you've allowed me ample time to dress your hair, miss,' Disher announced in a tone that clearly booked no defiance. 'And it isn't a h'ap'orth of good you flashing me that dagger-look, young lady. I never doubted his lordship's feelings about you,' she went on to reveal. 'But I wasn't so sure about your own, especially whether you'd be willing to give up much of your precious freedom and forgo many of your former practices. Well, it's too late for you to consider that now! Before too long, if his lordship has his way, you are going to be Viscountess Greythorpe. So you'd best accept at the outset that certain things will change. And must change! You must be impeccably turned out at all times, not just when it pleases you to make the effort. So you'd best begin right now!'

As a result of Disher's determination not to be found wanting in her duties as an abigail, it was almost mid-morning before Annis was able to escape the bedchamber. Impeccably attired, it had to be said, in one of the gowns his lordship had brought with him from Leicestershire, and without so much as a single strand of silky brown hair out of place, she looked every inch a lady of quality.

As she knew the Viscount had every intention of spending the morning catching up on estate matters, she knew precisely where he was to be found, and entered the library to discover him, as expected, busily at work behind his desk. All the same, there was no mistaking the spark of pleasure that instantly sprang into his eyes when he raised his head to see who had entered his domain.

'I'm sorry to disturb you, Dev,' she apologised after unblushingly returning his welcoming kiss. 'Ordinarily I wouldn't have dreamt of doing so, because I know how busy you must be after your time away, only…only I thought if I delayed, I might think better of it and change my mind. And that wouldn't do at all.'

'That sounds decidedly ominous,' he remarked, after listening to the somewhat garbled explanation for the interruption. 'And be assured I shall never be too busy to see you, if there is something of import you feel you must relate. Let that be clearly understood

at the outset.' Although there had been a decided twinkle of amusement in his eyes, there could be no mistaking the sincerity of his
tone, especially as he added, 'Now, what has occurred to cause you
some disquiet?'

'I'm not unduly troubled, Dev,' she began by assuring him,
'merely a little concerned over someone's well-being. You see,
during your time away, I discovered who it was who shot you a
few weeks ago.'

Not even by the slightest upward movement of one of his expressive black brows did he betray surprise. Nor did she betray her
admiration for his perspicacity when he said, 'And for some reason
you do not choose to disclose the miscreant's identity.'

'I'm more than happy to do so, providing I have your assurance
that you will take the matter no further.'

His lack of response was sufficient to assure her that she had
failed to win his wholehearted support at this stage. And small
wonder! Had their roles been reversed she wouldn't willingly forgo
the opportunity to be avenged on the person who had inflicted
bodily harm upon her. Nevertheless, she still believed she would
win his support over the matter if she was to reveal one very salient
fact. 'Given that your local Justice of the Peace is none other than
Lord Fanhope, Dev, I do not suppose that you would take the
matter any further, especially in light of recent events.'

Within a matter of seconds his lordship's eyes had turned ceilingwards, confirming his immediate understanding. 'In God's
name!' he burst out. 'Don't tell me that wretch Charles was at the
bottom of it!'

'In so much as he issued the order, yes,' she confirmed.

His lordship was totally at a loss to understand, and it plainly
showed. 'But why?' he demanded, not unreasonably. 'What have
I, personally, ever done to him to engender such antipathy?'

'From what I understand, he was motivated by neither spite nor revenge,' she assured him, quick to set him right on this matter. 'He merely wished to—if I might resort to vulgar, modern-day parlance—bring you up to scratch, as it were.'

If possible, his lordship appeared more confused than before, and Annis bridged the distance between them to place her hands gently on his shoulders and laugh lovingly up at him. 'Incredible though it might seem to you, my darling, there were others besides myself who had taken it into their heads that you meant to marry Caroline Fanhope. Charles believed it was your intention at some point to propose to his sister. Sheer madness it might have been, but all he was endeavouring to do was to speed matters up a little, simply because he does surprisingly have a genuine fondness for at least his sister, if for no other member of his family. He believed that if you were brought to the Hall, weakened by your wound, and awoke to find Caroline playing the part of ministering angel by seeing to your every comfort, you would be so overcome by feelings of admiration and gratitude that you wouldn't delay in naming the day.'

'Good gad!' he muttered faintly, almost sending Annis into whoops. 'You'd best tell me everything... You have my assurance I'll take the matter no further.'

It wasn't until after luncheon that his lordship set off on horseback for Nanny Berry's cottage, accompanied only by Rosie, who had once again taken to dividing her time between bearing her beloved mistress company and seeking out his lordship in the hope of an extra jaunt in the fresh air.

Annis declined to join the outing, even though her best habit had been included in the trunk brought from Leicestershire. His lordship wasn't quite sure whether her refusal stemmed from a genuine wish to be with Sarah in order to involve herself more in the arrangements for the forthcoming party, or the fact that she considered on this first occasion, as he privately did himself, that it would be far better if he saw Master Fletcher by himself in order to make up his own mind about the man without her trying to influence his judgement in any way.

He had already promised he had no intention of bringing charges against Jack Fletcher, and he had no intention of going back on his word; whether he would find employment on the estate for the man who had had the impudence to shoot him was a different matter entirely. Nevertheless, as he arrived at the row of recently lime-washed, well-maintained cottages, and secured his mount to Nanny Berry's gatepost, he was determined, at any event, to keep an open mind.

Before he could even begin to make his assessment, he was obliged to spend a little time with the elderly woman who had been one of the few people to show him any real affection during his childhood. News of his engagement, undoubtedly related by the servants at the house, had already reached the tiny hamlet, where several of the estate workers and their families resided; and Nanny Berry was determined to leave him in no doubt of how delighted she was personally, and how wholeheartedly she approved his choice of future Viscountess.

She wasn't slow either in singing the praises of the young man who, in a matter of a few days only, had transformed the sizeable patch of ground at the rear of her cottage from the weed-choked wilderness it had become during her convalescence into a neat and orderly garden once again, ready for planting those precious vegetables needed to help sustain her throughout the year.

No matter what Master Fletcher's faults, fear of hard work, evidently, did not number among them, and within minutes of making his acquaintance his lordship decided to forget past indiscretions and give him the benefit of the doubt.

'Well, you young rogue, are you prepared to work for me, now that Miss Milbank will not be leaving the Manor?'

'Aye, sir, that I am.'

'From what I've managed to discover about you already from my head groom, I think you might make the ideal replacement for my gamekeeper when he does eventually retire in a year or two. Your skill with firearms is in no doubt,' his lordship, continued, smiling wryly. 'The future Viscountess Greythorpe seems to take the view that the injury I sustained would have been a good deal worse had it not been for your expertise. Therefore, not making full use of your undoubted natural abilities would be a waste. In the meantime, though, I believe you will be of greater value working in and around the stables. I want you to take up the duties of Miss Milbank's personal groom.' His lordship was suddenly serious. 'She is not to be permitted to ride anywhere, not even across the estate, unattended.'

Jack regarded his new master keenly for a moment. 'Is there something queer going on, sir?'

'I wish I knew for certain,' the Viscount admitted. 'Colonel Hastie paid me a visit yesterday. He swears he caught sight of that showy chestnut of Fanhope's being ridden along a country lane earlier in the day, and asked me whether your old master had returned, so I sent a brief note round to Lord Fanhope this morning. Seemingly he hasn't, or if he has he's certainly staying well clear of the ancestral home.'

'Might the Colonel have been mistaken, sir?' Jack suggested, not unreasonably. 'His fondness for brandy is widely known. And his eyesight ain't perhaps as good as it once was.'

'Had he said he'd spotted your old master himself, I might have had my doubts. But he said he recognised the horse. And where horses are concerned, Hastie doesn't make mistakes.'

Jack frowned. 'But why would he return, sir?'

'I was hoping you might be able to enlighten me.'

Jack paused in his stoking of the bonfire to rub a hand back and forth across the stubble on his chin. 'Well, he don't visit no woman round these parts as I know to. Keeps a mistress in Oxford. And it don't seem likely he's wishful to see his family.' He returned the Viscount's steady gaze for a moment before adding, 'Happen you might be right, sir, and it would be as well to keep an eye on Miss Milbank for a while. I'm not saying as how he'd go out of his way to harm her. But if he got a chance for revenge there's no saying that he might not take it, if he were in one of his moods.'

As this was precisely what had been preying on his own mind since the Colonel's visit, Greythorpe nodded in agreement. 'We can't be certain that Fanhope is back, of course. It might be that he changed mounts before setting off on the road to Oxford, and has arranged for the stabling of the chestnut at a tavern hereabouts, and someone was merely exercising the animal. But it's as well to keep our eyes and ears open for a while. Stay here for the rest of today, and then see Wilks in the morning.'

As the Viscount chose not to cause his future bride unnecessary distress by informing her about Charles Fanhope's possible return to the area, Annis retired to bed that night in a state of blissful ignorance, and in a mood of almost complete blissful contentment.

Louise having been invited to spend the day with the vicar's eldest daughter, Annis had been more than happy to remain with Sarah, ensconced in the small parlour, discussing arrangements for the much larger party. Naturally enough, now that it was to be her very own engagement ball, her attitude had changed dramat-

ically, and Sarah, although more than willing to help, had been
only too happy to take a far less active role and to allow Annis to
make the final decisions on decorations for the ballroom, and
those all-important dinner and supper menus, of which Cook had
thankfully approved.

They had discussed too at some length Sarah's plans for the
future, and this had proven to be the only slight flaw in what would
otherwise have been a perfect day.

Although delighted by the engagement and by her brother's
choice of future wife, Sarah, it seemed, was determined not to
remain at the Manor once the marriage had taken place, and nothing
Annis could say had managed to sway her from her resolve to set
up home for herself somewhere. Bath, clearly, was now at the top
of her list. Consequently she was very much looking forward to
meeting Lady Pelham and her half-sister the following day.

Annis too was very much looking forward to their arrival, but
for a very different reason. She was keen to catch up on their news.
From what she had gleaned from her godmother's most recent
letter, there had been a decided cooling off in Helen's feelings
towards Mr Daniel Draycot, and although she couldn't say for
sure that the relationship had definitely come to end, her godmother had certainly given the impression that she no longer
viewed the opportunistic Mr Draycot as a major problem.

Smiling to herself, she snuggled down into the comfortable bed,
wondering how the pair of them would react when they discovered
her standing in the hall, waiting to greet them. In her last letter, she
had suggested that, although invited, she wouldn't be remaining at
the Manor for the party, so they certainly wouldn't be expecting to
find her here. And they certainly wouldn't be expecting to be told
that she was Viscount Greythorpe's affianced bride!

'Oh, I can hardly wait to see their faces, Rosie! And what the

deuce are you doing scratching at the door? Surely you don't need
to go out again?'

Seemingly, though, that was precisely what she did want, for she
continued to whine, demanding attention, until Annis, very reluctantly swung her feet to the floor. 'You are not all joy, you troublesome cur,' she scolded, knowing full well that she would be obliged
at this late hour to deal with the matter herself. She hadn't heard a
sound for the past half an hour, which suggested strongly that all
the servants had retired. 'Why didn't you avail yourself of the opportunity when James the footman took you out an hour ago?'

For answer Rosie merely wagged her bobtail in joyful expectation, while Annis slipped on her dressing gown, slippers and finally
her cloak, for there was no saying how long she would be obliged
to wait. Then, picking up the bedside candle, she made her way
towards the back staircase, used mostly by the servants, from where
the quickest access could be gained to the side entrance leading to
the stable-yard.

By the time she had let Rosie out of the house, Annis wasn't
feeling nearly so aggrieved, and felt sure she would have forgiven
her pet completely for obliging her to leave the warm comfort of
her bed, had she not waited what seemed a full ten minutes in vain
for her return.

Likely as not, the dog had picked up the scent of a rat or some other
creature lurking in the shadows and was enjoying the sport, Annis
decided, taking the extra precaution of arming herself with one of
the lanterns, conveniently left on a side table, before going in search.

There was no immediate response to her soft call and whistle.
Then, when almost halfway across the yard, Annis thought she
detected what sounded suspiciously like a thud, immediately
followed by the faintest of yelps, emanating from the direction of
the largest stable block. Ordinarily she would not have attempted

to venture further, most assuredly not in the dead of night when every object cast a dancing shadow, eerie and threatening. Yet it was so unlike the dog not to come when summoned. By the time she had arrived at the stable block, she was already beginning to suspect something was very wrong. When her eyes focused on the dim flicker of light beneath the door and the two drawn-back sturdy bolts, she was certain there was a presence within with two legs, as well as the several with four.

Concern for her dog quickly silenced the tiny voice advocating extreme caution, and she entered to discover, as expected, a familiar figure holding a candle aloft. Only the light wasn't safely enclosed behind the glass of a lantern, but dangerously naked and casting its bearer's large shadow menacingly across the stone wall.

'What in the world do you imagine you are doing here?'

Chapter Fourteen

His lordship raised his eyes from their contemplation of the amber liquid in his glass to check the position of the hands on the handsome ormolu timepiece taking pride of place on the library's mantelshelf. The ladies had all retired some while ago, and the servants, including Dunster, had undoubtedly done likewise.

And it was high time that he retired too, he told himself; except it was only on occasions such as this, when alone and at leisure, that he could sit back and reflect on his great good fortune, and once again silently bless Providence for ensuring a very special someone had crossed his path on a certain bitterly cold day towards the end of February.

Having been obliged to leave the ladies to their own devices for much of the evening, he had managed to complete several tasks, which now left him free to play the gracious host to Lady Pelham and his sister Helen when they arrived on the morrow; a highly pleasing prospect, and one that he was very much looking forward to. It was just a pity that he had been obliged to deny himself Annis's delightful company for most of the evening. As usual, though, she had understood perfectly and had been uncomplaining. Yes, he had been blessed, truly blessed the day Miss Annis Milbank had walked into his life!

Yet, how could it be, he wondered, that two people of opposite sexes, not to mention differing backgrounds and diverse upbringings, could rub along together so remarkably well, in such perfect harmony? The empathy between them was something to behold, quite out of the common way, and had been almost from the first. He would not go so far as to say that he never failed to know precisely what she was thinking or feeling, or that there had never been the odd occasion when her reaction had been puzzling, not what he had been expecting, but these instances had been rare indeed. For the most part he knew precisely what her response would be to any given situation. Why, how many times in recent weeks had their eyes met across the parlour of an evening to enjoy a fleeting moment's shared and silent laughter when his sister had fallen into one of her twittering moods, or Louise had uttered something foolishly ambiguous? The answer came hard on the heels of the question—countless! And long may they continue to do so!

Darling Annis, bless her, had freed him from the shackles of a strict and, for the most part, loveless upbringing, where simple pleasures were frowned upon and displays of emotion forbidden. She had encouraged him to smile quite openly again, and to laugh at the absurdities of their fellow man whenever and wherever he chose; whilst he in turn had removed the thin mantle of resentment of his class that had clung to her when first they had met.

Yet a further smile came effortlessly to his lips as he raised his glass in a silent toast to the woman who was to become the future Viscountess Greythorpe, an event that could not occur soon enough as far as he was concerned. The devious stratagems he had adopted to keep her a resident under his roof had proved to be successful, and wickedly satisfying, it was true. Yet he couldn't deny that her continued presence at the Manor had sorely tested his powers of restraint, not to mention his honourable inclinations. It was perhaps just as well that Lady Pelham was arriving on the morrow, for his future Viscountess was possibly going to require more than just the protection of that eagle-eyed companion-cum-maid of hers before the precious knot that would irrevocably bind them was blessedly tied!

Tossing the brandy down his throat in one satisfying swallow, his lordship rose to his feet, and quickly went about the room extinguishing the candles, before collecting the one left burning to guide him safely up to his apartments on the first floor. It was not unusual for him to be the last member of the household to seek his bed. It was not unusual, either, for him to detect the odd sound as he departed the library and crossed the chequered hall towards the stairs. It was none the less most unusual for him to hear the unmistakable loud creak of a door and encounter a draught of sufficient strength as almost to gutter his candle.

Evidently someone other than himself was about at this late hour, he decided, then checked, one foot raised in readiness to make the ascent to the upper floor.

Common sense told him that in all probability it was merely Dunster, late about his duties, meticulously checking doors and windows. Yet when no further sound reached his ears, not even so much as a footfall, one of those tiny seeds of uneasiness, sown shortly after Colonel Hastie's most recent visit, rapidly began to germinate, obliging him to satisfy himself that all was as it should be.

Having resided at the Manor for the greater part of his life, his lordship knew his ancestral home's every nook and cranny, the position of each and every stick of furniture, and the precise placement of every object of value or otherwise. It was by no means unusual to find a variety of candles and lamps on any one of the tables positioned by each and every entrance. But to discover a naked candle burning at this late hour, and in a porcelain holder that was normally to be found in a certain chamber on the floor above, most certainly was not the norm.

His uneasiness increased at an alarming rate when he discovered the door unlocked. He could almost have wished to discover an intruder lurking in the shadows of the passageway behind him, but didn't even bother to turn his head to check, for he knew he was quite alone. This was no forced entry. A resident of the house had merely wished to attain access to the yard. Unfortunately he had a fairly shrewd notion of precisely who that certain someone was, and precisely why she had found it necessary to be wandering about at such an ungodly hour.

Annis, ever considerate to the feelings of others, wouldn't have dreamed of rousing a servant from his bed to attend to the needs of her dog, when she was quite capable of dealing with the matter herself. Nor would she have wished to risk disturbing any member of the household by wandering through the main body of the mansion, and had therefore eschewed the use of the main staircase and front entrance, where the smallest noise echoed about the lofty hall like a fearful death-knell.

Of course, by making use of the back stairs and the side entrance to achieve the objective, she was oblivious to the fact that he himself had been up and about, he thought grimly, taking the time to light yet another of the lanterns before setting off in hot pursuit. But she would soon discover it. And to her cost! He had to put a stop to any further midnight wanderings, no matter how valid the reason. Rosie would just need to remain in one of the outbuildings overnight, at least until he was certain in his own mind that Charles Fanhope posed no threat.

By the time his lordship had reached the middle of the yard he had been forced to accept that his worst fears had been thoroughly justified. He had heard that gleeful, childish laughter too many times in the past not to be quite certain of precisely who it was standing on the other side of the largest stable's door. And he very much feared his unwelcome visitor was not alone.

Annis wasn't slow to recognise the inane cackle either, and was even quicker to recall precisely when and where she had heard it before. Why it had taken all this time for her to identify the culprit she could not imagine, especially as the Viscount himself had reminded her where and when, and in front of whom she had mentioned her particular fear of confined spaces. It just went to prove that she hadn't been quite herself in recent weeks!

'So, it was you who kindly bolted the icehouse door, knowing full well that I was within.'

Now that she had recovered from the shock of discovering Lord Fanhope's heir in the stable, her initial fear began to ebb, though she remained decidedly wary. She was not standing close enough to detect any telltale odour. Nevertheless, the glinting eyes and the fact that he seemed to be swaying slightly, like a well-nourished sapling in a moderate breeze, suggested that he was not perfectly sober. As she knew quite well that certain gentlemen when in their cups were wont to give way to their baser instincts, she thought the wisest course might be not to antagonise him.

'Might I be permitted to know what I did to earn your disapprobation? After all, at the time we'd met only once,' she reminded him. She already knew the answer, of course, but had quickly decided that encouraging him to talk while displaying no hostility might just persuade him to reveal his purpose in coming to the Manor.

'You ruined my plans for my sister.' Apart from the ugly curl to his lip, his behaviour remained, thankfully, unthreatening. 'But for your meddling, I'd have had them announcing their engagement by now.'

Annis lowered her eyes momentarily, lest he should recognise the speculative gleam lurking there. Clearly he had not heard of her own engagement to his lordship, and, given her present, vulnerable position, perhaps the wisest course of action was to allow him to remain in ignorance, and continue believing, quite erroneously of course, that there was a possibility of a union between his sister and the Viscount. It might be as well also, she told herself, not to furnish him with the knowledge that Jack Fletcher was now in the Viscount's employ.

She didn't suppose for a moment that his purpose in coming to the Manor at this time of night was to seek an interview with the Viscount. All the same, she didn't think it could do any harm to allow him the opportunity, should he wish to avail himself of it, to air his grievances. He might then become malleable and might even be persuaded to leave without any undue pressure being brought to bear, and without any further unpleasantness taking place between them.

'I'm afraid I do not perfectly understand you, Mr Fanhope,' she lied. 'How did my arrival here interfere with your plans for your sister's future?'

He opened his mouth, then closed it again almost immediately, evidently having thought better of freely admitting to ordering Jack to shoot his lordship. 'Your coming here has caused nothing but trouble,' he muttered sulkily.

'That wasn't my intention, sir,' she assured him with total sincerity. 'I came at my godmother's behest, to act as her ambassador by conveying certain information concerning his lordship's half-sister, that is all.'

'Then why have you remained so long? Were you hoping to

catch Greythorpe for yourself?' The unpleasant curl grew momentarily more pronounced before he spat out accusingly, 'But for you I would still be at Fanhope Hall.'

'Believe me, sir, when I tell you that I attained no satisfaction whatsoever from what took place that night. But do not expect me to apologise either. You were quite ready to cheat Thomas Marshal out of a deal of money, and others too, if what I have learned since is true. I cannot be sorry that I was instrumental in bringing such a despicable practice to an end.'

This seemed to afford him no little amusement, for he laughed out loud. 'If you suppose that, madam, you are in error. You have merely curtailed my rewarding—er—occupation for a while.'

'Do I infer correctly from that that you have not returned with the intention of making peace with your family, of mending your ways and doing your father's bidding?'

'You do indeed. I merely returned to collect one or two items that I had inadvertently left behind in my haste to depart the Hall, which will enable me to live comfortably until I can establish myself on the continent.' He took a moment to slide a hand beneath his voluminous cloak and pat his jacket pocket lovingly. 'One of the servants at the Hall has always been susceptible to a bribe. I didn't even need to set foot inside the place.'

It would have afforded Annis the utmost satisfaction to swipe the smugly satisfied smile off his face, because she didn't doubt for a moment that someone, somewhere, would be made to suffer in order to keep him solvent. His despicable sort wasn't above resorting to blackmail.

'Your family is most concerned about you. Have you made no attempt to make contact?' she asked, hoping the contempt she felt was not evident in her voice.

His shrug of indifference was not totally unexpected. 'I might possibly write to Caro at some point in the future. But as for the others...I shall see them soon enough, I dare say, after I have come into the title. My father can't last for ever.'

His complete unconcern that the members of his family were being made to suffer and would continue to do so as a direct result of his selfish actions came as no real surprise to Annis either, though she was finding it increasingly difficult to control the rising contempt for someone whose sole concern was only for himself.

Wholly selfish, and totally lacking compassion, he was a prime example of the very worst of his class. He was the type who wasn't above resorting to the most underhanded means to attain his own ends, and wouldn't concern himself unduly either over the misery, physical or mental, that might need to be inflicted on his fellow man in order that he remained cocooned in comfort, able to command any luxury. Notwithstanding, she felt equally certain that he was in no way naturally violent by nature, and would therefore do his utmost to avoid confrontation, or involving himself in actions that might ultimately bring about someone's death.

Convinced she had his measure at last, she didn't hesitate to ask, 'So why do I discover you here at the Manor? I cannot imagine it was to thank his lordship in person for the assistance he rendered your estimable father in what turned out to be a vain attempt to locate your whereabouts.'

'What a clever little puss you are, Miss Milbank!' He allowed his eyes to wander over her in a slow appraisal that bordered on the insulting. 'Now that I come to look at you more closely, I can see you are not without a—er—certain charm.' He frowned suddenly, suspicion clearly writ across every plump contour of his face. 'Perhaps Greythorpe might be interested in you, after all. He seems to favour females with brains. I myself am attracted by purely physical attributes.' The frown deepened. 'And never to interfering baggages like you! But for you I wouldn't be in this predicament now!'

Annis successfully suppressed the strong urge to gloat. 'So why are you here?' she asked again in an attempt to divert him from the main grievance he held against her. 'It wasn't to seek shelter and spend a night sleeping on straw, I'm sure.'

Her stratagem worked. He merely looked impatient now. 'The idiot in whose care I left my horse succeeded in straining one of its hocks whilst out exercising the animal, and I was forced to ride here on the most misbegotten nag that ever was shod, one of which it succeeded in losing on my return to the inn. Hence the need for a fresh mount.' He paused to brush the remains of an unsightly cobweb from his cloak. 'I could of course have deprived old Colonel Hastie of one of his choice hacks. But I decided, instead, to avail myself of Greythorpe's favourite hunter, as the Manor was just that fraction closer.' His smile was not pleasant. 'And you, my dear Miss Milbank, shall assume the role of groom and make yourself useful. It will be some recompense for all the trouble you've caused me.'

'Be damned if I shall, sir!' Annis snapped, quick to resort to her late grandfather's colourful language.

'You'll be sorry if you don't,' he warned, smugly satisfied, as he took a step aside to reveal what he had successfully hidden from view behind the folds of his voluminous cloak.

Annis's look of defiance was instantly replaced by one of acute dismay. The shock of discovering Charles Fanhope in the stable had thrust all thoughts of her pet's possible whereabouts from her mind. In an instant all that changed.

Without a moment's consideration for her own welfare, she brushed past Fanhope, almost rocking him on his heels in her haste to reach the injured creature at his feet, and dropped to her knees.

Only when satisfied that Rosie had been rendered unconscious by a blow to the head, and was not dead, did she concern herself once more with the man towering above.

'You should be thanking me, Miss Milbank, not favouring me with that disdainful glare. Think yourself lucky that I attained enough satisfaction at rendering the nasty brute unconscious, after it had had the temerity to attempt to take a bite out of my leg.'

Although he might not have been perfectly sober, he succeeded in swooping down to retrieve the stout piece of wood that had proved such an effective weapon against Rosie's attack before Annis could reach out a hand to grasp it.

'Now, Miss Milbank, if you do not choose to receive the same treatment as that damnable cur of yours, you will do my bidding. And be quick about it!'

He might stop short at committing cold-blooded murder, but Annis wouldn't have put it past him to strike a female, especially one he disliked as much as her, and reluctantly rose to her feet.

Since her arrival at the Manor, she had paid frequent visits to the stables. As she had never failed to bring along a few tasty morsels, the horses were always pleased enough to see her. His lordship's prized hunter, not usually at his best with strangers, had quickly grown accustomed to her frequent visits, and, although slightly skittish at the unusual disturbance at that time of night, he didn't take undue exception to her entering his stall.

It was while Annis was securing the bridle that she first detected the sound—faint, it was true, but discernible none the less, and definitely coming from the stable-yard.

She risked a surreptitious glance towards the door, as she led the powerful hunter from its stall. By his total lack of reaction it was safe to assume that Fanhope hadn't detected the sound. It could, of course, have been made by a rat out scavenging for food. On the other hand, it was possible that a stable-worker, perhaps even Wilks himself, alerted by the sound of voices, had come to investigate. If this was the case, the least she could do was attempt to hold Fanhope's attention to enable the possible investigator to slip, unnoticed by her companion, into the barn.

'Are you sure you are equal to handling Assaye? Greythorpe's a fine horseman by any standard. Even he finds the hunter a mettlesome creature on occasions.'

'Your solicitude for my well-being is quite misplaced, Miss Milbank,' he told her with such condescension that she came perilously close to forgetting her resolve and administering a well-aimed slap to the side of his chubby face.

It crossed her mind, as she watched him turn to place the lighted candle on the shelf behind him, that throughout her life there had been few people whom she had disliked more than the Honourable Charles Fanhope. Had it not been that her regard for Lord Fanhope had swiftly become totally at variance to that in which she held his son, and that she did not wish him to suffer further because of the actions of this totally selfish offspring of his, she might almost have wished that the wretched creature would succeed in breaking his bullish neck.

Successfully thrusting the shameful half-desire from her thoughts, she continued to watch as he picked up the saddle that he must have collected from the tack-room himself before her arrival on the scene. Either he didn't trust her to secure it properly, or he was eager to be gone, because he chose to complete the task himself, leaving her free to transfer her gaze and watch, with ever-increasing joy, as the door slowly opened and that beloved being who had come to mean everything to her slip as stealthily as a cat into the stable.

'Grieve me though it does, Miss Milbank, I'm afraid I must

inflict a little discomfort upon you until the morning,' Fanhope announced, with what she considered a fine disregard for the truth. 'As I'm sure a clever little puss like yourself must appreciate, I cannot have you raising the alarm the instant I ride out of here, thereby revealing to one and all my presence in the neighbourhood, before I'm able to put some miles between us. Therefore it behoves me to tie and gag you, and I do so hope you will not foolishly attempt to prevent me.'

'She might not...but I most certainly shall!'

Annis experienced the almost overwhelming desire to erupt into laughter at the look of shocked disbelief that momentarily swept across Fanhope's features at the sound of his lordship's smoothly suave tones.

Unfortunately her moment of satisfaction was short-lived. As Fanhope swung round to face his lordship, his cloak billowed out, brushing against the hunter's flanks. Assaye took exception to the flapping garment, and attained his revenge by performing a neat side step that knocked Fanhope off balance, sending him crashing against the shelves along the wall. The lighted candle he had placed there himself only a short time before, and several earthenware jars and bottled of varying sizes went crashing to the floor, their contents quickly combining as they trickled towards the pile of straw and hay on which Rosie lay, oblivious to what was going on about her.

Whatever the various jugs and jars had contained might have been quite innocuous on their own, but, mixed together and subjected to the naked flame of a candle, they proved to be a lethal brew. One moment all that could be heard was Fanhope's succession of curses, as he succeeded in standing upright once more, the next there was a whoosh of air as a long wall of flame shot many feet into the air, igniting not only the pile of hay surrounding Rosie but also the more substantial pile in the corner of the stable, and even reaching upwards to the wooden joists of the attic area above.

All then seemed confusion and panic. Annis darted along the stable to rescue her dog, while his lordship tried to calm his now rearing and terrified prized hunter, leaving Fanhope, unobserved, to wield the stick he had used to such good effect on Rosie. Before Annis had realised what he was about, and could scream out a warning, he had brought it down hard across the Viscount's broad shoulders.

How his lordship managed to recover so quickly after receiving such a vicious blow, and just how he succeeded in avoiding falling beneath Assaye's dangerously stomping hooves, Annis could only wonder. Scooping Rosie up in her arms and racing towards the door, she was helpless to offer any form of assistance, but gained a modicum of satisfaction from witnessing the Viscount easily ward off a further blow from Fanhope, before she raced out to the yard.

Once she had placed Rosie gently on the ground, and at a safe distance, she wasted no time in raising the alarm by striking the triangular-shaped piece of metal suspended from the stable wall for all she was worth. Only when Wilks's gruff voice, emanating from his sleeping quarters, drifted across the yard, and several lights began to appear at various windows in the Manor itself, did she satisfy the steadfast determination to return to aid his lordship.

Once back inside the stable, one glance was sufficient to assure her that she could do nothing whatsoever to stop the fire from spreading. In the short period she'd been away it had taken too much of a hold. The rafters above the attic area were already alight, and she feared it would not be too long before the roof caved in. Thankfully his lordship had fared rather better during her brief absence.

Despite having been almost felled by Fanhope's vicious and totally unprovoked attack, the Viscount had succeeded in gaining the upper hand, and now held his uninvited guest securely by his lapels, and was doing his utmost to reason with him, assuring him that he had no intention of dragging him back to the Hall, and that he was free to take himself off as soon as he chose, albeit on foot. Unhappily, though, all his assertions appeared to be falling on deaf ears.

Either Fanhope wasn't prepared to exert himself by walking back to his place of refuge, or his brain was too befuddled by the brandy he had consumed earlier in the evening to appreciate the immediate danger he was in, for he continued to struggle like a wild, unruly child, clawing frantically at the Viscount's hands, while screaming abuse at the top of his voice, until finally his lordship ran out of patience.

Unfortunately Annis chose that moment to begin leading the horses to safety. She darted forward to undo Assaye's reins from where the Viscount had securely tied them to the wooden post of his stall, just as his lordship drew back his arm to deliver a blow sufficient to render his uninvited guest incapable of struggling. Annis reeled under the impact of his lordship's elbow catching her squarely on the left cheekbone, and only Wilks's timely arrival saved her from ending in an undignified heap on the floor.

Only vaguely aware of the injury he had inadvertently inflicted, his lordship successfully placed a flush hit to Fanhope's fleshy jaw, the force of which sent the younger man tottering backwards dangerously close to the edge of the inferno. Either he feared his lordship would follow up his advantage without mercy, or he foolishly considered the fire less of a threat, for he swirled about, shocking everyone else present by taking a frantic leap through the burning hay.

How he managed to reach the rear door to the stable without being engulfed in flames, Annis could not imagine. Lady Luck, however, chose that moment of all moments to abandon him completely. There came the sound of an ominous creaking and a moment later, as she had feared, the floored area of attic directly above his head came crashing down, instantly burying him under a lethal pile of flaming straw and timbers.

The horses, though terrified, were removed to safety without too much hardship and, blessedly, without injury to themselves or any of their rescuers. It took the combined efforts of all the outside staff and most of the house servants in order to prevent the fire from spreading to the other buildings surrounding the yard, and several hours passed before the Honourable Charles Fanhope's charred remains were eventually carried from the smouldering shell of the large stable.

Chapter Fifteen

Although tired and deeply saddened by the tragic events of the night, Annis very much resented being almost commanded to remain in bed the following morning, and would certainly have showed her mettle and rebelled had it not been for the fact that she didn't wish to add to the heavy burden of concerns now plaguing the one who had issued the order. Fortunately, the tedium was relieved by none other than the temporary gaoler himself, who paid a surprising visit midway through the morning.

Without even bothering to wait for a response to his lightest of scratches upon the bedchamber door, the Viscount walked brazenly into the room, just as though it were a regular occurrence and he had every right to be there.

More startling still was the normally strait-laced Disher's reaction to the unexpected appearance of the visitor. Apart from dropping the slightest of curtsies and whisking up the breakfast tray, she departed without so much as uttering a word in protest, and even went so far as to close the door behind her to enable the room's remaining occupants to enjoy total privacy.

'Your influence upon my maid is something quite remarkable

to witness, Dev,' Annis informed him, after she was surprised still further by his plumping himself down on the edge of the bed.

'Disher and I understand each other well enough. I'm first and foremost a man, so it's unlikely she trusts me completely. But she believes I would remember that I was born a gentleman, should I be tempted to take advantage.'

Despite the tragic events of the previous night, Annis managed a teasing smile. 'Would you, I wonder, if I so far forgot myself as to place temptation in your path?'

Lowering his eyes, his lordship focused on the bodice of his love's modest attire. The nightdress might cover every inch of her from neck to wrist and ankle, but it quite failed to disguise the shapeliness of the slender figure beneath. Even the magnificent swathe of lustrous brown hair that cascaded like a silken veil about her head and shoulders and down below her breasts, effectively becoming an extra barrier, only added to the allure. He longed to reach out and curl several strands about one finger, but dared not trust himself the liberty of even this modestly provocative gesture.

He too had been able to thrust the unfortunate happenings of the night to the back of his mind, if only for a short period. Now they returned with a vengeance. 'My reason for wishing to be private with you at least stemmed from the purest of motives. I came here, first and foremost, to inform you that I have already paid a visit to the Hall.'

'And?' she prompted gently, when he fell silent, turning over in his mind what had been a most painful but necessary task.

'And I decided that you had been absolutely right last night when you had said that it would benefit no one, least of all any member of the Fanhope family, to learn the complete truth.'

Unlike his lordship, Annis made no attempt to control an impulse, and so reached out to stroke his cheek gently. She felt that he had grossly underrated himself a short while before. He wasn't just a man, but a highly honourable one who found any form of falsehood distasteful. Yet, at her instigation, he had been prepared to abandon his principles and resort to the despicable practice himself.

'So the polite world will soon discover that Charles Fanhope is no more. It will be believed that he lost his life, late one night, when he came to the aid of his neighbour, helping to rescue a string of superb horses from a burning stable. If he is remembered at all, then it will be as a young man who cared little for honour during his short lifetime, but who at least attained some at his death.'

She sighed deeply. To be able to bury Charles with their heads held high was little enough recompense for the members of his immediate family who had already suffered greatly. 'Be assured, Dev, no one will ever discover the truth from me. Nor from Wilks either, you can be sure.' She regarded him keenly for a moment. 'But did Lord Fanhope believe you, do you suppose?'

'Truth to tell, no. I do not imagine he did,' his lordship answered at length. 'But he was grateful, you may be sure. And relieved, too, I think. As you are very well aware, he has never been under any illusion about his elder son's true character. He even freely admitted to you that he always considered it a great pity that young Giles was not destined to step into his shoes. Well, Fate has finally decreed otherwise. And I too cannot be sorry for it. I just wish it might have been brought about in some other way—not here at the Manor, not after everything else that has happened in both the recent and distant past.'

Annis knew precisely what was passing through his mind, and once again experienced no compunction in reaching out to touch his cheek. 'Rid your mind here and now that you are in any way culpable for what took place last night.' She raised her fingers now in a dismissive gesture. 'As well blame me, his family, your father's ill advice of years ago for the way things have turned out. Person-

ally, though, I think nothing can be gained by attempting to appor-
tion blame.'

'You're right, of course,' he agreed, after the briefest of moments.
'It is fruitless to speculate too on the what-might-have-been, if
only… We can only move on from what is, from where we are.'
He stared down at her and the deep sadness instantly faded from
his eyes. 'And what is so sublimely perfect now is that I have you
to share my life.'

Completely forgetting his resolve to behave, he reached out and
drew her against him. Careful though he was to avoid the bruise
she had sustained, as he trailed his lips across the intelligent brow,
and down the uninjured side of her face to capture her mouth, he
felt her flinch slightly and instantly released her.

'Oh, my poor darling,' he murmured, all gentle solicitude. 'Does
it cause you much discomfort? I wouldn't have had it happen for
the world, you know that. We could always summoned the doctor.
He might be able to give you an alternative salve to the one I'm
certain the excellent Disher has already administered that would
offer more relief.'

'What…? Summon Dr Prentiss over such an insignificant thing
as a tiny bruise?' Annis was appalled and it clearly showed. 'I
would never dream of permitting such a thing, when his services
might be required elsewhere for those in genuine need!'

'A—er—little bruise?' his lordship echoed, thereby instantly
arousing her suspicions.

'Pass me that mirror!' she ordered, then promptly let out a tiny
squeal of dismay when he did so, and she saw for the first time the
livid mark that completely encircled her left eye. 'Little wonder
Dish has kept me well clear of every looking glass throughout the
morning. Oh, this really is too bad,' she went on, aggrieved, and
quite oblivious to the fact that his lordship was having the utmost

difficulty in containing his mirth. 'I did so want everything to be perfect when I meet the members of your family, not to mention your friends, and half the cream of society, if what Sarah tells me is true. And now I'm to attend my very own engagement ball sporting a black eye! It really is the outside of enough! Everyone will suppose I'm little removed from a street urchin, instead of a properly brought-up young lady!'

Needless to say his lordship's inability to retain his mirth did little to console her. 'I shall take leave to inform you, Deverel Greythorpe,' Annis said with careful restraint, 'that, for someone who, by his own admission, laughed only seldomly before I entered his life, you appear to have developed a very perverse sense of humour in a very short space of time.'

For answer his lordship kissed her soundly, and withdrew, his laughter echoing after him down the whole length of the long gallery.

It was a sound frequently heard by his four offspring throughout his lordship's long and very contented life.

* * * * *